Willow's Crush

Willow's Crush

~A Willow's Wounds Book~

Stephanie Fields

Copyright Page

Cover Design by Donna Cook
Editing & Formatting by Nicole Mullaney

Ebook edition
ISBN 979-8-9916717-1-2

Dedication Page

This series is dedicated to my mom, dad and exes. Without all the trauma you gave me, none of this would be possible.

Book Playlist

(In story order)

Matchbox Twenty- Back to Good
When the Doves Cry- Prince
Yummy Yummy Yummy- Ohio Express
Ironic- Alanis Morissette
Cowboy- Kid Rock
Possum Kingdom- Toadies
Jagged Little Pill- Alanis Morissette
When I'm Small- Phantogram
Brooklyn Baby- Lana Del Rey

CHAPTER ONE

WILLOW

Here I go again, pretending to be someone I'm not. A wife in mourning.

Ha! Who could ever mourn such a piece of shit like Neil? *My ever so doting husband.* That's what everyone keeps on saying, anyway. If they only knew the real him. I don't say anything though because he's dead— I'll applaud my work silently—and that means I don't *have* to explain the things he did to me. What a relief!

"Willow, my heart is broken for you. Neil was such a good, genuine man" the lady with the long, thick eye lashes said to me this morning as she took my order. I remember her serving us coffee in downtown Chicago on the square, when Neil was still alive and we'd go there together.

I looked at her name tag because I had forgotten her name. To me, she is just the coffee lady. "Thank you, Julie." A little tear trickled down my cheek. The one I forced out. I wiped it away ever so gently and sniffled a little, for show. I learned that from Neil. He was really good at that shit.

"He really was such a good, genuine, kind man," she insisted.

Did you wanna fuck him, Julie?

"Yes, he was," I agreed instead of saying what really popped up in my mind.

She handed me my large vanilla latté with two extra shots of espresso and *no milk.*

"And he died saving you? Just wow." She batted her way too long, fake eyelashes at me like it was a fairytale, minus the happily ever after—-in their eyes anyway.

"It's like all the stories I read in my childhood."

Rumor has it that some people believe he died saving me in a house fire while I was imprisoned by Brock, my side guy who turned out to be an *absolute fucking psychopath.* The police records clearly show my report that both Brock and Neil kept me hostage in Brock's townhome apartment. I don't argue with anyone who thinks Neil died saving me, though. Because technically he did and I am not the greatest liar. I mean, this is big. Really big. It sort of just presented itself to me by Chief Phil. It fell right into my lap, and I sort of went along with it. Hey. Case closed. Still, that doesn't change how fucking hard it is to hear someone, *anyone* talk about Neil in such a good light.

I blinked at her. No more tears fell down my cheeks. She probably thought I was showing jealousy—lucky for me because nobody likes an insensitive widow—- because of the look on my face that I could not hide. Okay, I know I'm supposed to be crying like *all the Goddamn time,* but I just couldn't hide this one. It wasn't jealousy that arose on my face this morning. It was disgust that I felt. Disgust at what the fuck she was saying about Neil. She just kept going on and on and on and it was just *a little over the top, Julie.*

She doesn't really know him, I reminded myself. That helped me feel a little bit better about getting through that conversation without downing an entire bottle of vodka afterwards.

She looked down, clearly uncomfortable under my gaze, then pushed her hands against the counter to perk herself up. With a sad smile on her face she said, "Like your knight in shining armor."

Her brown ponytail bounced and swayed side to side. I wanted to grab ahold of it and smash her pretty little face on the counter she laid her hands upon.

Gag. Me. I need vodka, pronto.

"Thanks again, Julie," I exclaimed my gratitude. *Wasn't that enough for her?* I held my latté cup up in the air like I was toasting her. Spinning on my heel, I made my way around the tables and got the hell out of there because I couldn't take it any longer. Usually, I'd sit in the lounge and make myself comfortable in the biggest fluffiest chair I could find, enjoying my latté and browsing my phone on all the social media platforms— Facebook. Instagram. TikTok. X, formally known as twitter.

Not today.

She literally called out to me as I was right at the door to leave. "Your next latté is on me! Shit!" She slapped her leg her apron was resting on. "No wait! I should have had this one on me."

She looked *so very* disappointed in herself.

I opened the door and the bell at the top chimed in my ears. *Ding ding ding.* That was my cue to leave. To leave that coffee shop and to leave Chicago for good.

"Come back!" Julie hollered. "I'll refund you!"

Really? How much more pathetic could she be? I did not go back over there just so she can feel good about herself and brag to the rest of the coffee shop later on that she paid her condolences to me by buying my five dollar cup of coffee.

No. Fuck that and fuck her.

"Don't worry about it!" I said, chipper, toasting her again with my latté in the air. I turned back around and I closed that fucking door behind me so fast I think I actually accidentally slammed it. Outside the door to the coffee shop, I dug around in my purse, the one I got on sale at Nordstrom rack. *A steal!* There it is! My sanity. I unscrewed the lid to the vodka bottle and poured a little in my latté.

That's much better.

The walk back to my old apartment complex was a nice one. Not only because autumn was just around the corner and the breeze felt cool and fresh against my skin, running its invisible fingers through my hair, but because this all made me think of the guy from the beach. The one who grabbed for my hat at the same time as I did after it blew off of my head. He, too, was cool and fresh against my skin. Fresh hands on my body— nice—ice cold to the touch—not so nice. It's all very bittersweet to me. I used to make him warm his hands up before touching me. After we got a little more comfortable around each other, he started to get annoyed with it. *Honeymoon stage equals over.* He'd place his hand on my bare back and my whole body would tense up. *Shiver.* Why was he always so cold?

"Rub your hands together before touching me again. They're freezing cold," I demanded. No more fucking asking these guys to do what I need from them just to feel comfortable.

"I have to every single time now? Really?" Except when he said it, it was in broken English, which I always enjoyed.

Yes, really. You asshat.

He eventually got sick of having to do that simple task, and I eventually got sick of *him.* Even after the ice cold touch of his hands bothered me so much he asked me quickly—a little too quickly—to go out of the Country to live with him. Men really do try to commit so fast. Neil proposed to me only four months after we started dating. Brock chained me up in his townhome apartment after seven months of what ended up being our fatal affair. And this guy? After just six and a half months? A whole different country?

"Vill oui' go here wiff me?" Diego asked me in that to die for foreign accent of his. God. I'm a sucker for those. While he spoke better English around other people, he let it all loose around me and I was totally okay with that. He asked me just four days ago, while browsing pictures of Dubai on his Chromebook. The bright blues and greens stuck out to me as he cruised the mouse up and down the screen. The image looked beautiful. Like a great vacation getaway.

You know what *else* stuck out to me? That Lifetime movie starring Sally Field, *Not Without My Daughter.* I barely knew this guy! I pictured myself as Sally Field, face covered and fighting to leave the country with my non-existent daughter. I have no idea what I was pregnant with when Brock kicked my stomach over and over and over to force my abortion— Huge shoutout to him for saving me from motherhood—but I would have fought for her. Or him. Whatever.

Diego wasn't from here, but he also wasn't from Dubai. His name meant *The Famous Bearer.* I looked it up on Google one time during a cozy night in with him. We lay in bed, each reading a book. Mine- a thriller. His- a historical non-fiction. I set my book face down on the nightstand table beside me. Looking at him, I asked "What would you call your son if you ever became a dad?" I wasn't asking because I want to be a mom. No way in hell. I was asking because I was curious if he'd call his son a junior and brand his name on him like that. I wanted to know if his ego was so big that he would have another Diego walking around, giving no originality. This, to me, says a lot about a man.

Diego said he would junior his son up. I immediately got the ick, but I looked up what his name meant anyway because I was curious. The meaning of his name stuck out to me, and I began to call him that as a long nickname.

Going to Dubai with him was tempting. Did I mention those bright blues and greens drawing me in to say *yes* to going to Dubai with him? Wouldn't that be something? Me in Dubai? The architecture there is something out of this world. It is definitely something to be admired. Dubai really is quite fucking stunning to be honest. But, I said, "No thank you," and I booted him out the door because I am no longer a 'yes man'. It is better this way, anyway. Even though—like they all do in the end—he continued texting me. Blowing. My. Phone. Up. But I was not responding anymore.

Ding! My phone chimed at me.

Diego, Cold Hands, The Famous Bearer
Whatcha doin'?

Really? Him again? Go away, Diego, Cold Hands, The Famous Bearer.

I am on a plane and on my way to New York City and I cannot have him tagging along with me. It is time for a new State. A new city. A new life. And a *very new me.*

CHAPTER TWO

HIM

There she is. *Finally*. I feel like I've been sitting here forever with my head down, hiding my face, waiting for hers to appear. I'm only, like, seven rows behind her. What if she bumps into me? It would all be over then. She would think I'm an absolute creep, just like her other exes. I'm nothing like them, though. I'm better than them. I always have been, and I always will be. When will she realize this? When will it click? When will the fucking light bulb turn back on? She has lost trust in herself. When she trusted herself, we were golden. Everything was perfect because she knew she was with the right person. The one who could protect her. Only I can. Only I can provide her with the security that she needs. Still, I hope she doesn't notice me. I have too much work ahead of me for any hiccups.

No. She won't bump into me. I bought the ticket to have the seat behind her on purpose, so I could watch her for a reason. But, what if she notices me here on the very same plane ride as her? What will she do? How will she react? *Stop!* She won't see me. I've put in too much work. I've studied her too much to get caught.

She's so easy to learn. She is usually far too oblivious to her surroundings. Taking in all the beauty around her. Stopping to smell the flowers. Dancing to the tune of the music playing. It's a good thing. To appreciate all that is in front of you. To live in the moment, instead of worrying too much about what the future holds. She's in her own little world. I could probably walk right past her with the baseball cap and my head pointing downwards, and she still wouldn't notice.

God. I feel just like Joe Goldberg from that Netflix series, YOU in this stupid ass baseball cap. Willow devours that show each time a season comes out. My disguise! I'm invisible! Only in the cap, though. Only in the cap. It's so easy. If she gets up and walks by me for any reason at all, I'll just pull the cap down over my face and stuff my nose in a book or pretend to be a sleeping passenger with the cap covering my face. Thanks for the tips, *Netflix Joe.* I truly appreciate it. I hope it works out in real life like it does in the movies because if not....

She turns her head, like she is just slightly looking behind her. Does she know I'm here? Shit. Fuck. Damnit. Did she see me? Could she feel my presence? *Stop it.* She's not superwoman. Close to it, but not quite with the same senses. I could see just half her face, with her blonde curly locks bouncing as she turned her head back to face the front and away from my direction. *Whew, close one.* See? I told you she probably wouldn't notice. She's too engrossed with the fantasies playing in her head about what her life in New York City will be like. I imagine she pictures a fairytale ending. Or a fairytale beginning. The beginning of something magical.

How could she have any type of a happy ending without me? I gave my all to her. Why wasn't that enough to keep us together? Her tune will change soon enough.

Her face has a soft, porcelain glow to it and just a dash of color so she doesn't look so washed out from her summer tan fading. Like she had pinched her cheeks and rubbed on lip stain that almost matches the pretty pink color her natural lips already are. Her freckles aren't really visible right now because it's not summer anymore. In the summertime her freckles become really pronounced, like a soldier standing at ease. *Aye, aye, captain!* Her ripe full lips seduce me. They always have. All it takes is one taste and I'm down on my knees for her. She licks them to keep from getting chapped. I watch as she rubs her upper and bottom lips together, pursing them to a kiss while gawking at herself in a vintage, rustic looking , golden compact mirror she holds in her hands up to her face. She turns the mirror slightly to see behind her without having to turn around. I pull down the cap again over my face, so she won't see me. She sensed me looking at her.

My God, I miss her so damn much already. And here she is. So close I can touch! I can smell! I can almost taste her! Like sweet honey and vanilla. I know that's her I smell. I know it is. I know because that is what she normally smells like. Her scent is strong and *fucking intoxicating.* I could bottle up her scent and take it with me everywhere I go. Like a security blanket. My obsession.

Is she getting up? Shit. She's standing. Looking all around the plane with her light brown bushy eyebrows furrowed in confusion. What, is she looking for the bathroom? I know where it's at. It's behind us. I can't help her out, though. I duck and pull my cap down forward—again, Thanks Netflix Joe!---over my face and hide in a book. A book I know for sure that the title and cover would never draw her attention. She has a love for thrillers. Not sappy love shit. The cover of the book I'm holding up is sappy love shit.

She just walked right by me and didn't even realize it. *Thank God.* Wait a minute. How could she not? Really? Don't we still have chemistry? Wouldn't she just be able to feel me here? I assumed our connection was strong enough to draw her right into me. Well, you know what they say about assumptions. If I assume I make an ass out of you and me, but that's something Willow has already done without any of my help. I can't think back to a time, during our entire relationship, that she didn't turn nothing into something. There was always something she had to make a fuss about. A look on my face that she didn't feel lived up to what I told her I was thinking. A sigh falling out of mouth that she thought was meant for her. A tone I used while talking that caused her to question me. All assumptions.

I turn my head in her direction to watch her walk away because *I hate to see you go but I love to watch you leave.* She's got on an oversized red sweater tugging at her ass while the black leggings show exactly what she's got packing back there. A dump truck booty is what she always called it, but I never thought that quite described it well enough. Her soft blonde curls fall at her shoulders showing how bare one of them is. A little porn for me. For all of us, really. She knows how much I love that sweater on her, and I know that when she wears it she thinks of me, so back to it… a little porn for me. Thank you, Willow. *Ah.* The way her name tastes in my mouth. *Willow.* My lover. My best friend. My everything. We could build a whole life together if she'd let me back in. Together, we could conquer the world. She doesn't even know it yet. Her eyes will be opened to it all soon enough. There is no question about that.

But really, Willow? Black sparkly UGG boots? Come on. You're not a teenager. Only teenage girls wear shit like that. It's not a good look on her. That's Willow for you, though. Childish at heart, in her very core. She steps out of my sight and I can finally breathe. How long had I been holding my breath? I just let it all out, everything I'd been holding hostage inside me from the moment I saw her stand. And this? Well, this long ass sigh I just released caused the jackass sitting next to me to roll his eyes and huff and puff, as if I interrupted his day. *We're on a plane, guy.* All there is to do are people watch, sleep, and watch shows.

What's he watching anyway? I lean back against the chair I'm sitting in. It's really not that comfortable. My ass is already starting to feel numb—- almost as numb as my heart has felt since the day Willow left me—-and I notice he's watching a rerun of Friends on Netflix on his tablet with his air pods tucked inside his hairy waxy earlobes. I feel like I just threw up a little in my mouth. I almost think out loud, Sure dude, so sorry to interrupt something you've probably watched twenty times already while jacking off to Jennifer Aniston. I roll my eyes at him. He doesn't notice this. I'm polite and do this when he's not looking at me. I don't need any problems with my neighbor. I'm forced to sit next to him for the next four hours or so. I gaze around the plane, hunting for my Willow. How long ago did she get up? Is she lost? Did she already walk by again?

She's back. I know she's back because I smell her sweet vanilla and honey again.

Baseball cap down and book up. Got it.

You know, I refuse to do this our entire relationship. This shit makes me sweat and I don't think Willow likes a sweaty guy. Who does? I'm tossing out this stupid ass baseball cap as soon as I get to New York City. *The Miller Grill Apartments*, door three o' eight. The window diagonal from Willow's!

CHAPTER THREE

HIM

Willow tucks the sweater she's wearing to cup her ass even more before she sits back down in her seat. She wants an audience. She always wants an audience.

She slips one of her blonde curly locks behind her ear and looks to her neighbor, the passenger sitting by her side, before she leans her head back against the chair. She looks at the stranger again, and I see her blush. My eyes drift to him. It's a guy, and she likes him already. I feel heat rising to my face. Suddenly, I notice I'm grinding my back teeth, so I relax my jaw a little. The betrayal I feel is raw.

That. Fucking. Bitch.

He turns his head to the side to face her. I gulp hard seeing his profile. A perfect God damn profile. Sharp jawline, stubble and clean shaven at the same time—oh, come on. Both?— thick dark hair, long eyelashes. He's wearing a gray fucking turtleneck. Preppy asshole. I see his cheek raise up. He's smiling back at her, and they're flirting already.

"You just visiting?" he asks. Their voices carry and I can hear every single thing they're saying to each other. It's evident that she is absolutely fucking cheating on me!

She blushes a–fucking–gain and says, "I'm actually moving there. I've got an apartment already furnished and a job waiting for me and everything!" She smiles a little wider.

"Everything is going to be just so perfect." She beams at him. I can tell she's eager to tell him more. She's ready to just pull the Band-Aid off and share with him her whole life story, but she doesn't. She leaves it at that. This bothers her, though. I can tell. I know Willow, and she loves talking about herself.

Grinning from ear to ear, she blushes. Yep. She does like him, and she is a very stupid girl to think everything is going to be perfect with him. As he grins back at her. I notice his white, straight teeth with a perfect fucking smile just like his perfect Goddamm profile. I hate him already.

"Same here!" he exclaims, obviously excited to have something more in common with her other than them both being on the same plane ride. "I'm moving from Texas. How about you?"

"Me too! I just visited a friend in Chicago." She lies. Why? Why does she lie about this?

"Nice. What part of Texas are you moving from?" Another way for him to get to know if they have more in common, but now he's keeping it cool and calm, like he isn't as excited as he was just one second ago. I can tell he's ecstatic, though. And while Willow is a very stupid girl, she's also a very smart girl and I know she knows his game.

Willow waves her hand in the air and tosses her eyes up, then smiles again. "Oh, a small town you wouldn't know. People say if you blink you miss it." She adjusts in her seat. She always adjusts in her seat when she's lying about something. "I'm moving to New York City for opportunities, ya know?"

"So, you're just a small town girl?" he asks in a sing-song way.

And I shit you not, they lean in together and sing the small town girl part from *Don't Stop Believin'* by Journey like they're lovers and best friends already. They lean in a little too close for my liking. I am pissed the fuck off right now and there is nothing I can do about it. She really is cheating on me. It hasn't even been that long. How could she do this to me? How could she do this to *us*? I thought I meant more to her. Was I just a fling, that she said, "I love you," to, without meaning it?

Willow wants a guy to listen to her talk about life, vent about her troubles, hear about her goals and desires. I can still be that guy. I can be even more than that. I'll show her. I'll show her real damn good.

CHAPTER FOUR

WILLOW

I can't start over and be a very new me in a new state and a new city with a new *crush*. This guy, though. This guy. He just might really be the one. Feeling all giddy inside, I fidget with my hands on my lap as the butterflies flutter about in my stomach. I can feel myself blush. Like I used to with Neil and with Brock when we first started dating. And, well, a few others I suppose, but that's beside the point. That was a long time ago. When I was a different person. I don't fall on the first date anymore. This isn't even a date. This is just a meeting. A crush. It's all fantasy of what could be. All because he smiled at me. Because he's hot. That's all it takes, and my imagination runs wild. It's always short lived, though. By the time they fall for me my bags are packed and I'm ready to leave. Still, I can't help but wonder. The what ifs drive me insane sometimes.

Wait. That's bad. This is bad. Why am I like this? I am always like this at the beginning of something new with a new guy. High expectations and confusing lust for something else. At least this time I'm noticing it quickly. This all makes me feel nervous. We're still on this plane. I need to get off this plane. It's crowded and my anxiety is rushing in. It's not too crowded, though, because I do like that my elbows brush up against this guy's elbow every once in a while. What's his name?

"So," I say, drawing out the 'o' sound. "What's your name?"

"Bryan. And you?" He leans into me. He's flirting with me, but I can't. I can't.

"Willow," I tell him, even though I wanted to lie. I had plans of giving myself a new name. A brand spanking new me. It just came out like word vomit, though. My name. I'm so used to just saying it when someone asks. I told you I'm not a good liar. I can still be a new me without a new name, though. Everyone thinks my name is pretty, anyway. They always say that right after I tell them what my name is. Like I came up with it myself and dreamt it to life or something.

"Now that's a pretty name." He leans back away from me in his seat and rubs the stubble on his chin as he studies me.

Up and down. Up and down. His eyes unclothe me. "Wow. It suits you, too. The name Willow," he utters.

I love the way he says my name, and I'm suddenly really, really glad that I am not a good liar. He says my name like it's a breath of fresh air to him, and he's still staring at me, right into my fucking eyes now. I peer my eyes down because—Oh. My. Gosh.— And this one does not have a foreign accent. But I think, ah, there it is. Cliché of him to comment on my name. His eyes, though. He sees right through my soul.

He is trouble. I can just sense it in the air. The problem with that, is that I like trouble. Should I do this, though? Or should I leave him to be a stranger on a plane. I feel some type of chemistry between us, and did I mention he does not have a foreign accent? I'm a sucker for those. Those are red flags to me because Brock, Neil, and Diego, Cold Hands The Famous Bearer all had foreign accents. I really do need to stay away from the red flags. So maybe, just maybe…

Whew. All of a sudden, it's hot and stuffy in here. I start to fan my face with my hands.

"Would you like a bottle of water?" A young-ish woman that looks to be in her early forties appears right beside me. Her face is that young, old looking kind and wise around the eyes. Blue eyes. Bright and welcoming, like my mom's without the welcoming part. She has dirty blonde hair and her cleavage is showing just a tiny bit. I guess this helps her with tips. I thought that was only in the bars and restaurants. She is really pretty. I am certain she gets good tips. She smiles wide at me. Like she does to all the passengers on the plane. I think I will tip her good because dammit she is working hard, just like me to fit into this God forsaken world that tears us women apart.

"Sure. Yes. Please," I answer. "Thank you," I add as she nods her head at me and hands me a sweating bottle of water, already cold to the touch.

This reminds me of him again. Diego, Cold Hands The Famous Bearer!

Ugh! It's like he is in my head sometimes. Get out of there! I scrunch up my nose and slap my hands in the air to wave him away. Then I shake my head. I forget people can see me doing things sometimes and realize I must look insane.

"You alright there?" Bryan asks.

He's already concerned about me. *For me*. I like that, but it reminds me of when Brock pretended to be concerned after I opened up to him. Just look where that landed me. Pregnant without my consent and chained up for three months in a townhome apartment where only the 'old folks' lived—as he said and he was right—with not a soul to hear my cries for help. So, I think I won't open up this time.

"Mmmhhhmmm," I managed to get out.

My lips press into a tight line as I think about the sixty one text messages——and counting——I have received from Diego, Cold Hands The Famous Bearer since boarding the plane. I haven't opened up any of them yet, so I don't know how much he's begging me to get off the plane. To go to Dubai with him instead. Calling me a bitch, slut, whore. The standard names men call you when they don't get their way. I don't care to read how many apologies there are after and in between the name calling. I can't handle it. It's all just a little too much for me right now.

When I left for New York City, and he left for Dubai, our goodbyes didn't turn out the way I envisioned. I pictured us hugging. A long embrace. Breathing each other in one last time. We didn't have a relationship full of fights. I figured we could thank each other for the time we spent together, then go our separate ways.

He, apparently, had other plans in mind. He got down on one knee. I thought he might propose. My heart sank to the pit of my stomach. I wasn't going to say yes. I have learned my lesson. Grabbing my hands with his sweaty palms and his face scrunched up in an ugly form, he begged me to stay. "I'll do anything. Please don't leave me." I had to shake my leg to get him off me. Like a dog humping somone's leg. Annoying. A nuisance.

I push my head against the seat and maneuver around to get comfortable. I reach my hand to my heart to grab the charm on my necklace, and I remember that it's not there. It got lost in the house fire at Brock's townhome apartment when I finally got the courage to escape him. That same apartment he kept me chained up as his prisoner. His "wife". The "mother of his child". His "best friend". All the words he used to describe me. Like I consented to having chains wrapped around my wrists day and night. Having to depend on him for necessities to survive. That's the way he wanted it, though. Depending on him to live another day. He just didn't think I would win. And in the end, I did. I won. And I still win. He's dead. I am no longer his prisoner.

The necklace I wear now has a different texture and when I feel it, I'm brought back to the thoughts of the charm I had before. My forever lost crutch. Never to be seen again. I press my pointer finger and thumb over the flat, smooth surface of the heart shaped charm on this necklace. I move the chain holding it back and forth, back and forth, and slowly fall asleep.

CHAPTER FIVE

HIM

Willow has her head—those soft spiral curls—sprawled about on Bryan's shoulder. That should be *my* shoulder she's sleeping on. He's holding his shoulders stiff, staying completely frozen. Still as a statue. He doesn't want to move a muscle. I'm sure he doesn't want to move because he knows that will wake her up and then she won't be touching him anymore. I guess he'll take what he can get from her right now. Beggars can't be choosers.

I used to be right where he's at. In the very beginning of me and Willow. Taking what I can get. Hoping for more on each date. The less attention she showed me, the more I wanted her. The more attention I showed her, I looked like a desperate asshole. I learned quickly. I enjoy the chase, though. It's a high. It's foreplay to me.

But now I'm putting in all this effort when she's giving me competition. A sloppy competition at that. I bet he couldn't even make her cum. She's probably thinking of me right now.

I know she didn't mean to lay her head on him. Accidents *do* happen. She was asleep and her head just… fell. We're in a tight space, after all. She didn't mean to cheat on me this time. Not like this. No. She's my good girl. And I can't blame him for letting her sleep on him. I would too. That doesn't change the fact that I still want to sneak up behind him—an empty plane besides us three; me, Willow and Bryan—and tilt his head back to slice his throat wide open.

The plane begins slowing down causing me to snap out of my daydream of slicing open Bryan's throat. Have we really been flying long enough to actually…

"Ladies and gentlemen, welcome to New York City. The local time is three forty five PM. For your safety and the safety of those around you, please remain seated with your seat belt fastened and keep the aisles clear until we are parked at the gate." A flight attendant wearing too much makeup to cover up her age—why do women do that?—breathes into the intercom just above my head.

Her voice is soothing. Like she knows she has to talk softly to get people to quiet down to listen closely to what she is saying. That's really the way to do it. To get people's attention. To get what you want. Quiet. Shhhhh. Talk ever so quietly. So, they have to shut the fuck up to hear what you're saying and do as they are told.

Willow catches my eye again, but really, when does she not? She's the reason I'm here. She's the reason I'm on this plane. She's the reason for everything. She turns her head to the side to face Bryan, her new muse, and smiles at him with a desperation to finally get off this plane. She smiles at him like they share a secret already. An inside joke, perhaps. Like they aren't complete strangers. It's a flirty smile. How could she move on from me so fast? She licks her lips. The same lips I want to taste, and more than ever right now. I want to right now. Right. Fucking. Now. It would remind her of who she really wants and who she really needs. Me.

In the wild, the lion lurking to catch its prey would pounce on anything in its way. Running fifty miles an hour, teeth bared, sharp and ready, slobber dripping from its mouth with hunger and a tunnel vision focus to snatch up what's theirs. And they get away with it because they are animals. I am not an animal and neither is Willow, but Bryan is in the way. I really wish the same rules applied to us as people just as they do to animals, so I could pounce on him and devour what's mine right here, right now.

She licks her lips at him. *At him.* I remember when I first met her. She smiled at me like that, and her smile was a beautiful smile. Then she licked those pink, delicious lips at me. Some people say it's the eyes that hypnotize. With her, it was the smile. Innocent. Pure. Full, tasty lips ready to be fucked and sucked. I was immediately hooked on her. Hooked. On. Willow. And now?

Now? She's got a new focus and his name is Bryan. I already hate him. He is preppy. He is pretty. He is taking my Willow away from me.

Not. Gonna. Happen. Bryan. The plane pulls to a complete stop and that same soothing voice comes back on the intercom, escorting us out the door. I take my time 'looking' for my luggage, so my back remains facing her at all times, until we are finally off this plane. I'm a safe distance from her. I know she won't realize I'm here. I'm too far for her to notice me. I grab my luggage and pull it down. The compartment hits me on top of my head. The blow was hard, hurting more than I imagined it would. "Ouch! Goddammit!" I accidently belched louder than I meant to. I keep facing the direction of the luggage and away from her, in hopes that if she hears she doesn't recognize my voice and confront me. She would definitely know I'm here because she is. I wait a few minutes before I check on her. When I turn around she is gone. She's off the plane. I head to do the same.

God. Finally, Fresh air. Room to roam freely. My ass is more numb than my heart felt since the day Willow left me high and dry. But it's not completely shattered and broken into a million pieces anymore because there she is, and here I am. Here we are together. Together in New York City, where the oyster shells were used to pave Pearl Street in the eighteenth century— fun fact— and there are over eight million people here. It's easy to blend in with any crowd whenever and wherever I want, so she doesn't catch me checking in on her when it's needed, which is always because Willow seems to get herself into some seriously sticky situations.

I keep a certain distance behind her. Willow and Bryan walk together because of course they do. Unfortunately, this isn't like it was on the plane, though. I can't hear what they're talking about, but I'm sure it's going something like this. "So, where's your new apartment?" Bryan asks, anxious to find out how close or far apart they live from each other. I know what he has in mind. Fucking her. That's all he cares about. Me, on the other hand? I actually give a shit about her feelings. Will he wake up in the mornings before she does to make her a cup of coffee and bring it to her in bed? No. He won't. He has only one thing in mind.

"The Miller Grill Apartments," Willow will answer. She will tell a complete stranger the exact apartment complex she lives at because she has no boundaries for herself and she is a very stupid girl who trusts strangers too easily. Too quickly. Far too quickly. This is how she ended up with the most untrustworthy, psychotic, stalker types of men. The kind of men you don't want your daughters dating. Not your sisters. Not your mothers Not your grandmas. These types of men don't give a fuck about her boundaries. They lack empathy and don't care who they hurt as long as they get what they want. They usually end up stalking and hurting her. That's not what I'm doing here. Before you base me in that category. I am simply watching over her. I'm protecting her. Especially from men like that. Predators.

I shudder. She deserves better than that. Willow needs a man who will do what I'm doing for her. She deserves to be protected, loved, guarded, and cherished. These are all things I'm willing to do. She just has to open up her heart again to me, to allow me back in.

Willow and Bryan walk side by side, as her name brand purse and small luggage bag covered in book patterns bump up against her back every time she tugs at the straps to hold a little tighter, like they'd leave her if she didn't hold on with all her strength. Like she should have tried more with me. The two bags don't match. They clash, making her look like two separate identities. It's as if there is a name brand Willow, who needs the approval from others, and then there's bookbag Willow who hides her face getting lost in the pages of Gillian Flynn, Lisa Unger and Carolyn Kepnes.

Yes. I know her favorite authors. I also know her favorite body lotion and her favorite latté choice. I bet Bryan won't remember any of those things even if she tells him. The small things. The important things. Those things you can surprise her with to watch her eyes light up and her smile widen with excitement knowing she was thought about on no occasion at all other than because she is who she is. Just because she is Willow. Because she deserves to be thought of at all moments, big or small, and receive gifts for being a very special lady.

When Willow gets to the door at the entrance of the airport Bryan opens it for her and bows his head with his hand spread out like he's a door man with a crush. A crush on Willow. She bats her eyes a little at him, blushes—so much blushing—and shyly thanks him with her head tilting down just a little bit. Oh boy. What a gentleman. Spare me. This is the bare minimum a man can do for a woman. I hope she's not buying into this bullshit nice guy act he's putting on for her right now. It's all an act. That's all it is. An act to get into her pants.

She rolls her eyes just slightly when he doesn't see, though. Yes. That's my girl. Her reaction tells me she knows he's just playing the nice guy right now. She knows he won't always be opening the door for her. Because while Willow can be a very stupid girl, she is also a very smart girl, and I don't think she's going to fall into his arms or bed as quickly as he's hoping she will.

CHAPTER SIX

HIM

Because I know where Willow's apartment is—since, well, I live there too—I decided to go take a little detour so we don't run into each other on our very first day at home. *Our home.* God. I love the sound of that. It makes my heart skip a beat and tightens my chest. In a good way. In a happy way. We're back together. Finally.

Waving my hand, I flag down a taxi.

"Where to?" The driver asks. Oh, he's got that New York City Yankee accent like no other. Definitely born and raised here!

I'm going to a place called Stereotypes Camera Shop on Shuffle Field Drive, but I don't tell him this. Instead, I show him the address on my phone like someone too old to be at a bar showing a picture of their kids or of their nine million cats as a conversation starter on their cell phone to someone who really doesn't give a shit. He's used to all kinds of people, so he doesn't seem annoyed by me not speaking. He nods his head as if to say, "Got it!" and he turns back around to face the steering wheel.

He's got orange-red hair standing up like a perm on top of his head. His full, bushy beard is the same bright color as his hair. He's wearing a button up long sleeved khaki shirt that's too small for him. Showing his hairy—yes, the color matches his perm and beard—chest and protruding belly through the openings in between each button. He shuffles some in his seat. Seeming not to care what other people think. I know he can feel his shirt tightening around him like that. The buttons are about to pop off. He moves his arm up and pushes his sausage finger on the GPS system's speaker button.

"409 Shuffle Field Dr," he commands in his New York City Yankee accent.

I notice a blue baseball cap laying across a laptop in his passenger side seat, and it reminds me that I'm still wearing this stupid fucking baseball cap on top of my head. It got me through it, though. Thanks, Netflix Joe! I pull it off my head, and damn that feels good as the air conditioner hits the beads of sweat dripping on my forehead from the baseball cap. Into my hair the cold air flows. The relief of removing the cap is great and all, but it has begun to feel like a sense of security. I debate on whether I should keep it or lose it. What will I do to feel safe while I'm watching over Willow? I won't get rid of it just yet. I'll think about it for a little bit first. I can't be too impulsive in anything I do when it involves Willow.

With a shake of my head, I let my hair fall into place and scruff it around a bit while looking in my phone camera like it's a mirror. I all of the sudden feel like a bitch doing this. Who really gives a shit about what my hair looks like? I mean, it's not like I have anyone to look good for. Not since Willow left me. So, I stop fidgeting with my Goddamn hair like a schoolgirl and exit the camera on my phone. Instead, I pull up Instagram and I go to my search bar. @Willow1986 is already there, and I click on it. Then I click on her latest update, and zoom in.

Willow is sitting on the living room floor surrounded by moving boxes inside her old Chicago apartment. She holds her hands high up in the air and a big, cheesy grin folded across her pretty face. Her hair is wild, wavy and a little all over the place like she had been too busy packing to keep up with it. She looks happy. Too happy. Her sweater is black and fall colored floral patterns wrap around her upper body. The walls behind her are light blue and so very blank and empty. *Empty just like my soul since the day Willow left me.*

Everything had been taken off the walls and only the Moroccan— fancy way of saying colorful shit—curtains draped to the floor to her left with a brown suede sofa pressed against the empty—empty just like my soul since the day Willow left me— light blue wall sitting behind her along with the pile of moving boxes. Her caption read, "Starting over and you won't be able to find me! (wink face) And I'm selling what's left. Sofa is $300. Barely used! Curtains are $50. All from a non-smoker's home. First dibs get first dibs! Porch pick up only. (green heart emoji)" She signs every online post she makes with a green heart emoji claiming it to be hers. That green heart emoji is hers just like her actual beating heart is mine. I claimed her heart long before Bryan came along. Mine. I scroll down to read the comments.

"Omg! How exciting!" @sherryfelton pretends to be happy for her, even though she is probably, most likely jealous because she doesn't have the guts to start over and move across the country like Willow does.

"WHAT?! Where are you going?" @melindatrikes wants to know because dammit she is just bored and nosey.

"You're leaving me? (sad face)" @morganall pleaded even though they barely even talk to each other.

"Safe travels, honey. You're going to do fascinating things with your life!" @PauleenTilliesMom says because she wants to adopt Willow and replace her with her dead daughter, Tillie. *Oh, come on.* Who doesn't know that story? She plasters it all over Willow's social media pages. Comparing the two—Willow and Tillie—as if they are the exact same person. I know she struggles with the pain of losing her loved ones. I, too, struggle with the pain of losing Willow. But Pauleen is a nut. She's obsessed with Willow. Literally, the woman is obsessed. Sometimes, I get nervous about what lengths she'll go to, just to have Willow in her life.

Willow is nice about it, though. She is always too nice about it, if you ask me. She responds with hearts and sad emojis and all the right things to say to a wacky ass old lady in mourning of her dead daughter and dead husband. Yet she refuses to seek therapy while she takes way too many pills. When will Willow stop feeding into her delusions?

"I call dibs on the sofa!" @chystalr commented without asking how Willow was, where she is going or why. Typical, only caring about the material items and what Willow can do for her.

"Sexy!" @Jeremy says because he is straight up an asshole and thinks that will get her attention. *Fuck off Jeremy.*

More and more and more comments and likes keep piling on. We get it. You all just love her to pieces. Well, so do I but you don't see me on there blowing up her Instagram and harassing her like this. Get a fucking life of your own to be excited about, people.

Willow hadn't made a comment back to anyone — yet — and had only hearted each comment she got on the post. Heart, heart, heart, heart!

"That'll be thirty dollars," the taxi driver interrupted my thoughts with that New York City Yankee accent of his. And boy, was I in a trance. Reading into the life of Willow is a catchy little story. It's my favorite story to read. I get lost in the book of Willow. What she'll do next. What's going on in her mind. What she likes to share with the world while I'm seeing firsthand the things she does day to day. And what she keeps to herself. It's breathtaking. I get lost in it all.

Oh shit! We're already here? I didn't even notice the car stopping. Ran smooth as silk on this ride to the camera shop. The image of Willow didn't help. I look again. Her stomach showing a little with her hands held up high in the air in this picture had me in a tunnel vision of sex. I took a screenshot of the full picture and tapped the 'x' button to exit Instagram.

The taxi driver had turned half his body with his head facing towards me, staring me down with his big doe blue eyes. He reminds me of a cartoon character. Thirty dollars is a lot of money for a damn ride to a camera shop, though. I tip him well, too. Ten bucks. Forty fucking dollars for a one way trip? Shit. He got a steal out of me! My new at home job might not pay enough for me to be hailing fucking taxis all the time. I might need to actually get a car. I've gotta have a way to get around and go with Willow when she leaves. What if she just decides one day, on a whim, to go shopping, and I'm not prepared because I have to depend on a taxi, and wait for them to arrive? It'll for sure blow my cover. She'd see me. I'm buying a car.

I decided to let go of my sense of security because I won't be needing it anymore. We're in New York City. A place easy to blend in with the crowd. I leave the baseball cap I wore—goodbye Netflix Joe!—in the taxicab. It was a five dollar hat that I bought at a secondhand store in Chicago. Someone else will be happy to have it. One man's trash is another man's treasure, so the saying goes.

It's time to focus on what's really important. Willow. Willow is not my trash and she is absolutely not going to be Bryan's treasure.

CHAPTER SEVEN

HIM

I live on the first floor of The Miller Grill Apartments because Willow lives on the first floor of The Miller Grill Apartments. I'm lucky. My window is diagonal from hers. I can see right in her whole fucking living space from my window. I'm thrilled with how this worked out in my favor. I did my homework right. When you do your homework, stay up late to study, and pay close attention to every little detail, you get an A on the test. I got myself an A plus on this one.

At the camera shop I picked up a 200-500mm zoom lens for my Nikon camera. I zoom in so I can get a close up vision of her place. She's changed the way she decorates her flat this go around. All the details that make her who she is. Or, at least, who she wants people to see her as. Willow is sort of a plain jane person on the interior, but she shows much different on the exterior.

Her last apartment was Moroccan style. She had fancy colorful doorknobs on every single cabinet and drawer in her kitchen. Light blue, dark pink, burnt orange walls. Chandeliers that fell from the ceilings colored in light blue, dark pink and burnt orange just like her walls, but the opposite of colors. If the wall was dark pink, the chandelier would be burnt orange. If the wall was light blue, the chandelier would be hot pink. And so on and so on. Each room was like Easter day had thrown up in there. My eyes had to adjust to it every time I walked in, but Willow absolutely loved it. Every last bit of it. She shows an eccentric exterior like that. She likes to show her taste, leave her mark everywhere she goes, and she loves to be adored and receive compliments by the dozens. The more attention she can get, the better she feels about herself.

Me, on the other hand. I enjoy the simpler things in life. I'd rather blend in with the crowd, not stand out. Give me black. Hand me down the bare necessities, and I'm as happy as can be as long as Willow is by my side.

Now, Willow's apartment is all hippy dippy type of shit. Which is not that much different than the Moroccan style she was trying to pull off in Chicago. She did pull it off, and now she'll pull off the hippy dippy style in New York City because while Willow is a very stupid girl, she is also a very smart girl and she's always able to fade into whatever scene she is trying to imitate. She's like a chameleon fading into the crowd of the bark from a tree it sits upon to hide away from predators crunching leaves through the forest as it makes its way and moves past her. *Crunch.* She turns back to her natural color a little too quickly though, thinking it's safe. She gets snatched the fuck up before she even realizes it.

The view inside the depths of Willow's apartment is like catching a glimpse of what she's like without having an audience. Willow always intends to have an audience. Except inside her home. You can't get any more private than that. She intends to gather fans based on her performance. When she doesn't know she has an audience and is being her authentic self, I become her number one fan of all time.

If she only knew, that when she's not trying so hard, that's when she's the most beautiful. When she wakes up in the mornings, not a lick of makeup covers her face. Her hair is knotted and messy from a hardcore night of sleep. Tossing and turning in her bed. Walking to the kitchen to grab a bottle of water with sleep still in her eyes, yawning without covering her mouth. Alone, she lets it all hang out. The real, raw Willow with nobody there to put on a show for. I live for this shit. I set my alarm each morning to wake up at the same time as her, so we wake up side by side. Literally. And always, we always have a full day ahead of us together.

We've been living in our new apartment for a few days now, and Willow has got her apartment all decked out. Colorful tapestries hang on her new walls. She's even got one in big, bold words that reads, "HIPPY DIPPY DOO YOU, BOO," and I wish I could *do you, boo*. To be able to caress her naked back as she lay on her belly, with the thin sheet covering only her ass and down. Feeling her soft bare skin. Every inch. Every curve. Sliding inside of her to hear her gasp and moan just one last time. *Please, just one more time.* But I have to wait my turn again because right now she is focused on Bryan. But Bryan isn't worthy of her time. He's no good for Willow. He's the predator lurking, peeking through the leaves, hiding slyly while Willow thinks it's safe. Sweet, sweet, naive Willow. She doesn't have an inkling of what Bryan is capable of.

Bryan has got a thing or two to learn. I looked him up on Google after following him to his apartment only three blocks away from here. *Great.* They can just walk to see each other. It's that easy! My imagination runs wild at this thought. I picture Willow all dolled up, wearing my favorite sweater. The oversized one with the off the shoulder porn I like. Her soft, blonde curls will fall around her face and she'll wear red lipstick to make him think of kissing her. More will go through his mind. He'll feed her. They'll fuck. He'll think he has her forever. But it's not that simple.

It's not. It won't be and not because of me. Because of him. While doing my research, I found that Bryan has a long history of being handcuffed and thrown into a jail cell like an animal. *He is an animal.* Bryan has a temper. He doesn't know how to take no for an answer. Bryan is a predator. He's the guy your mom and dad warn you about when they tell you to lock your doors at night before you go to bed. He's the boogie man waiting to devour his prey. While Willow is a very stupid girl, she's also a very smart girl. I know she knows what he wants. Bryan wishes he could do you, boo, but he's not going to get to do you, boo. His rap sheet is longer than his one eyed snake. He goes to the bar within walking distance and drinks by himself. Poor Bryan. This guy is a walking disaster and a fucking loser. This guy is not for Willow.

CHAPTER EIGHT

WILLOW

I'm in a new state. A new city. With a new life. And I am a brand spanking new me. Plopped down on my fluffy, clean, white sofa in my new apartment, I think of all the opportunities headed my way! My new place is a studio apartment smack dab in New York City. It's so alive over here. It's not the country, but I still hear the birds chirping in the mornings. It is the city of all cities, so I also hear the hustle and bustle of people ushering each other out of the way to get to their nine to five jobs. A mix of both worlds.

I have a feeling that I'll fall in love with my new life. A fresh start. I'm still Willow, of course, but I can be whoever and however I want to be now. With no expectations or obligations to anyone but myself. I clock into my new job as a transfer Journalist from Chicago in five days. Just five days! I don't really have to work because the book that was written about my captivity with Neil and Brock brings in plenty of money to pay my monthly rent, bills and then some, but I have got to stay busy because I think I might get bored and get into a little bit of trouble if I don't have a job to go to. I know this about myself. I'm fully aware that I can be quite self-destructive. Just take a look at my past. Full of abusive boyfriends, neglectful parents, and bad decisions.

Maybe I'll actually start going to therapy now that I have a chance to start over and love myself the way I should have been doing all along. I'll have time for it. Choosing a part time job, I know I'll be able to have sanity and not work my life away, like so many of us have to do just to survive. That used to be my life. Now I will have plenty of extra time, but extra time means Bryan time now because I need to get my focus off Diego, Cold Hands The Famous Bearer who won't stop texting and calling me.

My phone chimes at me. *Ding!*

Diego, Cold Hands The Famous Bearer
Why won't you talk to me?
Ding!
What have I done to deserve this shit?
Ding!
What the FUCK is your problem?
Ding!
I fucking HATE you!
Ding!
You stupid fucking bitch!
Ding!
Willow, please just talk to me…
Ding!
Fine! FUCK YOU!
Ding!
I'm sorry!
Ding!
I don't mean any of that. I really don't. Please just talk to me.

Ding! Ding! Ding! Ding!

My heart pounds with anxiety as I read each text from him while the new ones just keep on coming in. I can barely get through reading one text he sends me before the ding sound echoes throughout my apartment, and the new text message covers the one I'm already trying to take in. *Please, just leave me the hell alone.* I get it. He's hurting. I suppose I'm to blame for that. The old Willow would console him, tell him what he wants to hear, and damn near submit to his instructions. That Willow is gone now. The new Willow doesn't ignore my gut feelings, people please, and put my feelings aside. I come first this time.

My palms sweat and that makes my phone overheat, so I set it down, face down on the coffee table. The coffee table I just put together in my new living room yesterday, in this new city, and new state, and new life to be a very new me. How can I be a very new me if my past keeps on knocking?

Ding! Ding! Ding! Ding! Ding! Ding!

Picking my phone back up, my heart pounds with the blood rushing in my ears. Fear creeps up my spine, like he could bust through my door at any moment and kidnap me to hold me captive. Have me chained up in Dubai. Just like Sally Field, just like I was with Brock. I put my phone on silent before I read his last text messages.

Diego, Cold Hands, The Famous Bearer
You broke my fucking heart Willow and you won't get away with this.
You stupid fucking bitch!

I block him. Then I unblock him because I'm scared of what he might do once he realizes he's been blocked. My overthinking gets the best of me sometimes. And sometimes my overthinking saves me. I realize how absurd this may sound to you but put yourself in my shoes. If he realizes he has no way of contacting me through texting, the possibility of him showing up at my apartment is more likely. That's my logic, and I'm sticking to it.

Instead of sitting around panicking over what ifs, I go ahead and send a text to someone else because my mom always told me that the best way to get over a guy is to get under a new guy. That's one of the best pieces of advice she's ever handed down to me.

Me
Hey you.

Bryan

How's the new apartment coming along?

Me
Why don't you come see?

Bryan
Oh yeah?

Me
Yeah.

Bryan
On my way!

CHAPTER NINE

HIM

I gaze down at my watch. Nine o' clock PM shines intensely in my eyes, like someone flashed the brights of their car in my face. Rubbing my eyes, I yawn. My reflection glares back at me from the face of my smart watch reminding me just how tired and shitty I look from all the hard work I've put into our relationship today, but I don't go to sleep until Willow goes to sleep.

Once upon a time we had a matching routine. Every night we went to bed at the same time and spooned each other until we fell asleep. I didn't mind being the little spoon sometimes, but I held her in my arms most nights. Running my fingers through her hair until I could hear her snoring. That was always the sign my job was done correctly. Willow would be fast asleep and my arm would go numb—almost as numb as my heart has felt since the day Willow left me—but I would stay laying in the same position. Not wanting to wake her from a good night's rest. I miss those nights. I miss Willow.

Willow has on fluffy, warm looking socks and has her feet propped up on her outside balcony ottoman. She's wearing a matching black and green floral patterned pajama set that is form fitting, showing her curves. Her hair is pulled to one side of her head resting at her chest, leaving the other side of her head empty. *Empty just like my soul since the day Willow left me.* She looks angelic as the balcony lights make a perfect spotlight on her. My beautiful angel.

The image of her dressed as a slutty angel on a crisp Halloween night, spreading her fake, white, wings full of the softest feathers runs through my mind. I entertain the thought some more and imagine her wearing a thin, velvet choker and lingerie that her tits and ass fall out of, leaving not much else to the imagination. As I have a handful of Willow's plump ass and one of her perky tits in my mouth I'm interrupted from my wet dream by a squirrel that hops from a nearby tree onto the ledge of my balcony, chewing on a nut. *At least someone is getting a nut around here.*

She holds her phone up to her face and the glare from the screen shows a glitter in her pretty almond shaped brown eyes. She smiles to herself as she reads on to whatever the fuck she's reading. Her sliding glass door opens. She turns her head, and her blonde curls bounce with her movement. They always bounce when she moves and so do her tits. *Those tits are mine.* She smiles again. Except this time her smile is wider than it was when she was just looking at her phone. I wonder what's got her smiling like this. I know that smile. That smile is the one she uses when she's feeling flirty. I move my camera and zoom in the direction she's smiling and I see him.

There Bryan stood. *Bryan.*

Willow? When the fuck did this happen? How did I miss this? How the fuck could she do this to me? It's one thing to flirt in a goddamn airport. It's a whole new level to invite him over to her place, though. I didn't think she would be so easy and sleazy. He's holding two mugs of hot, steaming liquid for the two of them. Probably not her favorite, like I would make for us. It hasn't even been enough time for him to find out her favorite drink anyway. Even if he had, I have a feeling he wouldn't care enough to remember it. It's very specific. She is very specific. Only someone who truly cares is going to put the effort into remembering special details that make her happy. He hasn't been around long enough to care. He'll just pretend to give a shit until he gets what he wants.

He hands her one of the mugs, and smiles at her. I can see she tells him thank you because I can read her lips through the bad ass zoom on this Nikon. Is this their first date? Willow in her pajamas at home. Bryan in another stupid fucking turtleneck sweater. He's making the two of them hot cocoa in *her* kitchen like it's *their* kitchen and bringing it out on *her* balcony like it's *their* balcony.

Bryan smiles back at her—smug—and I pull out my phone. I dig through my internet history and click on Mugshots dot com and find his smug mug. A skinnier Bryan just eleven months ago was detained for possession of a controlled substance and boy does he look fancy—so preppy--in his orange jumpsuit! Three months before that? Harassment charges. Ha! Someone didn't want him around them at all. A little fine print shows that he broke a restraining order. What a catch Willow chose this go around.

His face is slack in this mugshot, drained of whatever fight he had in him to be harassing someone who apparently did not want his attention anymore. My guess is an ex-girlfriend. It's always an ex-girlfriend. Isn't that the way it goes, though? Boy meets girl. Boy falls for girl. Boy harasses girl. Aren't there any real love stories left out there? Or do they all end up the same? In some type of travesty. A divorce. A death. A desperation to get the hell away from each other. Someone sure was desperate to get away from Bryan.

Six months before that? Harassment charges. In this mugshot, his eyes pierce the camera with anger and the glare from the flash gives him red, demon eyes. His chin tilts up and presses outwards like one of the police officers had just said something to him that he felt was unjustified. *It probably was justified to say.* Hell, at that point, the cops could turn a blind eye at an ass whooping from a jail bird, and it would be justified. Bryan doesn't seem to learn from his lessons. The consequences aren't enough to keep on the straight and narrow. He keeps making the same shitty decisions.

Three months before that? Assault causes bodily injury to a family member—another way of saying he beats up women—and... ding, ding, ding! You guessed it, harassment charges. Cocky, cocky, cocky as *fuck* is how he looks in this one. Like he is untouchable. Bryan knows no boundaries. Consequences don't matter to him. Clearly. He has nothing to lose, so who cares if his next step is to kill a woman? I don't put it past him. He's got a whole record proving he's definitely capable.

Jesus fucking Christ. Was it the same woman he was harassing or were they all different women? Either way, this guy is a walking red flag and Willow, well, has she ever fucking heard of Google? Because after all she has been through with the men she's dated in her past you'd think the first thing she would do is Google a man she has even just a slight bit of interest in. It's not *hard* to find these things out. Hello! We're in 2023, where everything is approachable right at our fingertips online, but she doesn't do that because Willow is a very stupid girl. Does she want this, though? Is this what she really craves? Dating the same man over and over just in a different disguise? She appears to go after the same type of guy over and over again. Did she google him, find these things out and just sweep it under the rug like it's not a serious fucking pattern Bryan has with women? Maybe Willow has a death wish. Does she want to be punished? Does she think she deserves this? She can't possibly value herself this low on the totem pole. No. She's gotta have higher standards and better boundaries.

Then again, Willow also has a certain type of pattern with men. Does she think they're the same? That they're cut from the same cloth? How could she even begin to categorize herself with a junkie woman beater who can't take no for an answer? While Willow is a very stupid girl she is also a very smart girl. I know she doesn't actually think she deserves this shit. It's only been twelve days since we moved into our new apartment, and she invites the junkie woman beater harasser over? Has she not learned anything after all she's been through? Does she really want more of it?

Feeling sorry for her only lasts a few seconds and is replaced by a rage like no other. I want to march over there and demand my justice. Instead of sneaking up behind Bryan and tilting his head back to slice his throat wide open, I want to do it from the front. So, I can look into his eyes as life drains from his face. I want to feel his body fall slack into my arms. My eyes will stay locked on his, piercing into his soul, and I'll smile as he takes his last breath while I drop him to the floor to watch a pool of blood surround him. The intense hunger of it all is a satisfaction that I'm unwilling to let go of. Witnessing his blood cover that ugly ass fucking turtleneck sweater. Leaving a stain of a life once lived. What a fulfilling fantasy. It's just not enough, though. A fantasy is just that. It's nothing real until you put it into action. I want to feel what it's like to win this game.

Afterwards, I'll go wash the mug he was drinking out of and put it back with the rest of her mugs in her cupboard. Willow loves her coffee mugs, so I won't throw that one away like I would want to, but I am not drinking from it. I'll grab one that suits me and join Willow on the couch, so we can both drink her favorite hot drink that I'll batch up for us. We'll watch holiday Hallmark movies together while Bryan wilts away. 'Tis the season!

Bye-bye Bryan.

But I digress. That is not part of the plan. I know this, and yet I know I will still fantasize about it every time I see Bryan because I know I will see him again. Willow doesn't know how to be single. She doesn't know how to just *be*. If it's not Bryan in her arms, it'll be someone else. I promise you that. She doesn't ever give being single a chance. Willow can't stand the thought of being in her own solitude. Some people are like that. Afraid of their own company. The misery that lies between you and your own thoughts is too much to handle. It's easier to fill the silence with a stranger sitting beside you pretending to give a shit.

I know I'll be seeing them both flaunt their new fling with each other right in front of my fucking face. Tonight is not the night that I wait for Willow to go to bed before I go to bed because Willow will be going to bed with Bryan.

I set my Nikon camera down on the couch side table, head to bed and pull out my phone as soon as I rest my head on the pillow.

CHAPTER TEN

WILLOW

Ding!
Diego Cold hands, The Famous Bearer
Is all of this because you met somebody else?

I sigh. Apparently too loudly catching Bryan's attention. As he gives me a look I can't quite decipher, asking, "Are you okay?" In reality, does he truly want to know if I'm okay, or does he want to know why I sighed? My lips go thinner and thinner. Disappearing into each other. The rawest answer I have would scare him off.

Why? No biggie. I only jumped straight into a relationship with a guy I met at a beach after a traumatic event that I hadn't really recovered from just yet. No back story there with the guy at the beach. Just pure lust mistaken for feelings. Now that I've broken up with him he won't leave me alone. I did this. I did this right after I recovered from a hospital visit after being found beaten and bloody in a field. The field outside of Brock's townhome. The same one he held me hostage in. I was beaten by Brock for gaining his trust and only to finally be able to escape. His hope was to halt me from ever leaving. Strangers found me bloody from Brock kicking my stomach over and over again with his steel toe boots to cause my abortion. The rights to my own body were taken away. I was forced into pregnancy by Brock. I didn't want to have a baby. I never wanted to be a mother. But it was my choice to make when and how I would get rid of the problem. He took all those rights away from me and turned me into a kept woman. I'm partly to blame for all of this.

I was stupid enough to think a man who would help me cheat on my husband could be a prized winner. And there you have it, I cheated on my husband. My husband, Neil, wasn't a good man. He also didn't necessarily deserve to die. Or did he? I struggle with that. I killed him. I locked him and Brock in the townhome that was set on fire. I walked away, and I never told a soul that I could have let Neil leave with me and let him live. But I don't say any of that.

"My ex." I shake my head and set my phone down away from me.

I curl my legs up in a ball behind me on the couch in my living room and turn towards Bryan. He's here for me. He's right here right now. He's real and in the flesh. He's actually here, listening with hopefully no ulterior motives. Don't we all have motives, though? I just hope his are more pure than the men in my past.

Bryan scratches the back of his head. Lusting over his clean, full, thick dark hair, I imagine grabbing ahold of it and pushing his face down in between my legs. Let him taste me. I'm heated in between just thinking about it. It sure would make me feel a lot better right now.

"That bad, huh?" Bryan asks.

He takes a drink of his hot cocoa and peers at me over the rim of the mug waiting for me to answer. I don't want to tell him too much.

"I mean, yeah. He's blowing my phone up. I broke up with him because I moved here to start over. I don't mean to sound harsh. I really don't, but he's not part of my new life. Ya know?" I hope he knows. I hope he gets it.

"Yeah." He sets the mug down on the coffee table. "I do get it, Willow. More than you realize." Is he just saying that to make me feel better?

Less alone. Or am I too jaded to believe someone could actually care? Bryan might give a shit. Maybe he's not just appeasing me.

"And no." He interrupts my inner battle. "I'm not just saying that to make you feel better." His eyebrows rise, like he's reading my thoughts.

He truly does get it. *Calm down, Willow.* It's too soon to get attached.

As he moves closer to me on the couch my heart begins to pound with a smitten feeling and a touch of anxiety. He's so close I smell the chocolate on his breath when he says, "Is there anything I can do to help?"

I tense up. I tense up because I know what I want him to do to help me right now. Touch me. Whisper in my ear that you're mine. Grab me by the throat and Demand that I'm yours. Kiss me softly, gently. Then kiss me hard. Tell me that you'll protect me. Now, feel how wet I am just thinking about this.

All of that, though... All those things I so badly want him to do right now are just temporary fulfillments. They're so untrue to the both of us because it would be too fast, and people don't mean anything they do when they act too fast unless it is just sex. I need to slow it the fuck down because it's getting heated in here by us only eye fucking each other. I'm not exactly ready for anything more than eye fucking. Yet.

"Well, I don't know," I say and fiddle with my necklace. "I think just having someone to listen to me. That helps me in a way. Ya know?" To gauge his reaction, I glance his way. A little sigh of relief comes out of me because I did good. I fought my urge to take him right here on my brand new couch in this new state, in this new city, in this new life because I am a new me. I smile to myself because his reaction is a slow, knowing nod. He gets it.

"So," I begin, drawing out the 'o' sound like I always do. Why do I always do that? "Anyway, what about you? You got any crazy, stalker exes I should be worried about?" I laugh about this like it's funny or something. It's not funny. I pick up my mug of hot cocoa but it's not so hot anymore, so I take it to the microwave to heat it up.

"She was a basket case."

Great. I roll my eyes as he strolls along behind me. Men who call their exes crazy are usually the real crazy ones.

"Uh. I mean…" He clears his throat. Clearly trying to come back from that. He probably realizes he's already messed up. "She just had a little bit of a hard time adjusting to some things," he continues.

Adjusting to what things?

"To the move." Okay, is he reading my fucking mind?

"I wanted to move here. She didn't. She wanted to stay in Texas. She was emotional about it. She started picking fights all the time." He carries on.

"And that makes her a basket case?" I pull my hot cocoa out of the microwave, so it would quit beeping at me.

"Well, no, not necessarily," he answers.

"But she did start to get violent towards the end." He looks away and shakes his head, mourning the memories of her.

Carefully, I sit my mug down on the counter to free my hand and place it over my heart. I feel bad now. "Oh, Bryan. I'm so sorry. I didn't mean to pry and bring up bad memories."

"No. No. It's okay. You're okay. You're a sweetheart." He gives me a half smile and that's when I notice he has a dimple on his left cheek. I love dimples. "Your empathy turns me on." He changes the tone in his voice to flirty.

"You aren't like her, are you, Willow?" He breathes the words into my ear as he steps up right behind me.

Skin on skin. He must have sensed the sexual tension from earlier and hasn't let it go, like me. My belly presses up against the kitchen island countertop. He rubs his hands up my bare arms just slightly, barely touching me with his fingertips. Just enough to give me goosebumps, and it literally sends shivers up and down my spine—the good kind, not like with Diego, Cold Hands The Famous Bearer.

"I don't think you're like that, Willow. I think you're better than that. I think you're the prize, baby girl," he whispers in my ear.

His chin hangs over my shoulder and he moves his face to my hair. I could melt. He breathes me in with a big gulp. *Gulp.*

"Show me who you are, Willow." He breathes in my ear again keeping his voice low and soft and so *Goddamn perfect right now*.

"I wanna know you." He whispers, as he grabs hold of both my arms, with his veiny hands. Tattoos cover both of them. They're the meaningful kind of tattoos, not the random patchy kind. His body remains pressed up against my back.

What part of me do you wanna know, Bryan?

I tense up again and he laughs a little, like it's a game. I suppose it is a game. He grabs my hips with his veiny, tatted up hands, and turns me around to face him.

"Look at me," he urges.

He grabs my chin to move my face in the direction of his and looks directly into my eyes. And—*Oh. My. Gosh.*—I am in a trance.

"Don't be nervous, Willow." He breathes, gently.

So gently, smooth. A smooth talker like Brock used to be.

"I can tell you've been through some things. That you're still going through some things right now. You're tense, but it's okay. I'm not going to hurt you. You can trust me."

Why would I trust him? I just met him. His eyes bring me into a trance, though. Like hypnosis.

Bryan–Do as I say.

Me–Okay.

They wander from my eyes to the crook of my neck. He licks his lips, then his eyes wander slowly down the rest of my body, and again he undresses me with his piercing green eyes. Up and down. Up and down. His eyes make their way–just as slowly as they did moving down my body–back up to meet my eyes. He makes an mmmmm sound like I am already tasty to him.

"You are something else, Willow. You know that, right? You are something special. You know that, don't you? I can tell and I can wait for you. I can wait for as long as you need me to. You have to know how special you are to me."

Why is he saying he can wait for me when I've only known him for less than two weeks? Like there's a beast inside of him that he has to tame. Isn't there a beast to tame in all of us, though? We just don't usually vocalize it. I see that as a red flag. Then again… I like this red flag because this red flag is turning me the fuck on.

So, with my chin held high and confidence flooding me, I say to him, "Don't be so sure that I want you to wait." Even though I think I said this with confidence, I'm not so sure *he* thinks I said this with confidence. Does he know that if he just barely touches me with his fingertips like that again that I will actually melt?

His—Oh. My. Gosh.—piercing green eyes light up. A flicker of fun goes through his mind. Like he just thought of what it would be like fucking me. He tilts his head to the side and wears a look of pure satisfaction on his face like this is a cat and mouse game. He is the cat and I am the mouse. Even though I know what happens when the cat finally catches the mouse, I fucking love being the mouse.

"No, Willow. I want to wait." *I think he knows I'll melt.*

"I wanna wait until we can't take it any longer. You know? Until the tension builds up way too much and we just have to unleash like *Goddamn animals* and fucking *devour* each other." He bites his lower lip and licks it like he wants to lick me.

"Willow." The way he says my name is delicious. Like an expensive slice of triple chocolate cake that my mouth waters for. I like the idea of teasing each other until we can't take it any longer. The buildup before the ultimate orgasm. He presses his body up against mine again, and I can feel him growing down there. I blush and look away from his eyes. He gently puts his hand on my face and glides his fingertips until they're under my chin. His hand is soft. He moves my face tilting it towards his, so he can look me directly in my eyes again.

"Look at me, Willow." He says my name like it's a breath of fresh air to him. The way he breathes my name, *"Willow."* I die every time he does it. He pulls me into him harder and breathes me in again, then takes in another big gulp. *Gulp.* He gently releases me without breaking eye contact. I watch as he backs up just a little bit and tucks his hands in the front pockets of his jeans —reminding me of Neil—and leans his back against the kitchen counter. He pierces my soul again with his—Oh. My. Gosh.—deep ass green eyes and I remind myself he is not Neil .

"Waiting and letting it all build up and getting to know you." He gives me a little crooked half smile. "And I mean really getting to know the real you is what I want with you. With us. *For us*. We don't have to move fast."

He doesn't know it, but this makes me want him even more right now. His patience to have me is more of a turn on than if he were to actually grab me and take me the way I want him to. The way I feel a hunger for him is animalistic.

God. I want to collapse right now. He is perfect. He is different. This will be good. This will be *so* good.

Stop that, Willow! I straighten up my body a little, enough to feel like I've gained my consciousness back, but not too much to make him think I'm putting on a show because I had indeed, melted into his arms. I won't be fooled again. I won't let lust be confused with something deeper. Focus. Focus. Focus.

CHAPTER ELEVEN

WILLOW

New York City is a lot like Chicago in the sense that there are so many activities within walking distance and so many people walking within this walking distance to be able to just blend right in. I like that people don't ask me about Neil here. I like that I don't have to force tears in a conversation around people who are *hashtag team Neil*. Chicago is no small town where everyone knows your name and history, but when you're known as the woman who fought through fire—literally—to escape being a prisoner of a sex crazed monster—-monsters, Brock *and* Neil— well then, you're definitely getting the spotlight of your trauma by everyone on the block you live on, and the square you shop in and dine at. The worst of all, your favorite little coffee shop.

"My condolences," is all I heard after Neil died—well, after I killed him— everywhere I went. He was a true haunting. Like a fucking poltergeist I couldn't get rid of. Like a ghost that doesn't show its face, but you can feel the presence lingering in the corner. Pitying glances pierced my way from every direction. I couldn't *breathe* in Chicago. I had to get out of there. I had to get away. Far away.

One of the reasons I chose to live at *The Miller Grill Apartments* is because I love to have a quaint little coffee shop within walking distance of my home. Just like I had in Chicago. I never did care that much for the big coffee chains. They're overpriced and all look the same on the inside and outside. A cute little coffee shop down the road from my apartment and on the square is what I live for.

I may be a brand new me, but I have my habits that I'm not letting go of. This coffee shop is just my style. It's got a vintage vibe to it. Chaise lounge chairs made of blue, green, orange and pink velvet to choose from as a little temporary getaway with matching ottomans to prop up my feet or if I decide, to sit on it without leaning against the back. I indulge in the luxury of this vintage vibe and my vanilla latté with two extra shots of espresso and *no milk*. The last time I stood inside a coffee shop I had to rush out to get to freedom, New York City. I had been followed by my past and it wasn't letting me go. This time I get to sit in the lounge and take in the beauty of all that surrounds me. I gaze around in awe. It's just like the pictures I saw online before I put the deposit down on my apartment. I'm right where I'm supposed to be.

I browse online, going through all the social media platforms to kill time and relax a little before heading into work. My first day at work as a Journalist in New York City! This will be one hell of a ride. I'm nervous and I can feel the butterflies fluttering around in the pit of my stomach, so I focus on what other people have going on in their lives, and what they're overly sharing with the world today.

On TikTok, Brandie McGee, who I went to high school with, is blowing the fuck up. I am so proud of her because this is what she has always wanted! She is going viral since she knows how to dance. Brandie *really* knows how to dance. The woman was hot. I gotta hand it to her and she's in great shape. Within each TikTok she posts her smile looks a little wider and her confidence shows a little more. I liked Brandie McGee in high school, so I silently congratulated her and clicked to heart her latest post. *You go girl!*

On Instagram, Harley Mitchell, who I also went to high school with, shows off the fact that she is now an influencer for *Shine Bright Like a Diamond*. A little boutique that carries over-priced bling purses, bling platform flip flops, bling shirts, bling blue jean skirts, bling baseball caps, bling gaudy jewelry, bling everything to s*hine bright like a diamond*. In every picture she posts she is posing like she is some sort of a celebrity model. She is pretty. But she's a snob. She thinks she is better than everyone else. The bitch always has. She is perfect for them to use as a model to advertise their apparel, but I didn't really like Harley Mitchell from high school so I definitely won't heart any of her posts.

On X, Preston Peterson—what a stupid name he changed it to, to sound, in his words, legit and more professional. How? How does this sound legit and more professional? His real name was Christopher Phiber. Both names are stupid! I might be biased because I don't like Christopher/Preston. Anyway... He lectures all of us about politics and how being a Liberal or a Republican is labeling yourself and setting yourself up for expectations that you can't meet and blah blah blah blah. He rambles and rambles. In every single one of his posts, he looks like a total douchebag with a shit eating grin thinking he knows better and more than everyone else. He was like this in High school, too.

On Facebook, Maria Moore, who I also went to high school with, never shows her face and only posts videos and pictures of her four little boys who *get into all kinds of mischief.* She posts so much about them. Never about herself. Her profile name may as well be changed to The Moore Boys page. I honestly wonder why she hasn't changed her profile name to that yet. *Yet.* With each post she makes, she types up an entire paragraph about their day–multiple times a day–and she doesn't use any punctuation. That drives me absolutely fucking crazy.

"My little Brandon got into the pantry today and ate all the sour cream pringles which are my favorite (sad face) and when I told him no don't do that, give them to me now, he just laughs and tells me no. Motherhood is so hard but these times make me laugh but how do I get him to stop telling me no all the time? - Hashtag boymom." Maria actually types out hashtag instead of using the pound sign like everyone else does online.

As any normal fucking human being should. She annoys me. I think she does it on purpose to agitate people. As if scrolling through your timeline on Facebook to see every other post is of the Moore boys isn't annoying enough.

Her kids are cute, but they're also bratty and it reminds me of how thankful I am to Brock for kicking my stomach over and over again to cause my abortion. I hate him, but I silently thank the dead piece of shit. *Salute.*

An alarm goes off on my phone and spreads across the Facebook post I was just reading. It rings nine twenty-five in my ears. That's my reminder to head to work in a taxi, so I can arrive at my first day of work at ten o' clock AM, sharp.

I exit all the apps on my phone to save battery. Smiling, I reach for my latté and book bag from the table sitting next to me and make my way towards the door until I notice a familiarity in the air that doesn't feel quite right. I hear a voice, two voices, talking about me behind my back. Quickly, I turn around and squint my eyes to peer around the room. When I see them, my heart skips a beat and sinks to the pit of my stomach. My body tenses up in a state of shock. A fight or flight. Silent, I freeze in the spot I stand in.

Brock and Neil sit together, right across from one another. Chatting it up like old buddies or something. Like they were friends when they were alive and this hang out session is second nature to them. They each hold a latté of their own, and they talk about me like I can't hear them. Like I can't see them. Like I'm not even here. Like they're the ones alive and I'm the one who is dead.

What the actual fuck? I glance around the room in hopes that anyone else is noticing this but they aren't. I'm the only one. Everyone else is just going on about their business. Drinking their coffees and acting like there aren't two rotting dead bodies talking to each other in the lounge area. Neil and Brock aren't transparent like people imagine ghosts to be. Loose skin droops from Neil's face. *Stretchy.* Pulling a piece of the malleable skin from his bones, his teeth chatter uncontrollably. Swollen blood red gums spring out of his mouth as he chomps on his words.

"She really does think she got away with it." Neil's voice booms loud thundering throughout the coffee shop like it's bouncing off one wall and hitting another. It's as if it's the only sound in the building and it demands to be heard by all. He has his legs crossed and propped on top of the green ottoman as he sits on the matching velvet green chaise lounge chair.

My phone dings and I quickly take a look, seeing a text message from Diego, Cold Hands The Famous Bearer. But I ignore him. I shake my head to make the hallucinations of my two dead exes disappear. I look back in the direction they were sitting together and they are still there. What? How? This cannot be happening right now. Nobody else can see this?

"Oh yeah she does, but she doesn't have a clue what she's got coming to her." Brock laughs, and that too thunders throughout the coffee shop bouncing off one wall and hitting another demanding my attention over Neil's and any other sound clanging in the background.

Except, instead of a laugh it's more like a cackle. His head tilts back and his mouth is unnaturally wide open like a joker or a clown. The skin on his face turns more red by the second. He sits on the blue chaise lounge chair, just across from Neil and they both roar with laughter together like this is some sort of joke. A sick joke. Neil's pupils dilate and the whites of his eyes disappear. Springing his head in my direction, it wobbles for a few seconds like there are no bones in his neck.

"Look! There the bitch is!" He calls out to Brock. The movement of Brock's head is fast—unnaturally fast—as he turns it to face me. It's like the girl on The Exorcist. Almost moving in a complete circle. Neil's cackle bleeds my ears like a thousand hyena howling in the near distance. He points at me and raises his eyebrows, then cackles even harder. Holding his hand over his stomach like he can hardly contain himself from laughter, he howls out and the stench from his breath dances towards me causing me to gag.

Brock wears those same steel toe boots he used to kick my stomach over and over again to cause my abortion. I still thank him silently. Even in this fucked up bizarre situation that's happening to me right now. I wonder if it's real. This can't be real. Brock's face is more red now than it was just a second ago. His skin begins boiling like the pot of noodles that sat on the stove in his townhome apartment—the one he chained me up in before I splashed the boiling noodle water all over his face the day I escaped. His face doesn't look like a face anymore because all his skin starts peeling off and dripping to the floor at his feet. Landing right at his steel toe boots. *Splat!* Another piece of his skin falls to the floor by his boots. The same ones he wore while he kicked me over and over again to cause my abortion. Swaying, I begin to feel dizzy. Foggy headed. The room spins. I drop my latté. Vanilla with two extra shots of espresso and *no milk*. It splashes on the floor.

Splash!

A woman rushes up to my side, with a soft soothing voice. But I can't hear what she says to me. I feel just like I felt the day I escaped Brock's townhome apartment. I feel *just* like I felt that day. Fuck. The haunting followed me all the way to New York City. It's like my body remembers what happened whether I want to forget or not, and it reacts the exact way it did that day. A reflex. A response. A torturing return. *Mother fucker.* All of my senses are heightened to their peak except for my hearing.

On high alert I feel the room still spinning and I can't catch a grip on anything around me other than her shirt as my knees buckle then fall weak. I clutch even harder onto the woman's shirt who has a soft, soothing voice but I still can't hear what the fuck she says to me, and I really wish I could. My legs wiggle some— like the noodles in the boiling pot of noodle water that I splashed all over Brock's face that day—as I slowly fall to the floor. Just like my latté. Like I did the day I escaped Brock. Five months pregnant and running from a skinless monster is something straight out of a nightmare, but that was real life for me. My belly felt like a swimming pool. The whirlpool plopped up and down as I jolted towards the door before he kicked me to the floor. Tasting the carpet and too weak to pull myself up, Brock drove his steel toe boots right in my stomach. Just as soon as I thought he was done he'd hammer his foot again and again until clumps of blood poured out of me. Reaching between my legs to feel what the wetness was, I shook, knowing it was blood. Our baby was dead.

I look over to the lounge chairs that Brock and Neil were sitting in and find them both gone. Poof! Just out of sight, but not out of mind. I'm halfway to the floor, still holding onto her shirt and she pulls me up. She bear hugs me to keep me from actually falling to the floor. The concrete floor. That would have been bad. I can survive a lot of things, but my dead weight dropping on a concrete floor is probably not one of them. I wrap my arms around her neck and I can't help it as I rest my face in the crook of her neck and cry just a little bit. Not as much as I want to. And definitely not as much as I need to.

"Are you okay?" Her voice remains soft and soothing, and I finally, actually hear what she says to me.

Lying to her I answered, "Yes." What else do you say in a situation like this? Would you tell her that you saw your two dead exes–that you killed–sitting in the lounge chairs chatting with each other? Yeah. Didn't think so.

I wipe my tears away. These are real tears, not like the ones I fake when someone tells me they're, "Oh so sorry for my loss." All of my senses are suddenly back like they were never gone in the first place. She walks me to a chaise lounge chair with her hand on the small of my back, guiding me. She points me towards the green one. No. I shake my head and pinch my eyes shut. Pulling back from the green chair, I stayed clasped onto her arm.

"What's wrong?" She wants to know. She's eager to hear the story of why the crazy lady freaked out in the coffee shop. I can see it in her eyes.

She loves the drama of it all.

"I'd rather sit on the pink one," I whisper because I don't want to sit where Neil or Brock were just sitting.

"Is there someone I can call for you? Someone to give you a ride home? Someone you know that can pick you up and make sure you get to your house okay? Your husband? Boyfriend? Family member?" The lady who just saved me from falling to the concrete floor of the coffee shop asks.

There are too many questions at once, and I can't fucking *think*. I'm not feeling dizzy anymore and my heart isn't pounding out of my chest. I still feel anxious, though because *fuck,* I just saw my two dead exes conspiring about me like I wasn't even here. They were obsessed with ruining me while they were alive. Not much has changed. I thought this was over. Feeling more free than ever. I was tricked. What a nasty little game life plays with me.

Fuck. I'm supposed to be shaking hands with my new boss right now. I Reach for my phone to see the time and I know for sure that I'm going to be late for my first day at work at my new job. Seeing the time, I realize that I *am* already late for my first day. I lean back against the pink velvety lounge chair and let out a long hard sigh.

Peering down at my hands crossed over my lap—I'm too embarrassed to look into her eyes—I answer her million questions with a simple answer.

"I live just down the street." Clearing my throat sends a thunder to my head, giving me a migraine that I didn't ask for.

"I'll be okay." I lied.

I lie a lot. Sometimes, I enjoy lying to people. Like when someone asks about Neil. I get sort of a sick satisfaction agreeing that it was an accident. Sometimes, lying is necessary. Like right now. "I'll be okay" is so much easier to say than what's really going on in my mind. There are too many tabs open. I minimize them to move one.

"Darling," she pronounces. "Can I ask you to stay here for a bit before heading back home?" Leaning towards my face, she glances into my eyes, like a cop that's flashing a light in your face to check if you're sober.

"Maybe rest some." She nods her head yes to me.

I nod my head back to her. "Okay." I stay.

I lean back on the velvety lounge chair and prop my feet up. I don't pull out my phone to distract myself from the misery of life. Not this time. As my stiff shoulders begin to shrink back down, I let myself sink into the cloud as I deserve.

A few minutes later she comes back with the largest cup they have in stock and nudges my elbow. "The man sitting over there," she pauses and nods her head back like she's pointing to something, "bought this for you. He said it's for all your troubles."

I don't bother making a big deal out of it. It's a drink. Like a man buying me a shot from across the room at a bar. I'll drink it, but that doesn't mean I'll give him the time of day.

"Thank you." I show gratitude as I reach for the cup. "Do you mind thanking him for me?" I ask.

Nodding her head yes, she takes off in his direction. Towards the back door. It was a nice gesture, but I don't feel up to talking to anyone right now. Especially someone new. Smiling. Showing pleasure. All the niceties. I just want to drink my coffee and relax.

I take a big, long gulp–*Gulp*–from it and notice that it's my favorite drink. A vanilla latté with two extra shots of espresso and *no milk*. I sit up fast. A little too fast. *Slow down, Willow.* I look around the room to find the guy who bought my drink. *Whew. Take it easy, Willow.* I don't see him anymore but I wonder who this man could be.

Standing, I leave my book bag still sitting on the pink lounge chair tucked into the cushion that I was just sitting on, contemplating what to do next. I walked towards the part of the coffee shop she pointed at a few minutes ago. I don't see him anywhere, and I don't even really remember what the back of him looked like because I was too busy getting over what the hell just happened to me.

Finally, I realize that he's gone. He is gone. Gone. Gone. Gone. And so is my fucking mind.

CHAPTER TWELVE

HIM

While Willow is too busy cheating on me with Bryan, I am busy making sure that she is okay. She almost fell at *The Charming Coffee Delight*. The new–to us–coffee shop we now attend is right down the road from our apartment. She stood frozen in place. Her whole body was trembling with fright and right as her latté fell to the floor, I got a hold of the barista's attention in place of someone else that was ordering their breakfast. I beckoned her to help the poor girl out. The barista ran for her, ready to do something other than serve coffee to customers with a fake ass smile on her face. She dove in and slid to Willow's rescue right before she was about to fall onto the concrete floor.

Crunch!

Her head would bounce and crack open if she had fallen. Without a doubt. Leaving her in a pool of blood instead of Bryan being in a pool of blood, and that is just not part of the plan. I could not let that happen. Even though I'd love to bash her head wide open just to see all the little thoughts that go through her mind every second of every day. To put the puzzle pieces together— finally—of why Willow does what Willow does. And why Willow is the way she is. Let it all just spill out. Her brain matter leaves trails behind of all the little bits and pieces that make up Willow's thoughts right there for me to follow. Giving me all the answers to the million questions I have for her.

I would start with these: Does she still love me? Did she ever love me? Is she even capable of love?

Willow looked distraught after what happened to her. Sprawled about on the pink chaise lounge sofa and not even scrolling on her phone to take her mind to a different place, so I ordered her, her favorite drink. A vanilla latté with two extra shots of espresso and *no milk*. Before she could tell it was me that got her back on her feet, I went for the back door and got the hell out of there.

I took a nice little walk, because it felt good outside with a light breeze and dammit I deserved to enjoy it. Not too cold and not too hot. While checking out all the little shops on the square that I watched her go into yesterday, I decided to go into the one that meant the most.

I knew I could do this. I knew I could enjoy my time and window shop for a gift for Willow without running into her this morning because she was too busy coming back to life after her face went pale. Pale as a ghost. Ha! Isn't Karma a bitch?

My eyes drift to the time on my phone. I had less than an hour before logging into my at home job as a newsletter editor. For the most part I'm lucky I can set my own schedule and can even log in sometimes through my phone. Then, I could wait all day if I wanted to, to edit whatever newsletter that gets assigned to me. But today I have an oh so very interesting one that I wanted to start on right after logging in. It was Willow's! Well, not quite hers, but it was from the company she works for and the company I work for sent it to me to edit.

Isn't that fate? You can't tell me that's not fate and if you tried to tell me that's not fate, I'd think you're utterly fucking out of this world deranged.

"That'll be ninety eight dollars and twenty-three cents, sir." Sir? Surely I don't look that old.

I came here only to window shop and put something on hold for her on my checklist for later, but I found it! I found the perfect gift for Willow. I pulled out my wallet and grabbed a one hundred dollar bill, handed it to the clerk and waited for my change.

"Thank you for shopping at *Lucky's Charms* and I hope to see you back soon!" Another New York City Yankee accent—born and raised here voice—said to me from behind the counter. She clapped her hands together once, then cupped them. The slogan was memorized. It had to be. It was something she was brainwashed to say to every single customer during training. I could just tell. It was almost robotic. She had probably already said it ten times before I stumbled in there this morning.

***

As I step up to my front door, apartment three o' eight, someone with a deep, but boyish sounding voice interrupts me. I stop in my tracks while holding my keys in the doorknob to turn and go inside, wanting to be by myself. I am not prepared for small talk with neighbors. This isn't really my thing. I'm trying to keep myself on the down low here.

"Lucky's Charms, eh? Who are you trying to impress?"

I turn to face the stranger in my vicinity, who is apparently a very nosey ass stranger. He nods his head towards the bag I'm holding. I glance down at the bag. A white paper bag with black embossing showing off the name of *Lucky's Charms* written in black letters inside a black heart that swoops from the 'L' and ends at the 's'.

My eyes return to the nosey ass stranger sitting in an open apartment doorway on the floor, halfway inside and halfway outside, smoking a cigarette. Does he think he's *not* getting smoke inside? His dirty blonde hair looks actually dirty and it sticks out from underneath the baseball cap he's wearing—-backwards—-and much higher up on top of his head creating a cone head look to him. I could walk over there and just *plop*. Plop my hand right on top of his head and make the hat stick to it, so he'd actually be wearing it the right way. He looks like a poser or wannabe in his scrunched up white sock with black Nike slide-ons. He wears a colorful tie-dyed t-shirt and black faded jean shorts that look like they'd fall right off him once he stands up.

He laughs like he's high, and that's when I realize it's not a cigarette that he's smoking. It's a joint. He offers it to me like we know each other already. I decline, holding my hand up—the one that I grasp the *Lucky's Charms* bag in—and tell him, "No thanks."

"So, who's the lucky lady, my dude?" *My dude?* Oh boy. My neighbor is a lonely stoner who apparently meets no strangers. This will be just so much fun.

"It's for my mom," I lie and smile at him like I'm a big ol' momma's boy.

He laughs again. I don't really see what's funny, but I laugh a little with him to be polite.

"I'm close to my mom also, dude," he says, relating with me.

I can't help but think to myself, Yep. That's probably your momma's house that you're sitting halfway out of, smoking a doobie and you probably really are a momma's boy and I'll bet she pays your way for everything in your life and then…

He fumbles a little using his elbows to help guide him to standing up to come and properly introduces himself to me.

"The names Sandy."

Sandy must be short for his real name, but I don't press because I don't care to know him on a personal level. I also notice from the sound of his voice that he doesn't have a New York City Yankee accent. He sounds more like a Californian to me. But I have no interest in getting to know him, so I don't ask him where he's from or what Sandy is short for. I just want to go inside my apartment. He shakes my hand like a good friendly neighbor. I want to immediately wash my hands now because he doesn't seem like a clean person. My eyes drift back to his dirty blonde hair that actually looks dirty, and I doubt he washes his hands after he wipes his ass.

"Have a good one," I say and go back to unlocking my door. He remains standing behind me, smiling with his lips pressed closed. With his hands in the front pockets of his too big for him black faded jean shorts.

He looks like he will laugh again at nothing, so I nod to him and close the door behind me.

Click.

I lock my front door so he will get the point that I am not looking for friends. I have no desire for friends. I have one focus here. Only one. That's Willow.

Stepping into my kitchen I set Willow's gift–She's gonna love it!–down on the kitchen counter. Grabbing a glass from my cupboard, I pour myself a glass of sweet iced tea. I wonder if Bryan drinks sweet iced tea, like a true Texan. Shoving Bryan out of my mind, I head into my living room to get busy with work. My work isn't so hard. In fact, it's easy. I would hardly even call it work. Not when I get to do it all from home. The living room is my favorite spot to set up. Just one glance up, and Willow is standing in front of me.

My living room is blank, bare, and pretty much empty— *empty just like my soul since the day Willow left me*—because I don't plan on staying here forever. I'm not using or expecting apartment three o' eight at the *Miller Grill Apartments* to feel like home because home is diagonal of me at Willow's apartment. Home is anywhere Willow is. But I did indulge in comfortable furniture and a nice flat wide screen television set with Netflix, HULU, HBO, and anything else I wanted to watch. I've got it made over here. I really do. Comfort and complete access to a view of Willow's full living space. It's almost perfect. Pretending to wake up in the mornings with Willow by my side and go to bed at night with her lying next to me isn't exactly what I would call the dream life. It's getting closer, though. She'll be back in my arms soon. Willow doesn't really have a choice. We're meant to be together. Soul mates are what the kids nowadays call what Willow and I have. It's impossible for us to stay away from each other for too long. We go through withdrawals. It's that deep. Watching her through a thin glass isn't the perfect life, but it almost is.

Almost.

What would actually be perfect is having her right here with me, right by my side like she used to be. Smiling that pretty, perfect simper of hers. Smelling that sweet honey vanilla scent she has naturally just beaming out of her. Touching her soft, spiral blonde curls and witnessing them bounce right back into place.

So, no, I don't have it quite perfect just yet. Yet. The power of yet!

I open up my laptop and log in to get busy on editing the newsletter of the company where Willow works. Explain to me— If Willow and I aren't destined to be together forever—how out of all the editors on the team I am the one chosen to be editing the newsletter at Willow's work. This really is fate. I wish so fucking badly that I could let her know this, so she can see it for herself and realize that we really are meant for each other. This isn't just some coincidence to brush off. There are no accidents. This is fate. And she will know it soon. She will.

It takes me less than an hour to finish the editing of the newsletter for Willow and I send it back to them all polished up. Once the cat is out of the bag and Willow realizes it's me who fixed their newsletter to be ready to send out to all of their fifty-two thousand followers she'll be ready to let me come back. To come back into her life to edit and revise and fix all the mistakes she has made along the way and the ones she's currently making. Life will be so much better for the both of us. It really will be. I know it.

On that note I close my laptop because I am done with work for the day. Two hundred dollars for a one hour job and I get to spend the rest of the day watching Willow because she is at home now. I suppose the episode at *The Charming Coffee Delight* has given her oh, what a fright!

I move my laptop off my coffee table and replace it with my cup of sweet tea. The ice clinks inside against each other as I set it down. *Clink. Clink. Clink.* I lean back against the couch to relax a little bit and wait for my favorite show to begin because this is so much better than Netflix or HULU or HBO. This is the show I'm invested in day in and day out.

CHAPTER THIRTEEN

HIM

Willow walks into her apartment—diagonal of mine!—and she sets all of her belongings on the side table right next to her front door, relieving her hands of the no good, very bad day she's already had. It's only eleven in the morning and her day is already ruined. Poor Willow. *Poor, poor, sweet Willow.*

She leans her back against the wall and looks up to the air. Because I've zoomed in on her face with my Nikon, I can tell she's frustrated and relieved at the same time to be back home and away from the dangers lurking outside. She sighs, then pulls the sleeves of her fluffy burnt orange cardigan up to her elbows and glides to her record player like she is in a field of overgrown daisies. Arms out wide and hands spread to feel the velvety touch of the dainty little flowers.

Rushing to my back door I smile to myself. I slide it open just a little bit because hers is wide open and I want to hear the songs she listens to. She puts on *When The Doves Cry* by *Prince.* Her body flows with the music and her soft blonde curls bounce. The V-neck on her shirt slips a little bit and I zoom my camera lens in to catch a good look at her tits that almost fall out of her shirt. The sleeves of her cardigan keep falling. Pulling the cardigan off, she tosses it on the couch. She dances around her living room like nobody is watching.

But somebody is watching her and that somebody is *me*. I get hard while watching her, and she has no idea. The very fact that she has no idea turns me on even more. Unzipping my pants, I reach down to give myself a happy little ending. As she jumps around the living room, her perky tits bounce up and down along with her movement. My body quivers as I finish the deed. Willow stumbles a little bit, then straightens herself up and glances around her apartment as if she's making sure nobody saw her trip.

I can tell she is already drunk. I'm assuming she poured a little—or a lot—in her large vanilla latté with two extra shots of espresso and *no milk* that I got her. Add a touch of vodka and voila! She's got the perfect mixture of poison to set her up for a damn good time for the rest of the day, which makes it a good show for me. She sways back and forth in her living room, feeling the music, feeling the liquor. Loose body, flowy sleeves, red face and singing with emotion as Prince asks the million dollar question: *Why do we scream at each other?* When the doves cry!

Willow, oh Willow show me again what you sound like when the doves cry.

Willow doesn't know the answer to the million-dollar question her and Prince ask, so she grabs ahold of her hair with one hand and scrunches it in place. She holds an invisible microphone up to her mouth with her other hand as she asks the question over and over again. *Why do we scream at each other?* At this point, she is no longer just swaying to the music and letting it seep in slowly. No. Now she has taken it all in like medicine, like dope shooting up straight to her heart. It has taken full possession of her. She isn't just feeling the rhythm anymore. She *is* the rhythm, the music, the lyrics.

When Prince is done with his plea for communication, Willow picks up her cup from the coffee table and downs the rest of her vanilla latté with two extra shots of espresso and *no milk*, and of course, however many shots of vodka she's poured in there. Hell. It might actually be just straight vodka at this point. There are a lot of things I can tell you about Willow. I know everything about her, but how much vodka Willow is willing to drink in a day, I do not know. This I just guess. She can be unpredictable with her drinking and push the limit. Like a child left unattended in a candy shop. She indulges far too much.

Some of the liquid from what she just devoured drips down the sides of her mouth and she wipes it away with the back of her hand. Then she wipes the back of her hand onto her jeans. She grabs a small remote and points it at her not so vintage record player–although she likes to think it is–and puts on *Back to Good*. She belches out with *Matchbox Twenty* all the secrets she's been holding inside of her. All of her desires to be with me. I know she's singing about me and her. I know she feels lonely. I know she doesn't know how to get it *back to good*, but I can show her how to get it *back to good*. I know she doesn't feel good about how she left me the way she did. To wither away on my own. Ash to ash. Dust to dust. Wipe her hands clean of me. People don't listen to *Back to Good* by *Matchbox Twenty* unless they're missing someone special to them. That someone special to Willow that she is missing is *me*. It's evident. The way she pouts and whines like a little brat when she's alone. She misses me. Her heart is broken. That's why she drinks so much and gets to the point of sloppiness.

Willow kneels down, singing with all her might in her invisible microphone when I get a knock on my door. *Fucking go away whoever you are.*

Knock. Knock. Knock. Knock.

I set my Nikon camera down on my couch because you can't see it from my front door. I don't want anyone to see it. Stupidly, I opened the door without asking who it was. I really should have asked who it was or at the very least looked through the peephole.

"What's up, Sandy?" Why does he look like a shy, scared little boy right now? Oh! Momma's boy. That's right.

"Uh, hey dude. Uh, yeah. Did you, uh, hear that noise?" Sandy asks me as if there really was a noise. He looks around sheepishly trying to find where the invisible sound came from.

I shake my head no. No Sandy, I didn't hear a noise because there is no fucking noise and you are just bored, high and nosey as fuck.

He peeks his head around the corner of my door to catch a little glimpse inside of my apartment. He's just curious. He just wants to know the new guy living across from him. I don't blame him, but he's wasting my fucking time when I have the whole day to myself with Willow. I let him know this with my eyes. He clutches the inside of the pockets in his faded black jean shorts that are too big for him and pushes his shoulders up. He wears a look of confusion like he really did hear a noise, so I take a step outside my door, close it behind me, and wait.

I wait to hear a noise. After a few minutes of awkward silence—with this grown up man kid—I balk.

"I don't hear a thing other than music playing from someone's apartment or car," I finally said to him.

"Yeah dude. That's probably what I heard." He chuckles and pulls out a cigarette. "I must be just high and paranoid." He chuckles again and shakes his head in disbelief at himself. I roll my eyes when he's not looking at my face. "I get paranoid sometimes when I smoke." He chuckles a-fucking-gain nervously, and I find it annoying.

"Well…" But that's all I can really say to him because what the fuck?

I go back inside my apartment and once more—click—I lock the fucking door to show him that I don't want any Goddamn friends. This is a no friend zone. Stay the fuck away.

CHAPTER FOURTEEN

HIM

I step back over to my window. It's a sliding glass door window and always has the drapes—dark, navy blue, blackout curtains—wide open so I can see into Willow's apartment. Reaching over, I pick up my Nikon that was just in my grasp before I was interrupted by the boy next door and zoom into Willow's living room to watch her dance and sing a little more about how badly she wants to get *back to good* with me.

Except, now she sings about how it's *yummy, yummy, yummy* because she's got love in her tummy. She dances around the room again, rocking her legs back and forth like it's the sixties and she has a pure heart. Ha! We all know damn good and well that Willow does not fucking have a pure heart or she wouldn't have left me like she did- broken and dead inside. The last time we were in the same room together, she looked straight into my eyes as she broke my heart and slammed that door shut. Securing a lock so I couldn't possibly get back into her heart again. She knows deep down that we belong together. It's fate. We're soul mates. There is no halting when it comes to us. Our bodies fit together like puzzle pieces. Perfectly. What we have is raw, real, and nobody can fuck with that. Not Bryan. Not anyone.

I wonder who she's singing about having love in her tummy for. It couldn't possibly be Bryan. She barely knows him! That's Willow for you. Mistaking love for lust. Those four little letters all jumbled together. *Love.* It has a much bigger meaning than what she accepts from losers like him. Giving her every bit of myself wasn't enough. Clearly. She had to self-sabotage a good thing she had going on in her life. Leaving me was a result—part of her self-loathing. Poor, poor, sweet, stupid Willow. When will she learn? What will it take?

Snap the fuck out of it, Willow! Wake the fuck up! You've got love right across from you. Real, raw, authentic love. Settling for a fucking turtleneck bitch you met on the plane isn't going to make you forget about me. Drowning in booze won't do the trick either.

Her face looks more red now than it was before Sandy knocked on my door. And she looks like she's becoming a sloppy drunk. She turns around and smiles a big cheesy grin. I move my camera to gaze at what just made her so happy, and there he is.

Bryan. Again. Making her smile with his presence alone.

Bryan has a grin on his face, too, like victory will be his by the end of the night. Grinning, he brings her a cup of whatever he's concocted in her kitchen and she takes it from his hands without any hesitation. Within a matter of seconds, she tosses it back like there's a party going on and she is a teenage girl with no background of shitty men because Willow is a very stupid girl to trust this stranger handing her drinks, watching her get loaded, so he can take advantage of her when she can't think straight. He's a predator like that. I want to march over and pound his face in until it's black and blue and purple and dented and distorted and his pretty face becomes unrecognizable at last.

But I digress, again, because that's not part of the plan. Not yet. And actually, Bryan wasn't part of the plan, but here we are. Bryan and Willow. Willow and Bryan. And she's drunk. She's just sad and mourning the loss of me. She is just using him as a rebound from me. That's what I have to remember when I see Willow and Bryan together in her hippy dippy apartment with her HIPPY DIPPY DO YOU, BOO tapestry hanging in her bedroom area in her studio apartment that fits her just oh so well. Rebounds never last long. Sure, she might fuck him. They might even cuddle and share their shitty childhood stories with each other. Maybe they'll go on a few dates. *Maybe*. He'll never amount to me, though. She fucking knows this. He's a beta. He can pretend to be an alpha all he wants. That shit will only work for a short period of time before his mask slips.

Still, the thought of her fucking someone else sends my heart right to the pit of my stomach, then fills me with a fatal amount of rage. Clenching my fist, I set my camera down. Pacing my apartment, I talk myself down from the ledge. Kill him. Don't kill him. Kill him. Don't kill him. Like I'm shredding flower petals one at a time chanting she loves me, she loves me not. The fantasy of slicing his throat wide open flashes through my mind again, like it did on the plane. Wearing his blood would suit me quite well. Don't you agree? It would be too easy to get away with. He has no family. No friends. Nobody to search for a missing Bryan. Willow will get over him quickly, too. She'd just think he ghosted her and moved on with her life, locking arms with another sad, rotten piece of shit until she inevitably comes crawling back to me.

Goddamnit. Stop it! I have to pull it the fuck back together. I can't kill him yet. *Yet.* Swallowing the lump in my throat, I pick my Nikon camera back up and zoom in.

Willow plops down on her bed, laughing at nothing other than the liquor kicking in, and Bryan follows behind her. Like a sick little puppy dog in love. *In lust.* Bryan isn't mistaking love for lust, though. No. He knows what he's doing. Preying on a vulnerable drunk woman, he smirks to himself. As he bobs his head back and forth to the music, I can't help but to wonder what it would look like on a stick. Or, possibly, hanging on my wall like a trophy from a hunting game that I win. This time, Bryan can be the prey and get a taste of his own medicine.

An eye for an eye, mother fucker. Heat rises to my face as Willow grabs ahold of Bryan's shirt and pulls him towards her, then sticks her tongue in his mouth.

I can't watch this anymore, so I put my Nikon camera down and close my navy blue blackout drapes for the first time since I moved here. Taking a breath, I step over to my front door and slide my tennis shoes off my feet, putting on my steel toe boots. I grab Willow's gift off the kitchen counter, and I head out to Home Depot to buy some building supplies because I have another gift in mind for Willow.

CHAPTER FIFTEEN

WILLOW

I slept with Bryan. Okay, okay, okay. I know what everyone's thinking. It wasn't when I was drunk, though! He's not a bad guy. He didn't take advantage of me when he could have. I threw myself at him all night long and he declined with lust in his eyes and a hunger to fuck me. Don't you see? That's *why* I got so turned on the next day. Lying in bed beside him with his coconut breath in my ear and the lingering hangover from the night before as we had let ourselves get the most vulnerable you can get. Him gently caressing me with his fingertips only. I melted and gave in—I caved in. We were supposed to wait, I know. I'm weak. I wanted it—I wanted him and I had him. I made a move and took him. And I let him take me and damn, it was good. I'm not regretful. Judge me all you want.

"You're mine, Willow," he whispered in my ear as he moved inside me. I drank in the dominating power he wanted to portray. Moaning, I got even more wet for him. I've always been a sucker for a man who makes me beg for it.

"Ask for it. Tell me you want me, Willow. Tell me you're mine. Whose pussy is this? Tell me it's my pussy, Willow," he whimpered while teasing me.

It's been five days since Bryan and I had sex, and I have heard from him every single day since then. We literally talk all day long. Then again, it's not like I have anything else to do since I've been staying at home. I haven't left my apartment in six days.

Not since what happened at The Charming Coffee Delight because I won't, I'm a little scared. I called off my job for another two weeks just to be able to settle in. They understood because they thought that I should settle into my new place first before starting at a new job in a new state. That's actually what they offered me in the first place. It was their suggestion, and now I am taking full advantage of it.

I still want my coffee fix, so Bryan brings me my favorite drink every morning—a vanilla latté with two extra shots of espresso and *no milk*—and just like that he's got it memorized. My hero. But now I've asked him to buy me the k-cups and the mixture of all that it takes to make it at home, so I can have it anytime I want without having to leave. So, I can continue feeling comfortable in my home, and so—

Knock

My head turns towards the front door. With my brows furrowed, I wonder if I'm hearing things because I haven't invited company over. Bryan and I agreed on him coming over tomorrow, not today.

Knock

I stare at the door as if waiting for something to happen. Anxiously, I begin counting in my head. One Mississippi, two Mississippi, three Mississippi.

Knock

As the slow, daring knock beats through my front door, I freeze, unsure if I should answer it. I don't know who that could be, but the sound sent a jolt through my entire body. My gut alerts me that this is bad. This time, I'm more than just a little scared, but I stand up anyway. Slowly, I creep up to the door, careful not to make any noise. I look through the peephole after hesitating for a minute or two once the knocks stop, but I don't see anyone there. I go through the contacts on my phone and dial Bryan's number.

"Was that you?!" I ask way louder than I meant to and with frustration in my voice. I didn't mean to sound frustrated.

I hear shuffling in the background on the other end of the line. "What?" More shuffling. "Willow," he breathes like my name is a breath of fresh air to him even after the annoyance in my voice. "Hey? What are you talking about? Slow down," he says calmly.

Halting in my footsteps, I realized that I had been pacing back and forth and he could probably hear my breathing get louder and louder.

"Just tell me right now, Bryan!" I peek through the peephole again. Nothing. "Did you knock on my door?"

"What? When?" He truly sounds like he doesn't know what I'm talking about and I believe him. I think.

I check all the deadbolts on my front and back doors, let out a sigh louder than I intended, and sit down on my couch. "Someone just now knocked on my door and when I looked in the peephole nobody was there. Nobody else knows where I live but you. I haven't lived here long and I just…"

"I'm coming over right now," he interrupts, saying this like it's his place to be here to console me. Like we've been together for way longer than just six days. Not counting the two weeks before I slept with him.

"You don't have to…"

"No. I'm coming," he interrupts me again. I can hear the sound of the city in the background behind him; people chatting with each other, their voices muffled. I don't hang up. A raspy voice comes through, "Hey man, you got a few dollars to spare?"

"Here," he mumbles, giving him what he's got in his pockets, and I like that about him. I can hear the sound of change clank together as it falls into the man's hand.

"Thank you. God bless you, sir," the man shows gratitude.

Ding! Ding! Ding! The sound fills my ears letting me know he now has his keys in the ignition to come save me from this… situation.

"Really. I'm okay, Bryan. It's okay. I didn't call to interrupt your day." I say this because I mean it. I also say it as a test to see if he'll change his mind and if he changes his mind… well then he is not the one for me.

"Willow." He breathes into my ear, and again, it still sounds like my name is a breath of fresh air to him. "It's really no big deal to me. It's not a bother at all. I'm on my way."

He doesn't say bye to me. He just hangs up the phone because there is no bye with us. He's on his way here—on his way here to scoop me up in his arms and save the day. Another knight in shining armor.

***

Bryan gets here within a matter of minutes after we get off the phone. Instead of him knocking on the door to announce his presence, my phone rings.

"I'm at your door." He says softly. He does this so he won't scare me any more than what I already am. That's another thing I like about him. He's thoughtful. Caring about other people's feelings, he puts me before himself. Rushing to get over here to comfort me, he goes the extra mile to think ahead of how his actions might affect me.

I open the door and there he stands with a black overnight bag that looks more like a week-long bag with how full it is. Was he already prepared for me to need him? There's no way he just packed those things in the little amount of time it took him to get here. He's also holding a gift bag from the store I went window shopping in a few days ago. I realize now why he didn't walk and drove his car over here instead. Too much to carry.

"Uh. This was outside your door," he says more like a question as he holds the bag out to me. A white paper gift bag that reads, *Lucky's Charms* in black writing with a heart swooping from one letter to the other to hold the brand name inside of it. I remember that place. Swooning over the jewelry and little trinkets, I was almost talked into buying something by an associate who made it pretty clear they get commission off sales. How did Bryan know?

This is too soon. Way too soon. I reach my hand up to my heart to grab the charm on my necklace because the bag reminds me of what used to be mine. My forever lost crutch.

Shaking my head to snap the fuck out of it, I invite him inside. "Sorry. Come in." I move to the side for him to have just enough room to shimmy through. He hands me the gift bag, then goes straight to my bedroom area and sets his big black bag down on the floor beside the part of my bed he slept on the night that I drank a little bit too much.

He rubs his hand across the bed to smooth out the wrinkles of my sheets.

"We were supposed to wait, Willow." He looks up at me with those piercing green eyes that I have pretty much already fallen in love with, and just like that the attention is brought to him. Never mind that I was just creeped on by only God knows who. Maybe even him. I don't even know anymore because of what he just said to me, and he sure did show up a little too quickly after the three knocks with all his stuff. Now this gift?

He takes his place on my bed and gets comfortable after sliding off his shoes. Like he lives here with me now. I internally shake my head and tell him no, but the words don't come out and my head doesn't really shake to refuse him. He leans his back against the mountain of pillows on my bed. I hold the bag out and away from me with my pointer finger and thumb like it holds a disease inside.

"What's in the bag anyway?" He sits back up with his eyebrows furrowing in curiosity.

"I… I don't know." I look at him and he gives me a sad half smile and gets up to walk over to me. I know what he's thinking. He's thinking I'm weak or crazy or damaged. Broken.

"Bryan?"

"Yeah?"

"Is this from you?"

He pauses in his steps and looks me dead in my eyes. The desire for me that was there just a second ago is now gone and replaced with something else. Something a little too familiar.

"Are you fucking serious right now?" He throws his hands up in the air, like what I just said was the most ridiculous thing he has ever heard. "Don't you think if it was from me that I would just tell you that upfront?" he spouts as he shakes his head in disbelief.

He could have said anything else. Anything. But this is what he chose to say. *"Are you fucking serious right now?"* His words echo in my head. Inside, my heart pounds because he just reminded me of Neil. It's not pounding because of fear, but because of anger. Deciding not to vocalize my feelings, I am once again a silent wife. I'm not married anymore and he isn't Neil, but I am thrown back into that hole in the ground to rot away. Numbness arises to the surface now.

I slow my breathing down and try to gather my thoughts before speaking the million things going through my mind right now. Instead of telling him to fuck off or to not talk to me like this again, I stutter, "Well, I just. It's just." I let out another big, long sigh and set the gift bag down on my little kitchen island. I rub my temples because my head is starting to hurt.

Bryan lays his hands on his hips. He takes a deep breath, lets it out and then trudges closer to me. Lifting my chin up tenderly with his hand, he gently apologizes. "Hey. I'm sorry about that." He shakes his head like he's disappointed in himself. As he should be. "About getting snappy. I just hoped you would trust me by now. Ya know?"

By now? What? In two and half weeks' time I'm supposed to trust you? This has me flabbergasted. I barely trust myself. How am I supposed to trust someone I just met?

I decided that I need to speak up for myself now. "Uh hey—

Interrupting me, he makes a suggestion. "Let's open it together and see what's inside."

I wonder if he already knows what's inside.

"Okay," I say instead of what's really going on in my mind. "You open it." I frown. "I don't want to."

"Willow," he breathes. His voice is different now. It's not defensive and sharp like it was a few minutes ago. Maybe I deserved that. He was just trying to help and I accused him of being tricky. Now his voice is low, soft, and gentle like it was when we were on the phone. I feel a little better now.

"It's a gift for you," he reminds me.

So, I open it.

Slowly.

Slowly.

Slowly.

I tug and pull at the white and black glitter tissue paper until I get to a small black jewelry box. Diego Cold Hands, The Famous Bearer immediately pops into my mind and chimes on my phone at the same time. I jump, too focused on the gift. Tunnel vision. Everything else was a blur until I saw the box and heard my phone go off.

Ding!

Diego Cold Hands, The Famous Bearer
Willow. Are you there?
Ding!
Diego Cold Hands, The Famous Bearer
Will you please just talk to me?

I press dial to confront him, and watch Bryan crack his knuckles like he is ready to fight.

"How the fuck did you find out where I live?" I have him on speaker phone so Bryan can hear it all, so at least I'll have a witness for whatever else Diego Cold Hands, The Famous Bearer plans on doing to me.

"How do you mean?" He stumbles over his words because he is too comfortable with me and lets his broken English slip out because he doesn't have an audience to be sure he speaks perfectly for. He then corrects himself by saying it the way he would have said to anybody else the first time. "What do you mean?"

"You left a fucking gift over here that you had no business doing and if you come by my place again I'll call the cops. I will. I'll get a restraining order on you! I promise you, you don't wanna fuck with me Diego." I yell this at him, forgetting I have neighbors that might hear my drama.

The last thing I need are neighbors checking in on me. Been there. Done that.

"No. Willow, I did not. Will you talk? If it's a gift, do you like the gift?"

He sounds like he's fumbling around and then straightens up. "Will you talk to me?"

"No. Diego. I won't talk to you. I told you we are done. I told you why and I am not repeating myself with you any longer. This stops right now."

Silence fills the air between us. Bryan pulls up his sleeves and clenches his jaw like Diego Cold Hands, The Famous Bearer is here within fighting distance. Maybe he is. I don't know anymore.

"Just leave me alone." I say that one last thing to him, and hang up, ending the call. He doesn't call back.

CHAPTER SIXTEEN

WILLOW

It's been eight days now since I saw Brock and Neil at The Charming Coffee Delight. I think it's time for me to buckle the fuck back up and take my stance against them.

I am alive. They are dead. I have won. They have lost. Fair and fucking square.

Straightening my shoulders up from the sinking they've been positioned in for far too long, I order my favorite drink. "I'll have a vanilla latté with two extra shots of espresso and *no milk*," I say to the lady with the soft, soothing voice that saved me from falling on the concrete floor the last time I was here. I look at her name tag because I want to remember her name and call her by her name every time I see her now because she is God sent.

When she hands me my latté I call her by her name. "Thank you, Chelsea."

Chelsea's orange apron fits on her plump body like a live-in maid you only see in movies now. Swaying towards me with her out of date flat black twinkle shoes, she grabs the whipped cream.

"You want some?" She holds the bottle to the lid of my cup, with her finger on the tip ready to swirl the load on top.

Politely declining, I shake my head no. Chelsea smiles and sets it down in the fridge. "Suit yourself. But me?" She lays her hand on her chest. "I gotta have my whipped cream."

Laughing with her, I make small talk. "So, how long have you worked here?"

I actually hate that question, but for some reason it's my go to. I ask this when I get my hair done, when maintenance comes by the apartment to fix something, when I'm at the bank waiting at the kiosk and it's too quiet. The mundane and niceties pouring out is like a slow torture. It feels like a lifetime waiting to hear the answer, deciding what to say next, holding my breath and letting it all out as I walk away. Shoot me now.

Without skipping a beat, she answers, "One year, two months, three days, and four hours." She doesn't even look up from the latté she makes for another customer when she adds, "I used to be a stay at home mom, but my kids are grown now and I got bored. My husband is rich." She boasts, shrugging.

"Well, *we're* rich. I work here for my own spending money and to have something to do. I get cabin fever looking at the same four walls every day. Ya know?"

"I know the feeling." *All too well.*

Chelsea makes all kinds of fancy drinks, and each time I go in there she creates a different design on top of my latté to surprise me. Heart swirls, my name swirled on top, flowers; I wonder what it will be next. I imagine a turkey for Thanksgiving, spelling out fuck off- the popular trend on TikTok, or butterflies.

Since the incident, we've grown a little close, chatting it up about everything and nothing. She has become my favorite coffee buddy, even though we really don't have that much in common. We just click like that, anyway. It's kinda hard not to. Once somebody comes to your rescue the way she did for me, it's an instant friendship. The bond was set in place the moment we locked eyes as she let me grab ahold of her shirt.

When Chelsea isn't looking and I notice that nobody else is either, I scrounge through my purse and pull out my little vodka bottle. Swiftly, I unscrew the lid—my medicine—and pour a few shots into my latté.

I've been visiting The Charming Coffee Delight almost every day here lately. Thankfully, I haven't seen Neil or Brock in here since the day they laughed me out of the building. I faced my demons and now they're gone. Things are going so so so much better now. Still, I wonder who that guy was that bought my favorite drink that day. When the timing is right, and I don't feel so insecure about my past to ask Chelsea, I'll finally bring it up to her. It's not that I'll be talking to her about my past, but people can sense when you're nervous. The subject revolves around my past. My stomach churns and my palms begin to sweat. Wiping the sweat on my jeans, I feel a bead of sweat drip across my forehead. *Great.* Grabbing a napkin to pat my face dry, I thank whoever has my back because she hasn't caught on yet. If she did, there would be questions. I don't have time to let someone pick my brain and dig through my past.

Get it the fuck together, Willow.

"Hey Chelsea," I say, urging myself on as I sip my vanilla latté with two extra shots of espresso and *no milk* with a touch of vodka. "Do you remember the guy who bought me a drink that day you saved my life?" I try with a little drama as a way to deliver what I'm needing from her.

"Oh, come on." Chelsea laughs and waves her hand like it was no big deal for her to help me. "I didn't *save your life,* Willow." She laughs again.

I laugh along with her and shift around in my seat at the bar while she stands behind it making a frappe for someone way on the other side who can't hear our conversation. That makes me relax in my seat, even more comfortable to carry on.

"Well," I say, drawing out the 'l' sound, like I always do. It's just me. It's what I do. I can't help it.

"Who was he? Is he a regular here? Have you seen him since then?" I ask. I'm about to burst with curiosity, even though curiosity killed the cat. She drizzles some caramel on top of the frappe she makes. I watch as she scrunches up her face in thought.

"Hmmmm. I don't think so." She looks up and directly at me with a little closed half smile on her face, but her eyes shine like she's intrigued. "You got a crush? You trying to find the man that saved you with a latté?" She swoons. "Your knight in shining armor?"

I freeze when she says this to me. She doesn't notice. Still smiling, she continues drizzling caramel on the frappe. She secures a lid on top of the cup, grabs a straw and walks over to the customer waiting on her caffeine fix.

My knight in shining armor was supposed to be Neil, saving me from my parents. Then it was supposed to be Brock, saving me from Neil. After that, it was supposed to be Neil saving me from Brock. Then it was supposed to be Diego Cold Hands, The Famous Bearer saving me from myself. Now, it's supposed to be Bryan saving me from Diego Cold Hands, The Famous Bearer. But, what if I'm my own knight in shining armor? What happens then? Because truthfully, I am starting to feel sick and tired of being saved by men when I should be saving my own damn self.

CHAPTER SEVENTEEN

WILLOW

I can do this. I can. I can. I can.

Pacing the floors of my small studio apartment, my mind drifts from what I'm supposed to be doing. I love this place and the style I chose to go with this time around. It's so….me. Focus Willow. Focus. Focus. Focus. I have just one thing on the agenda today. It shouldn't be that hard, so why can't I bring myself to do it?

Pacing back and forth, I distract myself with small silly little things. Anything to take my mind off of getting up the nerve to make the phone call. *The phone call.* It sounds like doom. I walk over to my coffee table and stare at my phone, moving the new charm necklace across my chin that my secret admirer—or hater— bought for me. My forever lost crutch. The exact same one I had before it got lost in the fire. Whoever got me this—which could be a number of people since everyone knew about my necklace because it was my signature—knew I needed it, and I do. Just like I needed it to be a gift from someone to make it more meaningful. Rather than buying it for myself. So, I use it. I wear it every day, and I don't give a shit what Bryan or anybody thinks or says about it. And trust me. Bryan has a lot to say about it, but I ignore him. I will keep on ignoring his opinions about it. It's none of his business anyway.

As I hold my hand hovering over my phone, needing to pick it up off my coffee table and make that call—doom—a ding chimes in my ears. I jump again, the sound startling me. Why? What the fuck is wrong with me? Before I call to set up the appointment I check to see what notification pulled my attention. I need to see what interrupted me, to see what it is that stopped me, even if it's just for a second, from making that phone call.

Mrs. Grey
Willow! I hope you're doing well in the big apple. Miss New York City, you are! We miss you so much! Come over for Thanksgiving?

I grimace. Her message makes me think of my mom and how she doesn't even know where I moved. Neither does my dad. *My lovely parents.* Mrs. Grey doesn't exactly know where I moved to, either. But she does know I moved to New York City. She just doesn't have my address or know the apartment complex I live at. At least she and Mr. Grey made the attempt to keep in touch with me. I try not to take it personally that my parents haven't reached out to me. They're the type to say, "The phone works both ways," when you're nine years old, wondering why they don't love you anymore because you haven't heard a peep from them in six months.

The fact that my mom and dad could know I moved by checking my Instagram, but not even bother to send me a quick text to ask where, is part of the reason I never wanted to become a mother myself. A parent. What a joke! I'd hate to end up like them. Leaving my child to feel like their endeavors in life aren't important. Maybe my parents don't even know that's how they've made me feel. Isn't that even worse? To not even know they've put those feelings to live deep inside you? So, to create a human being who goes through life feeling like this, even for just one day, without my knowledge that I'm the reason for it, is definitely not on my bucket list of things to do. Not in this lifetime. So again, thank you Brock for kicking my stomach over and over again to force the abortion I wanted to get in the first place. Salute. You huge piece of garbage.

My thoughts drift to Pauleen, the woman who had my back one hundred percent, through and through to all of the cops,

90

investigators, and news casters. The same woman that Neil—my asshole dead husband—deemed as 'the nosey neighbor'. The woman that lived next door to me and Neil who felt that she desperately needed companionship from me because I look just like her daughter, Tillie, who had been killed in a drunk driving car accident. Pauleen clung to me. Listening through the thin walls at my old apartment complex in Chicago was just her way of looking out for me. If she hadn't done so, and kept on eavesdropping, the cops would have thought Neil was a loving husband concerned about his wife's safety when I was in captivity. Pauleen saved my ass. Of course, we kept in touch.

Pauleen moved into the same apartment complex I moved to after Neil and Brock died in the fire at Brock's townhome apartment. She wanted to rent the apartment right next door to mine like we had at the one Neil and I lived in while we were married; while he was still alive. Unfortunately for her, that one wasn't vacant, so she settled for the one next to it. Fortunately for me, we were just two doors down from each other. I cared about Pauleen and wanted to stay in touch with her, but I needed my space and it was hard to set boundaries with her after she helped improve my life so much.

She would check on me almost daily. Whether that be a peep out her window to wave at me as I left, or a quick text message. And sometimes a full blown knock on my door bright and early in the morning, waking me up from a dead sleep. I guess you could say she had an unhealthy fixation on me. Most people said that and they still do, but I fed into it because she was so kind to me. Also, I felt bad for her; I felt *really bad* for her. Tillie, her daughter, is the spitting image of me. *Was* the spitting image of me. I look like I climbed right out of the framed picture that she hung above her fireplace and started breathing life back into Pauleen.

I played into our similarities on purpose sometimes. Dressed myself like her and wore my hair frizzier than what it already is to resemble Pauleen's dead daughter even more than I already do without even having to try. The look on her face when she came over for tea and girl talk, and she saw me wearing the new outfit I bought that Tillie was wearing in that picture, was priceless. She needed that. She really did. I provided that for her because it was easy. It was an easy way to make her feel like for just one day her daughter was here. Alive, in a way.

I needed it, too. I needed to be doted on by a mother. A parent. I really did. I needed to feel fully accepted, and on that day for that hour sharing hot green tea with bagels and cream cheese, sprinkled with girl talk, I felt it. It felt good, too. Pauleen has a natural mother's instinct for any young woman, in my opinion. When it comes to me, though? Tillie and I have an uncanny resemblance. Poor woman just wants her daughter back. She gets a little slice of that when she sees me.

Pauleen moved when I moved here because to her there just wasn't a reason to stick around there anymore. Now I'm the only one who knows where she lives because she is so alone, without friends and family to remind her that she's loved. Her new home is nowhere near me because she wanted to uproot to the country, not the big city of New York. All I have left from her are text messages here and there, and comments on my Instagram and hearts on all my posts to show she's still showing her approval and love for me. For Tillie. I'd be lying if I said I didn't miss her and her affection.

We used each other, Pauleen and me. We so obviously did. She used me as a short term replacement for her dead daughter, so she could feel somewhat sane from years of losing her mind after losing her daughter and her husband—that she actually loved— and I used her to feel a temporary unconditional love that I lacked for my entire life. In the words of Alanis Morrisette—*Isn't it ironic, don't you think? A little too ironic. Yeah, I really do think.*

I haven't answered Mrs. Grey's text message back just yet. I don't know what I'll be doing tomorrow, let alone on Thanksgiving day. I'll answer her later.

CHAPTER EIGHTEEN

WILLOW

The smell of stale and fresh cigarette smoke mixed together fills my nose. Behind the bar I sit at, deciding what to drink, two women wearing black, long-sleeved, low cut shirts and a lot of makeup with perfectly styled hair don't look up from what they're doing to ask what I want. I'm relieved because I haven't decided yet. They line shot glasses up in front of them racing with liquor. Kid Rock sings about being a cowboy baby playing on the jukebox that some young couple wearing matching I love my boyfriend and I love my girlfriend t-shirts apparently put on before I got there.

I watch as they stand and make an announcement, "Our song is finally playing!" Pulling each other close, they dance the way they should only at home. They should be where nobody can see them rubbing up on each other. They fade away shortly after their announcement because this seems like a normal occurrence to the regulars here. The couple turns back around to do what they were doing before the announcement—interruption—was made.

I pull my phone out of my purse and scroll a little on Facebook before ordering a drink because I still can't decide what I want my vodka mixed with tonight.

"Here you go." One of the bartenders with the black, long-sleeved, low-cut shirt sets a shot down in front of me. A little bit of the green liquid splashes out of it. She wipes the counter with a towel.

"This is from her." She nods her head back to point behind her and then turns her body to the side so I can see who she's talking about. I follow her gesture across the bar to the woman sitting alone. She sits alone just like me.

"Thank you," I say to the bartender for taking care of my decision on what the hell I should drink tonight. I don't ask her to tell the woman sitting alone at the bar 'thank you' for me, like I did to the guy sitting alone at the coffee shop the day I saw Neil and Brock sitting in the flesh. They were sitting there like they were really here. Like they were alive.

I'm here because I am actually and finally ready to talk to people. I don't know how long this feeling will last. But I'm ready to connect. To possibly make a friend that I'll want more out of than to just drink with or have sex with. If I don't, at least I got out and tried, which is more than most people can say. I'm ready for a true friendship with someone closer to my age. Not like Pauleen or Mr. and Mrs. Grey. Without stepping foot in here how could I find someone to trust and lean on without the expectations of sex involved? In other words, I'm not here looking for a man to take me home for the night, but a girlfriend. What better place than a bar to find a friend that won't judge you? We're all in here for a reason. Some have sinister reasons, like predators becoming vultures to their drunk prey. Others, like me, just need something simple. A friendship. A buddy to lean on.

Bryan is already starting to work my nerves and it took me bribing him with us time for me to have me time tonight. As if we don't have enough us time as it is. He is the only one I've been spending my extra time with. He practically lives with me now. I shudder at the inconvenience of it all. Another stage nine clinger to get rid of.

The bartender walks away from me and goes back to her job. She fake smiles at a man sitting alone at the bar—just like me and just like her, the woman who bought me a shot. Alone—he begins telling her all about his fishing trip and how he caught an actual shark one time. Years ago. He pulls out his phone to show her the picture. See? I'm a badass. I caught a shark. Go home with me. Have sex with me. She makes nice with him so she can get a good big fat tip, and the poor loser actually thinks he has a chance with her. I do not miss my days of bartending.

Placing my phone back in my purse, my eyes drift and I look across the bar at the woman sitting alone, the one that just bought my drink. I hold the green liquid shot in the air to cheer her and toss my head back to drink it all in one. Just like a shot is made for. It tastes sweet and sour at the same time. I wonder why she's here. I wonder why she's sitting alone at the bar—just like me— and I think maybe we'll have some things in common, maybe I'll make a friend tonight. I grab my purse and toss it over my shoulder.

Weaving around the chairs, I make my way to the woman sitting alone—just like me—in this hole in the wall bar that I found online to get lost in a world of people drinking their sorrows away—just like me—instead of calling to make an appointment for therapy. This is my therapy. At least for the night.

"Hey baby, come dance with us!" The couple wearing the matching I love my boyfriend and I love my girlfriend t-shirts yell out to me over the music as I walk by them. They both reach their arms out to feel my skin, and I smile a little at them to be polite.

"No, thank you." They don't press, like a lot of people do. They go back to business with each other as I continue walking towards the woman sitting alone at the bar.

Three women that look about my age sit together at a table. They look just as tacky as they can, wearing big, gaudy bling jewelry and each has a Karen haircut. They gawk at me with sneers on their faces, then turn their chairs and talk to each other quietly. Jealous bitches.

"Ey! Can I buy ya a drink?" A scruffy looking older man asks me right before I get to my destination, to the woman sitting alone at the bar. I look away from him and keep walking. He persists. "How 'bout a Miller Light, yeah?" Reaching out, he wraps my arm in his hand, holding me hostage in place.

"She's not interested." The woman sitting alone at the bar interrupts his little cat call. Except, she is not sitting anymore. She's standing right next to me. I glance over at her to make eye contact. She gives me a crooked smile. I like her smile. There is something devious about it.

"Come on." She nods her head to two free spots at the bar. I yank my arm away from the scruffy looking older man and lock arms with her.

The man shrugs his shoulders and tilts his head back to take a big swig of his foamy beer in a sweating cold mug. "Why don't you let her speak for herself," he suggests with a hint of frustration and sarcasm in his voice.

Laughing at this I shake my head a little because eww. "Yeah, I'm not interested." I hold my hands up like I'm showing free hands to a police officer and laugh again because no fucking thank you.

"Whatever," he grumbles and turns around to face away from us.

"Whatever is used when a man doesn't know what to say after a rejection," the woman who was sitting alone at the bar responds loud enough for the scruffy looking older man to hear. To my surprise, he doesn't reply. We head to our spots chosen by her, with our arms locked together again. We take a seat and she orders us each the same green liquid shot she ordered for me when I was sitting alone at the other side of the bar. I take a moment to look her over. She is fierce looking. Stunningly beautiful. She wears a sleeveless—even though fall has just begun and there is a chill in the air outside—plain black t-shirt that shows how tatted she is from her chest down to both arms, almost making a full sleeve on one of them. Some are in black but most are in color. Resist is tattooed on her left forearm, making my lips twitch. I can tell I already like her.

Her hair is dyed a fake, but classy looking red auburn color and she has it pulled to the side in a long Dutch braid. With her eyes painted a smokey gray lined with pitch black eyeliner in a point like cat eyes eyeliner. I like her style. She's got this whole 'Candace Stone from *YOU*' vibe going on. Does she have heart shaped sunglasses, too?

My new friend is wearing a matte desert taupe lipstick shade on her lips. I'm thrilled that I know that's what she's wearing on her lips because I have the exact same color at home. Maybe this is a cool way to strike up a conversation with the woman that was sitting alone at the bar who bought me a shot, and I don't really know why she did.

She interrupts my thoughts and quickly breaks the ice. I'm a little relieved that I don't have to start our very first conversation about how we both have the exact same lipstick color.

"You like those liquid marijuana shots?" She asks me, even though she already ordered us both another one. I think she knows that I liked it or she wouldn't have ordered us another shot.

I shake my head yes as she grabs one in each hand from the bartender, and hands one to me. "The music that's playing here sucks, so I paid through my phone—just by sitting here. How cool?!" She raves—"for better music to play on the jukebox,"

She rolls her eyes at a group of guys walking by that smile at us. Toadies start to ring in my ears, and the liquid marijuana is making me feel happy.

"Now, fuck yeah. Here we go. This is the shit I'm talkin' about," she sings while rocking her body side to side and bobbing her head. She leans her body into me and pats her chest with an open palm. "This is the song I put on." She smiles at me all bright and shiny. I like Toadies too. And we also have the same lipstick color, so I think I've made a new friend. I'm glad I came here instead of calling for a therapy appointment because this is therapy. Drinks, good music, fun redhead, and a hole in the wall bar? That's much more up my alley than sitting in a boring room with the same Van Gogh painting hung on the wall as every other therapist, recording my thoughts on papers, and asking the famous line, "And how does that make you feel?"

I dance along with her and sing all the words as the guy from Toadies sings Possum Kingdom and threatens to kill the woman of his dreams if she doesn't comply to be with him. We jam out to the music like it's an oasis because we finally have her playlist coming on and it seems we both have the same taste in music. Although, I have to admit that I get down a little with some Kid Rock.

***

Ding!

Reaching over to my nightstand to grab my phone, my head spins from the movement. I have a slight bit of a hangover from last night at the hole in the wall bar. With my thoughts still on the dream I had that's beginning to fade, I rub my eyes to adjust my sight from the sleep still lingering in my eyes, so I can read the text message that just came in. Bryan rolls over, still asleep next to me. He snores again and it starts to bother me. Reaching my arms above my head, I stretch and get out of bed, so I can get away from Bryan's loud snoring. I wonder when he'll go home and snore in his own bed.

With a sigh, I plop down on my couch, laying on my belly. I am now a little more awake than I was just a minute ago, so I can take in whatever message I just received. I hold my breath in hopes that it's not Diego Cold Hands, The Famous Bearer.

Mya
Wanna grab a coffee?

It's Mya, the woman sitting alone at the bar—just like me—last night. I hesitate for a minute because part of me feels like sleeping all day and it's not only because of a little hangover. I can handle hangovers all day every day. It's something else. It's like a dark hole that I want to throw myself into, to just rot. A dark hole like the one Neil tossed me in when we were married, except this time it would be my choice. My bed is the hole, and unfortunately Bryan lays on it. I sneak a peek over at him, still snoring and out like a light. He's off in whatever dreamland he's created to escape from reality. Not that his reality is so bad. Me, a comfy bed, and million fluffy pillows. His snoring roars throughout my apartment.

I can't handle this shit for one more second.

98

Willow
Okay.

I hopped off the couch to dig through my clothes for something comfortable and warm to wear ready to escape.

CHAPTER NINETEEN

HIM

Willow lays on her belly with her feet crossed in the air. Twirling her

luscious, soft curly hair. Like she is an innocent little schoolgirl—When I know damn good and well that she is no innocent any-fucking- thing—as she reads what's on her phone. She looks perfect, though, even after a night of drinking.

I watch as she peers over to the other side of the bed she lays on. The side that should be empty. *Empty just like my soul since the day Willow left me.* I zoom my camera lens in more to catch a glimpse of what caught her attention and—what-do-ya-know—it's Bryan. Bryan sleeps on his stomach, holding onto a fluffy pillow like it's a stuffed animal and he's a child. Zooming the camera in, I notice that a pool of his drool saturates beside his wide open mouth. God. I bet he is already getting on Willow's last nerves. How the fuck could he not?

Bryan has been there for over a week now. He's practically moved in with her. I know this isn't what she wants. It's most certainly not what she needs. Willow doesn't want to come home to a pretty boy every day. That'll get old for her. She'll get bored with him too easily and kick him to the curb, like she always does. I'll sit back and watch the show unfold. We'll call it a comedy because I'll laugh my ass off when she breaks his little heart. What she needs is a man. Someone to take care of her. A man that'll cook her a four course dinner, fold her laundry and put it away all organized by seasons so she doesn't have to dig too much for the right outfit, go down on her and make her cum every night, and wake her up in the mornings with a cup of coffee while she still lies in bed. What she needs is me. I'm the only one that would do those things for her, day in and day out, not just in the beginning to try to impress her.

Each morning I make myself a cup of coffee—would be two cups, but this bitch is playing—as part of my morning routine, and I zoom my camera lens into Willow's apartment to see if he's left yet.

Why the fuck is he always there?

She turns back to face me and types into her phone, lying on her couch now instead of her bed because she seems done with Bryan already. I told you. But this is different because she looks guilty. I notice how she swivels her necklace across her chin. She's nervous. She's guilty of something, not bored. She's got that look on her face. The one that shows what's going on upstairs. With her eyebrows raised and her pretty brown eyes widened, wearing the shade of guilt like she's already been talking to another guy behind Bryan's back.

I wonder…. Who is she talking to? Who has got her attention now? Is it another man? What have I missed?

CHAPTER TWENTY

MYA

"You can go. It's okay. I'll watch Ryder for you. You know that." My mom sits on the couch in my living room with adoration in her eyes as she watches my son yell out crash and boom noises when he makes his toy cars create a head on collision in the middle of the floor. She tells me this so I can go grab a coffee with Willow. Just like she told me last night so I could go grab a drink by myself. My mom is a saint, and I am a single mother. A complete single mother.

My mom stays in my guest house, and she gets to use any 'accommodations' at my house for free anytime she wants. The pool, the washer and dryer if hers ever goes out, the dishwasher, the oven, the internet, whatever it may be that she wants or needs at the time, she gets. She also stays in my guest house for free anytime she wants, so she has now taken up living there to help me with Ryder. It works out perfectly for the both of us. For Ryder, too. Him and my mom are very close. I don't charge my mom any rent money because well, she's my mom so I would never do her that way. Also, she cooks dinner most nights and breakfast each morning for our small family. She even babysits Ryder anytime I need a break, without any hesitation. In fact, he often prefers her company over mine. The little toot hurts my feelings with that, but hey, I'm not complaining. I enjoy my alone time. Besides, I can be moody, and my mom wears a smile on her face twenty-four seven, like she gets paid to. Sometimes I wonder what kind of pills she takes to make her so calm all the time. I know she's taking something. Nobody walks around smiling all the time, unphased by life's impossible demands.

Please give me whatever it is that woman is on!

After my husband, Ronnie passed away—committed suicide—he left my son and I his life insurance money. We are set for life. *For life.*

If I'm smart about the money I'll never have to work again. If I'm smart about the money, Ryder will never have to struggle when he's grown up. My husband came from a rich family and he made damn good money as a Defense Attorney when he was here and alive. Now I make damn good money just by staying alive. Painting colorful abstract flowers and mushrooms in my 'art room' with a pretty view of the green scenery and clear blue pool with an over the top fancy waterfall outside my big bay windows, while other moms work two jobs and go to school in hopes of making a quarter of what I receive from his life insurance money a year. It's not fair. I know it's not. But this is the way it is. I earned it and nobody can convince me otherwise. No matter how hard they try to. And they do. Trust me. They try to convince me otherwise.

I get lonely, though. I miss him and yet I don't miss him at the same time because he was a sad man. An angry man. A belligerent man sometimes. What can I say? He was just an unhappy person. But he was still my husband and the father of my son. That, above all, counts for something no matter how hard it was to be around him towards the end. Pushing the bad memories to the back of my mind, I'm brought to all the laughs we shared, the many meals we ate together, the countless times we kissed, the day we said our vows. It all just comes pouring in, like the tears on my cheeks after I lock my bedroom door to have a cry session without being interrupted by my son or my mom. When I can really let it all out. My heart breaks more each day that he's not with us. People are liars. Time doesn't heal the wounds of losing a loved one, and it doesn't make it any easier either.

We really had something going. At least, I thought we did. A family. A foundation. A life worth living but, to him it wasn't worth living. I have had to tell myself every day since then—since he swallowed a bottle of pills and finally succeeded at ending his life—that he was suffering with battles he didn't share with me. Or anybody for that matter. He was ready to leave this world, and I'll never know the whole reason why he chose to do that, to leave me and Ryder behind the way he did. While I might not understand that, I have to accept it and be okay with it because there is not any other way to handle it. There just isn't.

When I saw Willow sitting by herself at the bar last night, and the way she looked around observing to make sure her environment was right for her before she indulged in a world of booze, I could tell she was like me. Aware. Confident but not confident at the same time. Alone. Not just alone at the bar, but alone in her life. Alone in her thoughts. I thought to myself maybe I'll make a friend tonight. I think I was right. If life has taught me one thing in my twenty-seven years here, it's to trust that first feeling I get upon meeting someone. I learned the hard way. Ignoring my gut instinct about people has cost me jobs, friendships, and a lot of tears. I am a loner, and for the most part I'm okay with that. But it wouldn't hurt to have a friend or two to count on. Maybe someone that's a little like myself so I know what to expect.

When Willow sat with me, and I looked into her eyes, I strongly felt her energy. I'm not calling myself a psychic or anything like that, but everyone has it, the gift to pick up on vibrations and energy from other people. It's just a matter of whether you tap into it or not. I do. I can tell Willow is a fighter— just like me—and she knows what it's like to lose; to lose something, someone you love. She has experienced real love and real loss, just like me. Her eyes tell a story. A sad one. There's something different about hers, though. It's full of hope. And that? Well, you just don't see that every day. At least, I don't. Sadness and hope usually don't go hand in hand for most people. I like this about her. I have sad days all the time. Hope isn't something I allow myself to feel too often. Maybe it's a punishment. I do that sometimes. I punish myself when I'm too happy because how dare I when my husband is dead?

When someone you truly love dies, you can start to feel the energy and vibes radiating off anyone else around you—even strangers—who have experienced the same thing. Like a light beaming out of their chest and connecting to the one that's beaming out of your chest and then, boom! It's an instant connection. It's not something you have to try for. The connection is something that just happens because it's supposed to happen. It's a rare edition.

"Thank you, mom." I hugged her, wrapping her up in my arms and showing her that I appreciate her because not every mom with a young child gets a break like I do. Most people are too tired and drained from the demands of life to take their precious extra time out of any of their days to care for a needy child when what they really want to do is just rest. Not every mom has a mom like I do that loves her grandchild the way my mom loves Ryder. I know these things all too well. In my previous job, I used to work as a child protective services caseworker. I know the dark side, but I prefer the light.

"Come here, little one." I chase Ryder around the living room. He is four years old and always smiling because death hasn't changed him yet. One day it will, though. One day he'll really take it all in. Daddy is never coming back. Daddy is dead. Daddy killed himself. And he'll wonder for a little while—when he's in his teenage stage and thinks the world revolves around him like all teenagers do—if it was his fault. He'll play with the idea that he could have done something to prevent it. He'll think to himself that perhaps if he would have been a better little boy and stopped when his dad told him no or didn't throw fits or cry as much that maybe his dad would still be here. Those thoughts will go through his undeveloped mind hundreds of times. I'll have to remind him that daddy was sick. I'll lie and tell him that daddy did everything he could to stay with us, even though he didn't take the preventative measures I asked him to. But I'll tell Ryder that he went to all the psychiatrists, tried all the therapy and meds he could, prayed to God, and went to church on Sundays all in hopes of fighting the battle. Ronnie will be remembered as the man that tried it all. When he's older, and learns more about his dad and his suicide, and the decisions he made leading up to his choice in death, he'll start to wonder if he's like his dad. He'll want to know if the blood seeping through his veins carries the same as his dad's. Is it a disease? Is it hereditary? Will he die of suicide too? Is it inevitable? Is his mark already placed here, grave already carved with death by suicide?

For now, I'll revel in his innocence.

"Mommy will be back." I still talk to him in third person sometimes, and I think to myself how much I really need to stop doing that because it doesn't make any sense. I'm here right now. I'm the only parent he has left.

"Where are you going, Mommy?"

Ryder wants to know because if I say Chick-fil-a, he'll protest me leaving without him. He'll want to play on their indoor playground and make some friends. I make a mental note to take him there for a meal and playtime in the next few days to even out going out by myself two days in a row. I feel that mom guilt when I leave the house without him.

Tickling his belly until those high pitch squeals come out, I place kisses all over his pudgy cheeks. "I'm going to meet a friend for coffee."

He pouts, pushing out his bottom lip. For a minute there, I think he might go ahead and protest anyway and I'll have to cancel my morning date and spend it with him eating chicken nuggets and hearing kids scream. Sticking out his tongue, his cheeks rise as he scrunches up his face.

"Coffee is yucky!" He belches out.

Running off to grab more toys to sprawl about on the big playroom carpet, he doesn't skip a beat to tell me goodbye. "Bye Mommy!" Even though I know the mom guilt will pour on thick later on tonight when I'm lying in bed, remembering his sad face that lasted for a half a second this morning, I thank my lucky stars that he actually doesn't care because I have just a slight bit of a hangover.

"Don't forget to pick up after yourself," I remind him. I don't want grandma to pull out her hair by the end of my meeting with Willow, so I can continue going out and leaving him with my mom when I need adult interaction outside the walls here at home. Inside the same walls where I spend most of my days and crave conversation with someone, anyone that will understand me. Truly understand me.

CHAPTER TWENTY-ONE

MYA

Willow walks into the coffee shop, *The Charming Coffee Delight*, at her request. I can absolutely see why she asked me to meet her here.

"This place is gorgeous!" I rave as I meet and greet her at the entrance of the front door. She has on a sheer black floral long sleeved shirt with a black tank top underneath it, blue jean pants that tug at her hips and are fitted until they flare out at the bottom, and black boots that only show the points because her jeans are so long. Her hair is down and frizzy like a curly perm that has been brushed. She somehow pulls off this entire look. Everybody likes having a gorgeous friend, and that she is. A gorgeous friend. Envious of her beauty, I notice all eyes in the coffee shop are on her. Her look today is quite different from last night's oversized sweater and leggings, with her hair up in a clip showing a bare shoulder and her curls falling in her face.

"Isn't it though?" Willow beams. She's rockin' last night's makeup, which is basically no makeup anymore, and her cheeks are rosy.

"I actually made sure I had a cute little quaint coffee shop down the road from my new apartment before I moved here." She takes off her coat and lays it over the pink velvet lounge chair. Then she tosses her purse back over her shoulder. "I googled and saw the pictures and I just knew that I had to live close to this exact one." She looks around the coffee shop in awe.

"So, you live close by then?" I ask, starting up a conversation wanting to get to know her. I only live a ten minute drive from here. This is perfect for me!

She nods. "Yep. I actually live walking distance from here." She looks at my face and hers changes from a smile to guilt, with her brows in a curve. "Oh. I hope you didn't have to drive far. I didn't even think about that. I just really wanted you to see this place and it's just so comfortable and beautiful and—"

I interrupt because she's apologizing for no damn good reason. "Girl. No. Stop it." I laugh. "Don't even worry about it at all. Are you kidding me? If I knew about this place sooner I would have already been coming here." I sway my arms around like I'm presenting her with something even though she's the one presenting me with this place.

She smiles at me and bites her bottom lip. Pausing, she looks down and then back up at me.

"Okay then. It's settled. Let's go grab a coffee at the bar."

We take a seat on the stools but they don't seem near as comfortable as the lounge chairs in the back. Willow knows the barista by name and they chat a little as she makes our drinks. She introduces me to her barista friend, Chelsea. They seem like friends. Like the kind of friends you chat with over coffee, but not the kind of friends you chat with over liquor filled cups with a splash of something to chase while you're opening up about real life shit. Chelsea the Barista walks away to gather up caffeine and decaf orders as it starts to get quite busy in here. I'm unusually happy about this because now I don't have to be the third wheel. Even though something tells me I was only the third wheel for a few minutes because that conversation was more of niceties. Something tells me Willow doesn't meet up with Chelsea outside the walls of The Charming Coffee Delight.

She centers her attention on me and nods her head back towards the lounge chairs, the same ones she had draped her coat across earlier. "Wanna go sit over there?" she asks.

"I thought you'd never ask," I say, playfully. I grab my things and walk to the colorful lounge chairs with her.

Willow takes the pink one and I take the orange one beside her. Right before we can engage in any kind of conversation, a man that seems large and in charge with his aura radiating that he is the one in control here, walks up to Willow and kisses her cheek. Marking his territory.

"I've been looking all over for you." He takes a seat right beside Willow on the same lounge chair. "And I called you. *Twice*. You didn't pick up."

"Jesus, Bryan! You scared the hell out of me!" Willow shouts, quite loudly. With wide eyes, she glances around the coffee shop, an embarrassed expression covers her face. I don't think she meant to say that as loud as she did. She didn't realize she'd gotten so jumpy.

Bryan chuckles. "I'm sorry for scaring you."

After just a few seconds of awkward silence, the concerned look on his face turns to a scowl. "Ya know, Willow, I would really appreciate it if you tell me when you're leaving and where you're going."

I tilt my head sideways, keeping the thoughts to myself. Not your circus, not your monkeys, I remind myself. Still, it's hard watching Willow squirm, obviously feeling uncomfortable as Bryan tries to make her submit to him. I just get more and more pissed off with each thing said, but instead of showing that because clearly this is her battle and their argument, I just change the subject. I try for something light-hearted to ease the nerves building up here.

"So, Willow, where did you move from?" I take a sip of my latté. It's too hot to guzzle down like I want to. I cup it with both hands because they're cold and wait for it to cool down a little bit. "Oh! And why? That's an important one. Why did you move to New York City? Everyone has a reason to move here!"

They both suddenly stop their bickering. Bryan veers his eyes down at his shoes and cracks his knuckles. Willow clears her throat.

"Chicago," she answers. Just as she's about to answer why, Bryan interrupts her.

"I thought you told me you moved here from Texas." He gives her an accusatory look and purses his lips together. He places his hands on his thighs and waits for an explanation from her. He seems to enjoy an argument.

She snaps her fingers like she just remembered something. "Sorry. Yes. I *did* move here from Texas, but before that I stayed in Chicago with a friend for just a few weeks. Almost a month, actually." She adjusts herself in her seat. "And anyway, I called her apartment home during that time." She draws in a big breath, peers her head down, and clears her throat again. She seems nervous, but she made it through that lie. I can tell it's a lie.

"Ah. That makes sense," Bryan exclaims. At first I thought he said it in a sarcastic way and caught on really quickly, but then I realized he took in what she said, has already digested it, and it's just what it is. He won't put anymore thought into it.

But I can tell. I can tell that Willow is hiding something. Her phone dings and because she is already holding it in her hands she looks down at the text message. She shakes her head and then huffs in another big, long sigh, before tossing her phone on the empty part of the lounge chair she and Bryan are sitting on. Her phone continues to ding over and over again. Willow lets it. She tries to make small talk with me hoping to ignore whoever it is that's blowing her phone up.

"This weather is perfect, am I right? What were those little green drinks called again? Oh, liquid marijuanas. That's right! I really love your boots. Where did you get them?"

The small talk doesn't take either of our attention away from the constant dings chiming from her phone. She finally picks it back up, and her eyes become increasingly wider as she stares at the screen. Her hands begin to shake. Curiosity gets the best of me, and now I'm invested. Perking up, I lean towards her. I want to see what's on her phone.

Bryan peeks at her phone over her shoulder, at what has her distressed. He grabs the phone away from her with a yank, glaring.

"You're fucking leading him on, Willow." The accusation is enough to cause her to break it off with this asshole.

"That's it! I am so done!" She screeches.

Continuing, she spouts in one big breath. "You snore too fucking much. Goddammit. I can't get any sleep! You moved into my house without asking me. You're always there! I'm tired of seeing your face. You try to control me. Now you're embarrassing me in public. This is *insane*. I am done. Go home! To your house, not mine." She points to the front door of the coffee shop. A twinkle of anger sparks her brown eyes.

He grits his teeth as he stands and pushes her phone back into her hands, pushing it a little too hard. Then he looks around as if just remembering he's in public, and stomps away. Something tells me he'll be back, though. Something tells me he is not done with this conversation.

"Wow," I mumble without meaning to out loud. I notice she has tears filling up her eyes.

"I'm not crying because I'm going to miss him. I honestly barely even know him. I'm crying because I'm fucking mad." She pulls her phone up and puts the screen up to my face. "Does *this* look like I'm leading him on?" I squint my eyes to read what she's showing me. "Can I hold it myself to read?"

"Sure."

I take the phone out of her hand and hold it close enough to my face to read. I scroll a little up and see that it's just him texting her and she isn't participating. She has the guy that's harassing and threatening her saved as Diego Cold Hands, The Famous Bearer. After we talk about the complete bullshit that this guy is saying to her, I'm absolutely asking her why she has him saved under this extraordinary name because it's interesting to me, but I'm sticking with focusing on what's important right now.

"He's threatening you. This is a real threat." I hold up her phone, but I say this quietly so nobody can listen in on our conversation. "Is he serious or do you not take him very seriously and this kind of shit is something he's always saying to you or something? Either way, you need to block his ass!"

“I don’t know.” She sniffles a little. “I think he’s in Dubai right now. That’s where he said he was moving. He had asked me to move there with him. I am so glad I told him to fuck off.”

“Well,” I suggest, “You need to *really* tell him to fuck off because apparently the first time or however many times hasn’t worked. This is some serious shit, Willow.”

She pulls her shoulders up and holds them there. “Block him and then what? He creates another phone number and harasses me from that one, too? Been there. Done that.” She takes a big gulp of her latté. “It doesn’t work. It never works.”

“He just threatened to kidnap you! I’d say block him over and over if you have to.” I hand her phone back to her. “You might even need to go to the cops.”

“No!” she spouts. “Sorry,” she murmurs, her voice lower. “Sorry. Just…. no cops.” She gazes around the coffee shop again, seeming nervous. Fiddling with the charm on her necklace, she moves it back and forth across her chin. What is she hiding from?

“Gosh. You must think I’m a mess and you would be right to think that because I am.” She shrugs her shoulders and sets her phone down. “I really am and I can totally understand if after we finish our coffees that I don’t hear from you again.”

“Don’t be silly.” I wave my hand in the air to brush off what she just said. “I love a good soap opera.”

We laugh together at this, and she loosens up a little.

***

I know all too well what it’s like to be living a life full of chaos. Feeling alone in that sinking ship that people keep piling bricks onto to make it sink deeper and deeper into the ether as you fill your cheeks up to hold your breath. You hope that you have enough inside to keep you going so you can rise above the deep, blue water that you’ve let yourself fall into the bottom floor of, until you’ve fought against the waves and currents to take a big, long gasp of air and finally, *finally* you’ve caught your breath.

Finally, *finally* you've saved yourself before it was too late.

Sometimes you need someone—someone trustworthy and with good intentions—to dive down to the bottom of the ether you've sunk into. To grab your hand and swim above with you. To teach you how to take that big, long gasp of air to finally, *finally* catch your breath. And to finally, *finally* help you save yourself before it's too late. I can tell Willow needs that, and I can be that person for her. I really can. Because I needed that person and didn't get it. I can't watch her sink and not lend her my hand. Willow picks her phone back up after a few more dings spring out.

Ding! Ding! Ding! Ding!

"Block him." I remind her.

She does as I say. *Good girl*. She clicks on Diego Cold Hands The Famous Bearer. I watch her push the block button, and she immediately sighs in relief. Her shoulders sink, like she's been carrying the burden of him around for far too long. Making eye contact, I feel a connection that will surely last. It's not because she followed my instructions. I don't get off on that. It's because she knows what I've said today is true. She knows what's good for her.

That's my girl.

CHAPTER TWENTY-TWO

HIM

I knew I should have been paying more attention. I fucking knew I should have been paying *much* more attention than what I have the last few days because you leave Willow alone for just a few hours and she gets herself into shit. Just like a damn child that you can't take your eyes off of at the park. A child that you have to just sit and fucking keep your eyes glued onto or they'll notice you aren't watching and bam! They've hit another kid over the head with a toy shovel. Then that kid is screaming and the kid's parents are mad. And the other kids' parents are aware of the little kid that bashed another kid over the head with a toy shovel. Now your kid is the one other kids have to stay away from at the request of their parents, and it's all because you decided to have a little you time and take a scroll through your phone for just a few minutes. Those few minutes can change every visit you take with your kid to the park afterward. In fact, you might have to find a whole new park to spend time at, when really you should just teach your brat to keep their damn hands off of other kids. Teach your kids a lesson the hard way, like watching them have less friends because of their mistakes.

I might have to watch Willow learn her lesson the hard way or I can teach her it myself. Because what Willow has done is essentially the same. When will she learn the consequences to her actions equate to that of a child? Willow acts like a fucking child. Don't shoot the messenger. I just call it like I see it. That's all.

I wanted to see, though. I wanted to know. I had to know if she could be trusted long enough for me to get some more things done for our future together. To build her a gift that would take other guys weeks to do, but only took me days. That's how invested I am. Don't you see?

Not wasting time, I took a short trip back home to gather up some things for our life together and of course I had to rest before heading back because I am fucking exhausted after all the work I put into our relationship. And what has she put into us? Into our relationship? Nothing here lately. Not a damn thing. There is zero effort on her end of the stick. Fucking zero. She couldn't even hold herself together long enough for me to get some very necessary things done in order for us to move forward in the next steps of our relationship.

It was only a few days ago that I hadn't zoomed my Nikon camera into her apartment to watch her every move. These are things I have to do in order to make this relationship work. It makes me sick to my stomach witnessing her and Bryan wine and dine together like they're actually going to fucking make it as some starlet couple. It was only a few days. *Days.* That's all it took for her to fuck it all to hell and make a new friend. This isn't just any friend. I'm fine with her enjoying the company of another person that she wants to label as a friend, although I don't see the need in it when she has me. But this is an untrustworthy, controlling, brainwashing, manipulative woman that I wouldn't trust around my dog if I had one.

God. Save me your theatrics, Mya. Just block him, You're a strong, powerful woman and you can't let any man get in the way of that, Girl power, blah blah blah. Because Willow is who she is, she listened to her new friend and pressed that block button. What else will she do just because this Mya chick tells her to? That's what I'm stuck on. Why does she do what she tells her to do and she won't do what I tell her to do when she's only known Mya for a few days? Does Mya have some type of spell over Willow? Does she want her all to herself? How long will Willow take bullshit demands from a woman she doesn't even know?

The only good thing that's come out of everything that happened this morning, is her break up with Bryan. Had she not made friends with Mya, she would have kept that junkie woman beater around even longer. I know she would have. So, bravo Mya. Bravo. That at least gives me more of a chance—until Willow finds some other loser guy that'll cling to her like an extra limb she'll eventually want to saw off—to do what I have planned. The more she is alone, the more time I have for us. The more time I have to stick to my plan. To gain access to all that is Willow.

I put my phone back into my jacket pocket, grab my latté off the table in front of me, and toss it back to take a big swig. I realize it's empty—*empty just like my soul since the day Willow left me*—and I can't go order another one or she might see me here. Here in the same coffee shop as her and her new stupid friend, Mya. It would then be all over with. No doubt about it. There would be no explaining my way out of that. I have been very careful so that she doesn't see me. I've made sure we don't run into each other. I can't mess things up now. So, I stay seated and I wait and wait and wait for what seems like forever before Willow and Mya finally decide that they drank enough caffeine to get them started for their day out. They planned to spend the next hour shopping on the square—the same square we are at now, so I have to be extra careful walking home—before Mya heads home to her son and Willow heads back to her apartment to see that hopefully Bryan has packed up what little belongings he has there and has gone on his merry little fucking way. At least this way I don't have to kill him.

Mya makes an announcement to Willow that she needs to use the bathroom. Willow watches her walk all the way there. After her new friend has shut the bathroom door, she opens up her purse, grabs a little bottle of vodka and pours a few shots into her cup. She screws the lid back on the bottle and tucks it back into its place. She cradles her cup of latté vodka like a newborn baby. Hugging it like it'll wrap its arms around her and give her something back. Then she takes a big gulp and closes her eyes to relish in the moment.

Drink up, Willow. You're gonna need it.

I wait again. It's just a little bit longer before they leave out the front door of the coffee shop and I exit out the back door of the coffee shop to stroll the alleyway back to my apartment. Where the stoner across the door from me will probably be sitting halfway inside and halfway outside of the doorway, smoking another doobie thinking in his small mind that he's not filling up his momma's place with a skunk weed smell. I think I'll probably tell him that he's wrong about that when I see him again.

Pulling my jacket closed over my chest against the crisp air, it violates me with a piercing jolt. I rub my hands together and breathe warmth into both of them while they're cupped around my mouth. It's fucking freezing outside today. Looking above me, I notice the sky is gloomy. The sun is hiding from me. From all of us. It might rain, and I have too much shit to get done before the downpour. Walking faster, I take a peek down at my watch and calculate how much time I'll have before Willow gets back to her—our—apartment. It's imperative that I get this all done today. I don't have time to waste.

Walking the back alleyway, I notice a man who has more wrinkles than both of my grandparents put together sitting on the ground with his back leaning against the building and his legs propped up on a full trash bag sitting in front of him, like an ottoman. He holds his hand out to me and asks, "Do you have some spare change?"

Well, no shit I have spare change. Unlike him, I actually fucking work. I don't sit around on my ass and just wait for the next guy wearing nice shoes to turn the corner, so I can harass him for his hard earned money.

Going against my better judgment, I dig around in my pockets to gather up any coins I've tossed in there. The mixture of coffee and moldy muffins stenches my nose. The background noise is filled with cop car sirens and people chatting to each other as if there is no crisis happening around us. That's the city for ya. I find a dollar bill and three quarters in my pockets. I walk towards him to hand him the money, but his scruffy dirty mutt shows his sharp teeth and growls at me when I approach. The wrinkly man tugs at the mutt's leash.

"Now you just stop that!" He belches out and then starts coughing uncontrollably. He hawks a big loogie onto the ground. His disgusting mutt gets sidetracked by that and starts licking it up. I hand the man the money and I walk away as he's thanking me. I don't want to be around that pair for one more second. I am better than them. I bet he spends the money I gave him on drugs. Pathetic. At least I helped him, or at least I tried. Maybe he'll actually be a decent human being and put it towards a coffee, a pastry, or lunch at McDonalds.

Laughter fills the air as I'm walking past the next few buildings. A woman dressed in little to nothing—Is she not freezing?—leans against the wall while her muse kisses her neck and aggressively pulls her into him. She laughs. He laughs. They don't mind the smell of trash in the air or that they're actually fucking making out right beside a large trash bin, filling each other up, giggling like a couple of teenagers in love and staring into each other's eyes like they're in the honeymoon stage. Maybe they are. Nothing else matters but the two of them together. So, possibly they just haven't noticed the lingering smell of the trash. They're just focused on each other. That tunnel vision. I remember when Willow and I were just like this. Us against the world. Only we existed when we were together. Daydreaming about the love spell she's had me under for so long, I had forgotten I was just standing there, staring at them. My mind comes back to what's transpiring in front of me, and I wonder if she is a prostitute because of what she's wearing while it's this cold outside. The fact they're behind a building right beside a large trash bin is another factor. Only a whore would wear lingerie outside when it's cold. Only a whore would fuck beside a pile of trash.

Not realizing how long I had been staring, I wondered what the hell her problem was as she whispered something to her possible client while looking at me, snuggled into him as if he's her protector. I must have looked like a pervert, trying to sneak a peek. He turns to stare back at me, returning my death glare.

Embarrassed, I pull my eyes down to my feet. I keep walking and hear them behind me giggling again, carrying on with what they were doing before I accidentally interrupted them.

Skunk weed stench invades my nostrils, and damn that smells fucking sensational. I haven't smoked in forever. My eyes follow the smell to a couple of teenage boys that look young enough to have skipped school and hang in the back alley. One of them glides on his skateboard towards me. The others sit, watch, and laugh as they tell him, "Watch out!" when he gets closer to me. The kid isn't paying attention. He has his focus on his feet. On his skateboard, rather than his destination. I move out of the way before he can bump right into me, and he keeps on going. He never even looks up. He's probably one of those types of people that after he smokes, his mind races from thought to thought. Whatever he's actually doing while his mind races, he's doing without even really thinking about it. I know what that's like because I'm one of those types of people, too. That's why I won't smoke with my neighbor, Sandy, the dirty blonde hair *dude*.

I need to remain focused on the task at hand; Willow.

CHAPTER TWENTY-THREE

HIM

The walk back to my apartment is only a five minute walk, but the episodes that occurred on the way here made it more like a ten minute commute. Knowing that, it means I only have fifty minutes before Willow starts walking back home. Which means I only have fifty-five minutes before she arrives back at home. I count my lucky stars that Sandy isn't sitting halfway in and halfway outside his apartment door this time. I don't have time to make small talk and be forced into niceties. That means I can focus on doing what I need to do before she's home. I count my lucky stars again seeing that Bryan isn't there—halle-fucking-luja—and I can now find a way into Willow's apartment!

Thankfully, in New York City, nobody pays attention or cares about who is going in and out of your apartment or what door they're using to go in and out of your apartment because everybody is far too busy to give a shit the way they do in small towns like you see on tv. This will be easier than you think. Still, I wish I would have kept that stupid baseball cap that I left in the backseat of that taxi when I got to New York City and bought that zoom lens for my Nikon camera. It would be easier with that disguise. Joe Goldberg was onto something. He really was. Where is a damn baseball cap when you need one? I can't just hop Willow's balcony fence without having something to cover my face up without being so evident about it, like wearing a ski mask. I need something subtle.

I take a look around my apartment, going from room to room to come up with something—anything—that will at least cover my head. I finally find it. A hoodie. I peel my jacket off and pull the hoodie on. I toss the hood over my head and I don't put my jacket back on despite the protest of my body from the weather because I don't want anyone to recognize me by it later on. You can never be too careful. I grab a pair of black leather gloves and place them on my hands, so that no fingerprints are traceable, not mine at least. Then I grab the tile grip I ordered from Amazon to be able to get into Willow's back sliding door, and the syringes from my dresser. With a smirk on my face, I gaze down at my watch, acknowledging I have forty- eight minutes left before she starts heading her way back home. Making sure I have everything, I head on over to Willow's apartment keeping my head down with my hands holding onto the syringes and tile grip tight in my front hoodie pocket.

***

I don't glance all around me to see if anyone is watching when I get to Willow's balcony. That would look suspect as fuck. Instead, I jump over the wooden balcony the way people do when they're running from the cops, and they actually get away with it, whatever it may be, and then I look all around. My coast is clear. Crystal clear. Nobody has been watching, just as I figured it would turn out to be because everyone is too busy around here to care. People really should do better. Ya know? Care a little more about their neighbors. I could be a really bad man breaking into a woman's apartment to do the unthinkable, like rape, and nobody would bat an eye. I pull the tile grip out of my hoodie pocket and grab a hold of her sliding glass door. By instinct, I check first to see if it's locked and wam, bam, thank you, mam! It is unlocked! As I slide it open, I think of how Willow is a very stupid girl for leaving the door unlocked. Breathing in her vanilla and honey scent that I can smell as soon as I open the door, I step over the threshold. I'm in! I slide the door closed behind me and glance down at my watch again. I'm good on time. Thirty-nine minutes left before she even starts her way back home. That is plenty of

122

time to do this. I have three tasks to complete this morning while I'm here.

I checked every spot inside of her apartment where people would put an extra key. I'll make a copy because Willow is not sharing with me yet. I finally found it in her junk drawer in the kitchen, of all places. It was jumbled in there with old mail, old late electric bills from previous apartments, hair clips (of all things), clothesline clips, chip bag clips, so many different types of clips, used batteries, lids to plastic Tupperware, an old driver's license, and many other random things that conclude a kitchen junk drawer. Her junk drawer is so random that I don't even think she'll notice the spare key is gone. I may not even have to make a copy. This one will be my copy. I hold my key up in the air in front of my face and kiss it. Not the way I want to kiss Willow, but more of a peck. Happy to have found what should have been mine in the first place.

Since I'm already in the kitchen I move on to my next task. I pull the syringes out of my hoodie pocket and delicately lay them down on the counter in front of me. Willow likes going to The Charming Coffee Delight down the road from us, but she also likes buying the k-cups from there to make her own drinks at home when she's not feeling up to socializing. I pick up each of her k-cups and give them each a shot of morphine. I've counted nine to be exact. Nine k-cups and nine syringes. It worked out perfectly! Tell me that's not fate! Tell me that's not fate when I brought exactly nine syringes with me and she has exactly nine k-cups in her kitchen. Go ahead. I'll wait. You know this is fate.

My next task is not a tricky one at all, but I'm running out of time. I look at my watch again, realizing I have only ten minutes left before she starts walking home. I have got to find the perfect pair. Tiptoeing over to her bedroom, I look in the doorway. As fate would have it—yes, fate again—there they are! Lying on her floor right beside her bed. The perfect pair! Just like I have desperately needed for so long now, they're exactly like I have pictured them on her so many times. They're the same ones I have been dying to get a hold of, the ones I have been missing so much. I have been lost without having the scent of Willow with me.

Bending down, I pick up the lacey red lingerie that she probably wore last night under her leggings. I press them against my face and feel the softness of them. Then I breathe them in the way I used to breathe in Willow, and *my God*. I want to fuck her right now. The smell of sweet, sweet vanilla honey that lingers from her body is now mine to indulge in anytime I want. Anytime I need my Willow fix it's mine, because let's face it, this is a necessity. I put them in my hoodie pocket with the used syringes and the tile grip. Turning, I head on out of here and back to my apartment and I think to myself of how lucky I am to be the one that gets to call Willow mine.

CHAPTER TWENTY-FOUR

WILLOW

Glancing at my phone, It shows eight o' clock in the morning and I have to be shaking hands with my new boss at my new job at ten o' clock. Sharp. I am settled in my fluffy reading chair that sits right beside my window—back door to my balcony—and the sun beating in isn't too hot or too bright. It is just right. Shining in, it gives me just enough natural light to enjoy the nineteenth chapter of Gone Girl. Yes, I'm reading it again. It's my favorite book. This will be my third time diving into the fucked up little world that Gillian Flynn has created for the Dunnes.

Well, it's not so different from the one I was living before Neil and Brock died. Before they burned to death. I shudder at such an awful way to go, but they had to go. They had to die. It was me or them. I wasn't about to let either one of them win. Closing that door and locking it behind has been the best choice I've ever made. It was the smartest and bravest moment of my life. I don't regret it.

Me and Amy Dunne had the same goals in life. To escape our abusive, controlling husbands. Except, she went back to hers and hers wasn't actually abusive. She was the crazy one. I am not the crazy one. My dead husband was the crazy one, and thankfully I don't have to go back to him because he is dead. And actually, I had two crazy guys to escape. As luck would have it—or death, whatever you want to call it—I don't have to go back to either one of them because they are both dead.

Dead. Dead. Dead.

I applaud myself silently every time I think of Neil and Brock dying. Screeching out in agony behind a locked door as fire crawls up their bodies like bugs they try to swat —Neil standing there on the stairs, Brock lying on the floor—until it reaches their faces and eventually turns them to ashes.

It's been one month and three weeks since I moved from Chicago to New York City, and honestly? I'm not having as much fun as I thought I would. I pictured myself enjoying my own company with this place all to myself. Maybe making a friend or two. Just a small little group of friends that I can read books with and discuss each chapter before moving onto the next, drinking coffee and liquor with them. Not a mixture of the two. Coffee talk is way different from liquor talk. No men. No drama. No constant need to make sure others feel reassured in my life when I don't really even want them around me in the first place because they just radiate toxicity and bad energy.

Bryan gathered up his things from my apartment the day I broke up with him at the coffee shop in front of Mya. He had littered my apartment with his things like he lived here, too. I believe that's what he was trying to do. Move in with me even though he has his own place and I didn't invite him. Now that it comes to mind, I never even visited his place. I wonder if he even lived alone, like he claimed.

Unfortunately, Bryan waited until I was home to get his things. He could have gathered them up before I got back home. Bryan knew he left my door unlocked. My front and back doors were both unlocked when I got home, so he could have just come back here and picked up his shit and left. Instead, he waited until I got home just so he could try to talk me into staying 'his girl'. What a joke. I no longer allow men to guilt me into doing what I don't want anymore. I put my foot down. No matter what the consequences will be, whether that be a slap across the face, being pinned up against a wall, or chained up against my will.

Of course, I told him no. I also told him that we were never even official in the first place. I wasn't 'his girl' before, and I'm definitely not going to be 'his girl' now; not after what he did. The old Willow would have given him the benefit of a doubt. I would have sheepishly taken him back and given him another chance. Everyone deserves second chances, right? Wrong. The new Willow realizes who the fuck you are when you show me the first time.

I suppose he didn't like that too much. He got right into my face and yanked my arm. Leaving a bruise that I now have to cover up anytime I go somewhere. At least it's autumn. People won't ask why the hell I'm wearing a long sleeve or quarter sleeve shirt. That day was the last time I saw Bryan and it'll stay the last time I ever see him again. This might be a little tricky since he lives just a block away from me and knows the places I frequent. I've been lucky. I haven't run into him, and it's been almost two weeks. Bryan was such a waste of my fucking time.

So much for waiting until the buildup. We moved fast. Way too fast. Like I always do. That's why I pictured my life with no men this time around. One day we were cuddled up, eye fucking each other and waiting until the buildup. The next we were actually fucking each other and all of a sudden he was a different person. He practically moved in with me. The honeymoon stage was over before it could even begin. I was already over him the first time I heard him snore, and done with him before I broke it off, when there really wasn't anything to break off.

No. More. Men.

When I told Mya about him grabbing my arm and getting in my face, she was genuinely pissed off. I like that she cares about me. Like, actually cares, selflessly. I've learned that when a man 'cares' about me, it's because he actually cares more about himself. Oh, he cares about me alright. About what I can do for him. And that's really what it's about. Pretending to care about me. Pretending to love me so he can have me. Just so he can take me. It isn't real. It never is.

At least with Mya, I can already tell we have so much in common and that makes me feel safe. Like I know what to expect. When I visited her house for the first time, I had been taking in my surroundings of her home. Learning who Mya is even more than what she was already telling me about herself. By a glance here and there at the paintings hung on her wall. I noticed that each canvas has her signature written at the bottom in metallic sharpie. She's an artist. Buddha statues line up beside each other on her windowsill and they meditate together. Each Buddha is a different color creating a rainbow in a straight line instead of a curve.

Her bookshelf had caught my eye immediately, when I first walked into her den, but I kept myself from making the entire hang out session about books because I knew that once I started, I'd have a hard time stopping myself from grabbing each book like it's a library I'm visiting instead of her home. I wanted to be respectful of her time. There would be plenty of other times to come over and indulge in that side of her house. On that side of our friendship. The wall I faced during our conversation was the grand bookshelf. The entire wall, and even up to her high vaulted ceiling, were books! All books! She even has a wooden ladder with wheels making it easy to glide from one section to another. Every reader's dream. I gasped when I first laid my eyes on it. She smiled at me, proud of her home library, but I waited to talk about the beauty of it all rather than making a quick compliment about it, then taking a seat because that would demand much more attention than a subtle *this is beautiful.*

As we sat together, we chatted, and indulged in snacks and coffee, I noticed a book sitting on a table with a pair of reading glasses laid on top, right beside a green reading chair that is quite similar to the one beside my sliding glass window door. I bought my chair at a thrift shop and had to shove it into the back of a truck I borrowed from a friend, but I had a feeling she bought hers off of Wayfair or somewhere like that online, and had it shipped directly to her home. We aren't the same like that, but we are the same in so many other ways.

Gone Girl by Gillian Flynn was her last or maybe her current read. I could tell right then and there that we—me and Mya—are going to get along just perfectly. No question about it.

"Let me see your arm," Mya requested when I visited her house for the first time.

Ignoring her demand, I changed the subject. "Your son is beautiful." I expressed as he ran in and out of the room.

"Roar!" He belched, holding his toy dinosaurs in the air.

"Thank you," Mya responded, sitting up straight and showing her pride.

She opened up to me, telling me about her husband's suicide; a tragic story indeed. Mya is lucky she has her mother's unconditional love. She's such a great grandmother to Ryder. We talked about her former job as a caseworker for Child Protective Services and the secondhand trauma she gained from it. She told me about the small town she grew up in and how glad she was to move away from there. "The town is full of misogynistic assholes."

Since she shared so much, it was only right I told her about myself, so I told her about my upcoming job that I am finally going to start this morning and my hippy dippy decked out apartment. I claimed my parents are the complete opposite of hers, that I have never been married or pregnant before, and I'm waiting for the right guy.

What else could I do but lie?

After all this talk transpired, I finally opened up about what Bryan had done and she asked to see the bruises on my arm. "Let me see them." She was fuming.

I was wearing a short sleeve t-shirt and a light jacket that day to cover up the mark that Bryan left behind on my arm. I took my jacket off and pulled up the sleeve of my shirt to show her. Black and purple fingerprints cursed our eyes. Because I felt sick to my stomach—literally—every time I saw it, I dropped the sleeve back into place to cover up the ugly, sliding my jacket back on.

She shook her head in utter disgust. "I fucking hate men. I don't think I've met one man that doesn't abuse women in one way or another." She took a drink from her coffee. "You need to take pictures of it all and save any text messages and voicemails he sends you. Keep a log of his phone calls too," Mya suggested. "CYA," she added.

"What does that mean?" I was eager to know.

"Cover your ass." Mya winked at me and grabbed a cookie off the plate sitting on the coffee table in front of us. Her mother brought them in on a tray when I arrived and gifted them to us. The complete opposite of my mother. "Just in case," she said before taking a bite out of the cookie. Crumbs fell onto her shirt, and she dusted them off into her cupped hand. "Just in case things get out of hand and he contacts you again or starts to harass you." She glanced down at the tray in front of us. "Cookie?" She offered with her mouth full.

Without hesitating, I grabbed a cookie, still warm to the touch and fresh out of the oven. I took a big bite, leaving half the cookie to gobble up. Chocolate chip. My favorite. It made me feel warm, cozy, and welcomed. I decided that the tray of cookies would be my lunch for the day. Mya sat with her legs crossed, swinging one up and down while chomping on one cookie after another. She said nothing and waited patiently for my response. I swallowed my bite before I said anything back to her suggestions about Bryan.

"Yeah. I took pictures of the bruises. I'm taking screenshots and saving everything he sends me." I appease her. I took another bite, the last bite of that cookie. With a mouth full I said, "Just in case. You're right. Just in case." I grabbed another chocolate chip cookie and ate it all in one big bite. Then, I picked up another.

CHAPTER TWENTY-FIVE

WILLOW

Seeing *Gone Girl* on the table beside Mya's reading chair—that's just like mine!—kicked me out of the reading slump I had been in since moving to New York City. It prompted me to re-read it. The familiarity of it all brought me back to that place with Neil, my escape. And it brought me back to that place with Brock, my escape. I'm still in my pajamas and fluffy knee length socks, wrapped up in a blanket reading Gone Girl and sipping my coffee—a vanilla latté with two extra shots of espresso and *no milk* that I made myself this morning. A little jump start to my day!

My phone alerted me with a loud alarm that it was time to stop reading and face the real world, so I left my latté sitting on the small table beside my reading chair and placed the book upside down and flat on my coffee table to save the spot I was reading. Heading to get dressed for my first day at my new job, I begin to feel more and more sleepy. Hopefully, after consuming this much caffeine and getting ready for the day I'll wake up some. I've got a big day ahead of me. I can't be up there yawning in the boss's face while he's training me. I have to make a good first impression.

Smiling to myself in the mirror, I spread a little bit of lip gloss on and glob up my eyes with black mascara. Afterwards, I pick Gone Girl back up and take a sip of my latté. It's gotten cold, so I heat it up, and when it's just right, I take a seat again to have a little reading time with my latté and book before heading out to work. And you would think, wouldn't you, that with each sip I take I'd be waking up more? I mean, that's three after adding an extra espresso in one cup! But it's not doing the job. My eyes are heavy and my head is nodding. So, to wake my ass up for my first day at my new job in this new state and new city to be a very new me, I gulp down the rest of it in my pink cheetah print coffee mug. *Gulp.*

***

A grin that I can only describe as demonic looking violates the good dream I was having. The smell of garlic breath makes me gag. I can't get away from him. Frightened and wondering if this is real, I move my face away from his. Way too close to mine. He moans and as he breathes out I smell the garlic on his breath again, bringing bile to my throat.

How did he get into my apartment? How did he get in my bed? How did he come back? Why is he in my face? Is this a nightmare?

With his eyes hollowed out and black, a chill lingers down my spine and I freeze in fright. The holes where his eyes are supposed to be look uneven like someone had dug them out of the sockets with a spoon. Brock looks otherworldly. Like a badly deformed monster. He's like a real monster, matching on the outside to what was already deep inside of him when he was still alive. With one half of his face intact, the other half is skinless, showing red wet goo. The other half begins to drip. As it Slips and slides off, I watch it slowly fall onto me. *Splat!*

Part of the boiling skin, that once covered his face, drops onto my chest. My bare chest. It's hot and sizzling—sizzle—and the smell of my flesh burning takes over his garlic breath. The smell is too much to handle. Gagging again, I try vomiting over the side of my bed. I can't, though, because I'm too in shock to move. The burning pain on my chest only lasts for a second or two, although it feels like a lifetime. After I'm done screaming from the pain I pull my eyes down to see the burn mark and I notice that I'm naked on top, where my bra and shirt just were. I try to cover up. On instinct, I move my hands to cover my bare breasts so he can't see me even though he already has—many times—but

132

once again I can't move. I'm paralyzed. I am paralyzed with fear and something else. Something stronger than fear is holding me down. Like a weight heavier than Brock himself laying on top of me.

What the fuck is happening?

Icicles pierce my body. How can this be? His face, his neck, his chest showing from the few buttons that are open on his white polo shirt are all boiling, sliding off, and bubbling. *Pop!* One of his bloody bubbles burst and a few droplets hit my face. He smiles like he enjoys the feeling of his skin exploding. As he yanks my pants off me, I yell out for help and notice that my back door isn't closed all the way. I don't remember even opening it up today. Pulling my eyes back to Brock's boiling face, I notice that I am completely naked. The vulnerability. The paralyzation. The fright. I don't feel strong enough to fight back. I close my eyes and will myself to wake up. It doesn't work!

No. No. No. No. Please don't. I can't. I won't. I refuse. Begging him not to rape me only turns him on even more. He grabs a fist full of my hair and slams my head against the headboard. "Shut the fuck up and take this dick. This is your dick, Willow," he demands through gritted teeth.

My teeth chatter from the freezing cold that delivers from my calves gliding up and down my body, as he fills me up. He smiles at me like this is something I have consented to. Like we're doing this together. Like we're making love, a mutual bond. His hands have numbed me. They're ice cold. My chin quivers with fear and big fat tears trickle down my cheeks, making a pool in the middle of my neck in front of my throat.

My eyes flutter, trying to stay open, so I can see what he's doing, even though I don't want to. I really, really don't want to. I already know what he's doing and I can't push him off. I can't fight back. I'm still paralyzed. Not an inch of me can move at all. He pushes himself inside of me and I feel like my insides are ripping apart. Feeling the bones from the thrusts of his hips hit mine he tells me, "You're mine." Another soft thrust, if you can even call it soft when it's not wanted. "You're mine. Not anyone else's. Do you hear me?" Wrapping his hands around my neck, like I fantasized about Bryan doing, he whispers in my ear. "You belong to me." Another thrust, except this time it was hard. "This pussy is mine and I can get it anytime I want to." With his hand squeezing my throat harder, he says, "Tell me you understand, and I'll let go of your neck."

Refusing to give into him and tell him what he wants to hear, I muffle out, "Fuck you!"

He doesn't like that, so he grabs my hips and pushes himself so deep inside of me that I begin to vomit and have to turn my head to the side to not choke on it. He stops thrusting and wipes my mouth with my bed sheet. After I've stopped crying, thinking he was done, he grabs ahold of my neck and pushes himself into me again, demanding the same out of me. "Tell me you understand."

Because I don't want him to rape me harder like he already did and I want to get this over with, I tell him what he wants to hear. "I understand." He wants more. As if that wasn't enough. I guess he wants me to spell it out. As I begin to tell him, once again, that I understand, he interrupts me.

"Tell me. Say the words, 'I am yours, this pussy belongs to you.' Say it, Willow. I won't let go until you say it. Say it, Godammit." His voice echoes, loud like thunder in my ears. He gets frustrated because I haven't said it quickly enough. As his voice echoes throughout my apartment, I wonder if the neighbors can hear. Will they come running over and break down the door to help me? Will they at least call the cops? Or will they just turn the television up to drown me out? I don't dare yell out again, though.

"I am yours. This pussy belongs to you." I tell him through tears. He lets me go.

I gasp for air, believing perhaps I had just woken up from a nightmare and sleep paralysis had gotten to me again. As, that happens sometimes. The demon in the corner. This is the most extreme one yet.

It's just a nightmare. A bad, bad dream. The worst kind I've ever had before, I think to myself over and over and over again. My eyes slowly close and I am back asleep and Brock's ugly, deformed, skinless, boiling face with his garlic breath and hollowed out eyes are gone and out of sight, but when I awaken none of it is out of mind.

CHAPTER TWENTY-SIX

WILLOW

Squeak!

My bed squeaks as I sit up as fast and hard as I do when I wake up. I pat myself down quickly like an inmate getting frisked to make sure I'm wearing clothes. I look down at my body and—thank God—I am in the same clothes I was wearing before I fell asleep. The ones I had put on this morning to head out to my first day of work. A burnt orange turtleneck under a black suede one piece jumper and black boots. I grab my feet and I'm still wearing the black boots. It was all a nightmare.

Rubbing the sleep out of my eyes I check the time on my phone and *fuck me* I'm late. I am six fucking hours late to my new job in this new state and new city and I can just fucking forget about being a very new me. I check my text messages and phone calls, noticing I have one of each from my new boss.

New boss

I guess we missed you again today. I hope all is well over there?

Massaging my temples at the headache I woke up with, I press the dial button on the notification for a new voicemail to listen to my new boss fire me before I can even begin. "Willow. Hey. It's Richard, down at the office. We really want you on board with us, but we also need you to show up on time and if you can't make it on time, all we ask is you call or shoot me a text message.

Please get back with me and let me know you're okay. Talk to you soon? I hope?"

Click

***

"Just fucking great," I grumble out loud. I can't help but think about how this is the second time that I've been late to my first day of work at my new job without calling them ahead of time. This is something I don't think I can come back from. I doubt they'll want me after this. Come to think of it, I doubt anybody will want me in any kind of way after this. I feel ruined. Like rotten food to be thrown away. The nightmare felt so real.

Tossing my phone on the pillow next to me, I notice the vomit on my blanket. *Was this all a nightmare?* I think to myself as I swing my legs over the side of my bed and drop my feet—that feel way too heavy, like two cinder blocks have replaced them—to the floor to stand up. I feel wobbly and weak as soon as I do, but to my surprise I make it just fine without falling to my vanity sink to rinse off my face. I check myself out in the mirror before I do. Black crusted lines fall under my eyes, reaching my chin like I've been crying the mascara off. The vomit, crying, and my body feeling so heavy makes this all seem even more real.

All of a sudden I'm not too sure that my nightmare was a nightmare after all. For a split second I think it was real. Very, very real. I jog over to my phone. *Take it easy, Willow.* Slowing down, I walk carefully over to my phone. I check the time and… six hours? I slept for six hours? I don't remember laying in my bed. I don't even remember walking to my bed to lay down. What happened? Why am I forgetting what I've done? How am I losing time like this? Have I finally lost my mind?

I rinse the makeup off my face and wipe it clean with a hand towel. Gazing at the reflection in front of me, I see a lost, confused, traumatized woman looking back at me. I was tired. That's all. I was too tired to live today and instead of dying, I slept. My past is creeping in and I'm suppressing it while I'm awake, so

137

of course it's visiting me and demanding my attention while I sleep. It was just a bad, bad dream.

Even in death Neil and Brock—if it's only one of them it doesn't matter because it feels like both of them—are hunting me down. Kneeling behind big bushes. Laying low in ditches with their shotguns up to their faces glaring in the peephole waiting for me to be alone so they can shoot. Take her down, boys! Like I am prey. So, they can devour all of me before I can give even little bits of me to the actual worthy ones. The ones who won't tear me to pieces. People who will love me without conditions. I don't know how to tell who those people are anymore. Maybe I never have.

This isn't the way things are supposed to go. It's not the way things are supposed to be. I was supposed to have a fresh start in this new apartment. In this new city. In this new state. So that I can be a very new me. But they're dragging me down to the depths of hell with them. I refuse to let them win. No. *I win.* I won when they died, and I still win because they are dead. I just have to exorcize them out like a fucking demon possession and kill what's left of them in my head.

They're the ones who are dead. I'm the one still alive. They're the ones who died because of their choices. I am the one who is still alive because I am good. I'm a good person, and I deserve to live a happy and carefree life. They're gone and I can't let them win anymore.

I'm alive. I'm alive. **I'm alive**.

I win. I win. **I win.**

CHAPTER TWENTY-SEVEN

MYA

"So, tell me. Have you heard from him since you blocked him?" I ask Willow, even though I'm pretty sure she has because that's the way guys like that are. They don't take no for an answer and that brings my thoughts to Bryan. I wonder if she's heard from him, also.

She sets her latté down on the table in front of us and her phone dings at her. She ignores it and I wonder if that's him. I wonder which one it is. Bryan or Diego Cold Hands The Famous Bearer?

"Yes, girl. It's been three weeks and he's created two different fake numbers to text me from. I also have him blocked on all socials." She waves her hand in the air like she's slapping the thought of him away. "TikTok. Facebook. Instagram. X. Are you on any of those? Let's follow each other." She reaches to pick her phone back up.

"I don't really do social media. I prefer in person, text, phone calls. You know? I guess I'm a little old fashioned that way." I interrupt her from grabbing her phone. It's not that I don't have Facebook or Instagram. It's just that I don't spend any time on there, so there's really no point. I prefer to talk about things in person or the phone rather than see our daily updates before we can catch up. Seeing it all before we can talk takes away from the genuinity and gives us less to chat about.

"So, what about Bryan? Have you heard from him since you broke up with him?" I check the time on my watch. I notice we have exactly one hour on the dot left to chat before I need to get home to Ryder for my mom to go to her monthly hair appointment.

Willow rolls her eyes. "God no. At first I thought he probably won't shut the fuck up. That he'll probably blow my phone up. He's honestly a whiny little bitch and I wonder what the hell I ever saw in him. I really do. That was so short lived. But nope. He hasn't really been bothering me." She looks down, and picks at one of her nails, wearing a sad expression on her face.

"Be honest. Is he harassing you too, like Diego?" I want to know. I want to know this so badly because it seems like this woman has a slew of people just chomping at the bit to be with her at all times—obsession—and I worry about her. I really do.

"I wouldn't say he's harassing me." Her phone dings at her again and she points her eyes in the direction of it but keeps her face still, placed towards me. She crosses her legs, rests her elbow on her knee and plops her chin down in her hand, then lets out a long theatrical sigh.

"I wanna know, Willow. What do you call harassment? How many times has he contacted you since then? Since you broke up with him?" Sure, you could say I'm being nosey and maybe you'd be right, but we have grown to be close friends and I have already learned that Willow doesn't get what harassment really is. She plays it down because she is just so used to it.

"Literally only once since he came to get his things." She seems a little bothered by it. By him not blowing her phone up. "It's been three weeks." She's bothered by this because again this is what she is used to. Dating a guy. Breaking up with the guy. The guy then harasses her. It, in a sense, makes her feel loved, wanted, desired and cared for. Anything less than that and she doesn't feel worthy.

Ding! Her phone chimes at her again. She sighs once more and continues to ignore it. I get the sense that while this all fills a void that's empty inside her, I think possibly the harassment she receives from these men is also a bother and a turn off. It has to be. Willow doesn't know what she wants.

"Hey!" Her eyes light up and widen, along with her smile. "Let's go out tonight! Let's go to that same bar we met at!"

"Oh, Willow. I don't know, girl. That was sorta a one-time type of thing for me and my mom is already watching Ryder for me right now and—"

"Pleeeaaassssseee," she begs me with her hands in a prayer, showing puppy dog eyes and pouts her bottom lip out.

"Willow!? Is that you!?" A pause. "It *is* you! Hey!" A familiar voice calls out beside us. How could I ever forget his voice? He sounds like Matthew McConaughey. It's a very distinct accent.

We both turn and look to our sides to see Bryan standing there. Willow's jaw drops in surprise, and her phone chimes again. *Ding!* Bryan glances at it on the table in front of us and keeps a solid, wide, fake smile on his face. Willow glances at her phone at the same time as he does and I instinctively do the same thing. Although none of us can tell just by looking this far away who the person is on the other side of the screen, I can only guess that it's Diego. Diego Cold Hands, The Famous Bearer. It's not Bryan. He's here. Fucking right here, invading her privacy like I was just thinking that he would most likely be doing soon enough. I wonder what took him so long? What's his angle here?

Willow and I make eye contact. A knowing look. One that says what we're both thinking. What the fuck is he doing here? He's an outsider. He doesn't belong here. She adjusts in her seat and pulls the charm from her necklace up to her chin and moves it back and forth. Back and forth. Back and forth against her chin like she's rocking a baby to sleep and it'll finally calm down. Her nervous little fidget.

"Um. Hi Bryan?" That's all she can seem to get out. I can tell she wants him to go away. That she wasn't expecting him to show up like this. This makes her feel uncomfortable and brings her to think of the last time they were behind closed doors together. She pulls her hand up to her arm and rubs where he left bruises before.

He stands tall with his hands in his front jeans pockets, towering over her. "Fancy seeing you here, ey?" He says in a sarcastic tone because he knew she'd be here. He then heaves his upper body forward and laughs, a haunting one, gazing back and forth between me and Willow. "Amiright?" he carries on with his bullshit, as if neither one of us knows any better.

"You knew I would be here, Bryan. Don't act like that," Willow remarks, rolling her eyes at him.

"Oh gosh, Willow!" He takes his hands out of his pockets and pats his cheeks once, keeping them placed there like Kevin from Home Alone does when he puts aftershave on his face at only eight years old. "I really just had no idea you'd be here. An honest mistake. An honest bump into each other. Really." He roars out a sarcastic laugh that makes Willow lean her body away from him like he's a plague. And that really is what he is, a plague.

In the background, Phantogram sings all about Lucy being trapped underground and begging to be lended to the fire and thrown into the flames.

"But anyway, now that I'm here and you're here, how about we dance?" He holds his hand out for Willow to grab a hold of. She doesn't take his hand. "Shall we?" He persists. Her eyes bulge out of her head and she peers around the coffee shop, embarrassed. I feel secondhand embarrassment for her.

"Willow. You're being rude. I'm being a gentleman. Stand up and dance with me." She pulls her eyes down and away from him. Again, she moves the charm on her necklace back and forth across her chin. "Come on." He grabs her hand without her permission and tries to pull her up off the chaise lounge chair she's sitting on. The fucking audacity of this guy. Does he want to cause a scene? Because he sure is asking for it.

She yanks her hand away from his. "Don't touch me!" she yells, louder than she meant to. I can tell because she looks around the coffee shop with embarrassment sprawled across her face once again.

In the background, Phantogram asks her ex-lover to show her love and reminds him that he's got his hands on the button now.

"What do you want, Bryan?" I ask instead of waiting on Willow to say something else or take up for herself. Maybe set some boundaries. She is too tired to do it herself. Not tired in the sleepy kind of way, but tired in the exhaustion from dealing with people like this, type of way. Toxic people like Bryan. Like Diego. Like probably many others before she moved to New York City that I'm thinking of prying to get to know more about soon. I'm sure she's got tons of stories to share. She seems used to this kind of behavior by men.

Some people draw that kind of attention naturally to themselves. It's like once you meet one person like this, who clings to you and forces their way into your life, a whole slew of them come out of the woodwork just waiting to completely devour you and suck up all your energy to use as their own. It's like being a magnet for men—people in general, but mostly men—with severe mental issues. They're drawn to her and she's, unfortunately, drawn to them. I wonder what happened in her life to make this kind of toxicity attractive to her. Did it start with her dad? It usually does.

Willow is one of those people that naturally draws these types of succubus to her now and she will have to do something to make it stop. This has become way too normal to her. I wonder how long it's been this way for her. Actually, I wonder if it ever wasn't this way for her.

In the background, Phantogram has now damned Lucy to be underground forever and presumes that she is never coming back.

Bryan looks at me now, raises his eyebrows and pulls his face into a big, fake, mocking smile. "I don't recall knowing your name." He snaps his fingers like an idea just sparked. "Oh! But you were here the last time I was here with Willow. Yeah." He wiggles a finger at me and shakes his head up and down. "I remember you. You interrupted our date." I scowl at him. "But that's okay! Really. It's fine." He continues and waves his hand like it's not a big deal and he is forgiving. "But I was the rude one. I didn't catch your name." He holds out his hand to me—the same one he used to wiggle a finger at me and wave in the air afterwards—to shake mine. "Go on. Tell me. What's your name?" His hand is still held out to shake mine and he looks down at it, then back at me. "It's a pleasure meeting you. Really, it is. Any friend of Willow's is a friend of mine," he says in that same sarcastic tone he was just using. As he towers over me belittling me with a fake courtesy handshake, I make eye contact and he winks at me.

I wonder what the hell his problem is and why he's doing this other than to torture Willow. That's all it seems his efforts are for. To mentally torture Willow. It's so damn obvious that he gets joy out of making her feel uncomfortable. I wonder if he's ever had a normal relationship before. I sense some mommy issues underway.

I don't shake his hand and I don't tell him my name either. Instead, I stand up and unlike Willow, he doesn't tower over me while I'm standing. I stand eye to eye with him.

"This is called stalking. You asshole," I growl, scowling at him.

In the background, Phantogram repeats herself. 'Show me love, you've got your hand on the button nowwww'.

Bryan grits his teeth the same way he did the first time— the only time I met him. Sitting right here in this same spot. He says to me, "What the fuck did you just call me?" The sarcasm has drifted from his voice and face. It's now replaced with anger. He bows up to me like I'm a man his size. He is too quick to anger, so this will be really easy for me.

I grin at him. *My turn.* This is a public place and I am dying for him to forget that. Willow quickly stands up and walks away from the drama. In a hurry, she makes her way to the front bar where her barista friend Chelsea serves drinks to all the other caffeine addicted fools crowding the coffee shop. This is my time to shine and give him a little taste of his own medicine.

I gaze around The Charming Coffee Delight. This place is supposed to be our sanctuary. Our place to relax. And here this creep is turning it into a place that Willow and I will no doubt start dreading to go to after this. I take a mental note of the people who are busy with the sounds we make muffled from earphones drowning out any noise around them. Chatting with their partners and friends. Typing away on their Chromebooks. Hard at work or hard at play. Either way, not a soul is paying attention to us. This is just too easy.

"Pussy," I hiss at him loud enough for only him to hear. Then I tilt my head back, heave my face towards his, and spit right on his pretty, perfect looking little bitch ass face. Oooooh, how I want to do much more than just spit on it. So much more. I want to claw his eyes out. I hate men like him. Men who like too much of a chase. To the point of no return.

In the background, Phantogram carries her voice louder throughout The Charming Coffee Delight as she finally exclaims that she'd rather die than be with her ex-lover.

"You fucking bitch! You stupid fucking *whore*!" Bryan belches out after he's used his shirt to wipe my spit off of his face. His pretty, clean shaven, perfect, stupid little face. Ha! He lunges at me—Got him where I want him—and grabs a hold of my neck, both of his hands gripping tight and hard. So intensely. Pushing onto one of the chairs, he gets on top of me—I sing the praise of joy—. Straddling me and putting all of his body weight into my chest, I find it hard to breathe, but I rejoice! Hallelujah! He is going back to jail! Yes, I looked him up. What? Do you think I'm stupid? He was dating my best friend.

"Oh my God! Stop! Stop! *Stop it*! Bryan! Stop it now!" Willow cries. Literally. Tears coursed down her cheeks and her hands covered her mouth in shock. She bends her knees to be eye level with me and Bryan. "Get the fuck off of her, Bryan!" Willow screeches. Her voice sounds so tiny to me right now. Everything sounds so small and far away. She peers her eyes above us and into the crowd. "Somebody please help us!"

Even in a moment of panic she is polite, asking please. Please, please, please! She looks at us again, then back up above us and gazes all around The Charming Coffee Delight to see if anyone is coming to the rescue. I don't think anybody is. The place is packed with people. How is he getting away with this without someone stepping in to pull him off me?

All of a sudden this place doesn't feel so charming anymore.

Bryan's hands are still wrapped around my neck, pressed hard with his thumbs pushing into my throat. He has forgotten he's in public and will abso-fucking-lutely go down for this shit.

"She spit on my face!" He roars out loud to the people that have crowded us.

"She spit on my fucking face!" He roars again through gritted teeth this time as he shakes my head and it scrambles my brain.

I don't hear Phantogram anymore in the background, only the muffles of all the people I can see that have surrounded us demanding, pleading and questioning Bryan as he straddles me and chokes the air out of my lungs. Fuck pleading and trying to reason with him! Grab him and throw him the fuck off me! Nobody does.

He might actually kill me today.

Willow apparently loses all hope that he'll stop on his own accord and she hops on top of Bryan's back. Oh my gosh, the weight of both of them on top of me at the same time is almost too much to bear. It's like the dead weight of a three-hundred pound man decided to just *die* while lying on my chest. *Crack!* I think I heard one of my ribs break. Please, don't let this be the day I die. Especially at the hands of a man. I'll go any other way, but not like this.

She hits him on top of his head—Ah! That's the crack sound I heard! Go Willow!—Over and over and over again with her book bag until he finally gets the fuck off of me. How he hasn't lost consciousness from her banging his head with her book bag is beyond me. I think she has a hardcover book in there. And how I haven't lost consciousness from this motherfucking hulk smashing and choking me has to be only that of a miracle from above.

Also, Willow. The miracle of Willow. She just saved me. She saved my life. I owe her. She really is a best friend. *My best friend.* I've longed for a best friend for far too long. He could have swung her tiny body off of him with all his strength. She'd go flying through the coffee shop and no doubt about it, she would hit the floor and probably get a concussion. Yes, I owe her big time. Brave, strong Willow. She didn't stand up for herself, but she did for me. There's that fight! That's what it took, sadly. Willow is stronger and braver than she gives herself credit for.

I hope she feels a high off of that and becomes unstoppable when it comes to this prick from now on. I hope she keeps this fight when it comes to having her own back. She deserves to love herself. She is worthy of fighting for her own self.

Chelsea comes running, more like stampeding towards us, with her dark hair in a ponytail swinging side to side. When she finally gets to us, he is already off of me. She pants and peeves with her hands on her thighs like she's the one out of breath. Ugh. What a silly little bitch. Why did it take her this long to get here anyway? Did she have to finish making a customer's latté order before sprinting over? From what Willow has told me it didn't take her this long to save her from a fucking fall a few months ago. But go ahead Chelsea and top off that frappe with whipped cream. Add a little heart swirl while you're at it, bitch. Let Bryan here choke me half to death. No biggie.

She made it, though! She did make it here. Not in time. Nowhere near in time. Not even close. Give the girl a metal, though, because she made it!

You know how in the movies the bad guy keeps beating the ever loving shit out of the good guy after the cops have been called, and it takes the men in blue forever to get there? Then, once the good guy has killed the bad guy after a forever long fight, that's when sirens are heard and the cops finally show up? Yeah. That's what it's like. That's exactly what it's like. The cops probably stopped for a donut run on the way to the emergency, and Chelsea was probably shoving a muffin in her fat mouth before coming to my rescue. She could have at the very least called the cops. She didn't even do that! I knew from the moment I met her that she is a snake. She probably got off on the whole thing.

I don't know what Willow thought Chelsea could do anyway, and I don't know why the bystanders—even the men that could overpower Bryan—watched this all unfold before he could take my very last breath away from me, but Willow stopped him just in time because I was starting to see the light. This is why Willow is my best friend. This settles it. No debate about it.

"She spit on my fucking face!" Bryan screeches again in hopes anyone will be on his side. He sounds like a little boy trying to persuade his parents that his brother hit him first. But he started it! He tries to justify his behavior with a lie, I tell them.

"I would never spit on anyone. Especially not on anyone's face." I shake my head back and forth in protest of what he's accused me of. "Never." I reach for the bottle of water that Chelsea hands me. Chelsea to the rescue! "That's just disgusting. He's lying." I explain myself to everyone around me. Willow, Chelsea, Bryan, the people who have gathered to 'help' and all the ones eavesdropping in on our conversation.

Willow rubs my back in a circular, soothing motion. "Of course, we don't believe him," Willow reassures me while glaring at Bryan as he sits idly by, waiting for the police to arrive. A few male customers stand like soldiers with their legs spread in a v and their hands behind their backs. Watching him to make sure he doesn't try to make a run for it before the cops can show up and do their jobs. Their eyes threaten to tackle him to the floor if he tries anything else. Some of them give him daring looks. Try me, bitch. I've been dying to fight all week.

"Willow, I swear to God she spit on my face!" Bryan pleads as if he has any sort of a chance to win her heart or trust ever again. "Please believe me!" He sounds so urgent and so very fucking pathetic.

"You know what, Bryan?" Willow stands up and folds her arms together. She gives him a death glare. If looks could kill he'd be dead right now. Dead as a doornail.

"Even if she *did* spit on your face, that doesn't give you any reason or justification at all to fucking choke her. You could have *killed her.*" She tosses her hands in the air, then places them on her hips. "And you know what?" She smirks at him. "We're both pressing charges on you." She points her finger at me. "One for assault." She lays her palm over her heart. "And one for stalking."

Damn straight. Get it, girl.

Bryan sulks and rests his face in his open palms like a stupid, scared little boy about to get into trouble again.

CHAPTER TWENTY-EIGHT

MYA

I had forgotten the time and all about my mom's monthly hair appointment that was supposed to be today. Pulling my phone out of my bag, I see that I have two text messages and three missed phone calls from her. I checked the time and noticed it had been well over an hour since I last checked. She is definitely late for—had already missed—her hair appointment. My mom hasn't ever missed or been late to a hair appointment in all the years I had known her to go. Shit. I gather my things and head outside to call my mom back to explain what happened and apologize.

"Hey. I'll be right back," I announce looking at Willow. She begins to follow me outside because she is worried about me, so I let her know that I'm just calling my mom back and I remind her about the hair appointment she missed.

Willow halts in her movements. "Will you be okay, though?" I shake my head yes, and she nods at me like she understands.

I step outside of the coffee shop front door and the chimes from the bell above my head are too loud. Way too loud. I have a pounding headache. Probably from Bryan scrambling my brain. The crisp, cold air sends a jolt straight down my spine. I shiver and move the hair out of my face that keeps flying forward and smacking me. I stand at the window facing where Willow, Bryan, Chelsea and the soldier customers are so I can be within eyesight of them to help ease Willow's nerves because she's watching me like a hawk, grazing the charm on her necklace back and forth against her chin again. She's nervous. Rightfully so. Not just because of everything that happened, but Willow doesn't want to be in contact with the police. There has to be a good reason why. The headache creeping in gnaws at me like a dog with a bone. I pull a bottle of Motrin out of my bag and pop a few in my mouth. I guzzle down the water bottle that Chelsea gave to me and call my mom. She picks up the phone on the first ring with panic in her voice.

"Mya?" She gasps. "Mya? Honey? Are you alright? What happened? Where are you?"

She isn't used to me being a no call, no show. Not ever and especially when it comes to my son. Even when I was a teenager, while most girls my age were sneaking out to meet up and get sloppy drunk at parties or to make out with their boyfriends in their car parked down the road from their houses, I was the good one. I was always the good one. I never broke my curfew. I made straight A's in all my classes. I babysat the local kids. I tutored my peers after school. I was a trusted, reliable teenage girl. I was every mother's wet dream of a daughter. All the parents wanted their daughters to be like me. Like responsible, trustworthy, reliable Mya.

Why can't you be more like Mya? I bet Mya doesn't do that. Do you, Mya? My friends' parents would go on and on about me. Their intentions were good. They just wanted their daughters to make better choices and used me as an example in hopes they would change their behavior. But they gave their daughters a complex and pretty soon glances full of resentment were shot my way from the table in the school cafeteria; a table I was no longer welcome to join.

"Something really bad happened, Mom, but I'm okay now and I'm really sorry you had to miss your hair appointment." I apologize because even though I was fighting for my life while her hair was supposed to be getting chopped in the same style she's worn it since I was like, twelve years old, and colored to be her almost exact natural hair color that it already is, I just couldn't help but feel like a child again. Desperate for her approval at any moment that I wasn't perfect. Even if it was completely out of my control and this was completely out of my control, but I still—

Wee-oww! Wee-oww! Wee-oww!

Loud yelps from the sirens on the cop cars arriving at the coffee shop violate my ears and I jump right out of my boots from the sound of it all. It feels like a heartbeat inside of my head and I need this Motrin to kick in right now. The bright red and blue lights are saturated like photoshop would do to pronounce a color even more. It's brighter than the day. Blinding, actually. Like looking straight into the sun. I raise my hand like a visor across my forehead to fade the brightness.

My mom understands when I explain to her that I have to go inside and give my statement.

"Wait! Don't forget to let me know if you need to go to the hospital afterwards. I'm pretty sure you have to and I'll be there. Mya, maybe you should even if they tell you that you don't need to because I really think you need to, honey."

"Of cou—"

Who is that? I can't help but stare at him. He looks so familiar. His face. Well, the sliver of a face that he shows. His vibe. His energy is strong with a warped sense of darkness to it. Who is he? Why is he watching Willow the way he is? With lust and resentment at the same time. This has to be someone who knows her very well.

I mean sure, people are curious as to what's going on inside the coffee shop. The cops just made a scene and they just got here. But this is New York City. The cops are always making a scene and just getting somewhere to arrest someone. Always. Occasionally someone will stop and do a double take, but people generally just walk on by and go about their day as if nothing happened at all. Even if what had just happened was a woman being choked nearly to death. Only people who are new to city life stare through windows in situations like this.

He doesn't appear to be some newcomer to city life, though. A curious country boy from a small town that acts foreign when things like this happen. No. He's a city slicker through and through. It's the way he carries himself. I can just tell. You live here long enough and you will be able to just tell, too. His head tilts sideways and he smirks like he's intrigued and sure, you could say it's because of the show that was just put on by me and Bryan inside The Charming Coffee Delight but it's not. It's Willow he's looking at in this weird, fascinated, creepy kind of way. Everywhere she moves his eyes follow.

He is fixated on her.

And sure, you could say it's someone else who has his attention because there are other people around and how can I see exactly who he's looking at this far away? But it's not someone else. They don't have his attention. It's Willow who he focuses his attention on. She steps to the left, his eyes wander to the left. She walks to the right, so do his eyes. He's also trying to make sure he isn't able to be recognized. He's wearing a hoodie with the hood over his head and sure, you could say he's wearing it like that because it's cold outside. But it's the way he veers his head downwards and pulls the hood slightly to cover part of his face when anyone looks in his direction. Except me. He hasn't noticed me watching him yet. I look around me to see if anyone else is noticing this. Nobody else is. Nobody else notices. Am I just seeing things? Do I have some type of concussion from Bryan choking me? Surely, my eyes aren't playing a sick joke on me.

He pulls out his phone and captures a picture of Willow as she stands, waiting for the police to arrive.

What the fuck?

"Mya? Hello? Are you there? Are you okay? Sweetheart?!" I had forgotten I was on the phone and I can't tell you how many times my mom called out my name or how many beats her heart skipped because I wasn't answering back.

"Sorry, Mom. Yes, but I have to go now." I'm about to push the end call button, but I feel bad leaving her like that, so I add, "I'll call you back. I love you."

Click

With a twinge of panic, I storm towards the creepy guy in the hoodie watching Willow, in big steps like I'm galloping. I try to move quickly before he sees me and takes off. I've got to know who this guy is. More importantly, what kind of nerve he has to be so open about what he's doing. If he'll do this in broad daylight, what will he do at night when nobody is watching? My mind wanders in so many directions.

I no longer have a headache, so I guess the Motrin finally kicked in or maybe it's just replaced with all the thoughts swirling in my mind. I want to confront him. I'm feeling triumphant with a hero complex. Like I can do anything. I hope Willow feels like this, too. I feel like I can pick up a car with one hand and save someone stuck underneath. Maybe this is adrenalin. Taking a step closer to him, I notice that he doesn't look so taunting anymore.

The creepy guy in the hoodie changes his facial expression from a smirk to a serious one. Like a deer caught in headlights. I follow with my eyes to what has stopped him in his tracks like this and that's when I see them. Right. The cops are here now. Instead of giving him my undivided attention like I want to, my eyes drift to the blue gang headed towards the coffee shop door.

A scrawny man in a cop uniform with a handlebar mustache holds the door open for a heavy set woman wearing a matching uniform, with pitch black hair high up on top of her head in a slick neat bun. She reminds me of the principal from Matilda. When I turn back to face him, he's gone. What? How? Where did he go? I spin around fast and glance all around me like he can just snap his fingers and end up behind me or something. Like he can teleport. For a second I thought of chasing where he was to catch up with him to ask why he was taking a picture of Willow. So maybe I can snap a picture of him and show it to the cops and to her. So, we can perhaps figure this out together and get one less creep off the streets.

I wonder if this is Diego Cold Hands, The Famous Bearer. I'll have to get her to show me another picture of him to compare to this guy in the hoodie, even though I barely saw his face. I'll never forget the pointy nose and beady eyes or how tall he seemed to be. Still, it would be nice to have a second look.

I don't go chasing after him, instead I choose wisely and head back towards The Charming Coffee Delight because it would be such a charming little delight to watch Bryan get handcuffed and escorted out the door with his head hanging low. Like the little bitch that he is. I hope they slam him to the ground after they handcuff him when they see the marks around my neck. Surely he left marks. I gaze at my reflection in the window of the coffee shop and hold my hand up to my neck. Red and dark blue are already starting to form and I wonder how dark they'll end up being. It's only good when they're dark in front of the cops. After that, I'll just be upset every time I see them and need to buy special products to fully cover them up so Ryder doesn't notice them. So, nobody does. I already went through this once before. I refuse to cover up for another man again. Pulling the collar of my shirt down, I take a long gaze in the window in front of me. Memorizing what to say isn't so hard when Bryan has made himself look so bad.

I'm wasting time. I need to go in there and make my statement to the police. I need to show them these marks on my neck that are growing by the second and have Willow pull up her shirt sleeves to present to them the marks on her arm that he left three weeks ago, and they still are black and blue. That's how hard he grabbed her. I need to make a Goddamn performance in there and get this asshole put behind bars for a long, long time.

My judgment about the guy in the hoodie may have been cloudy anyway. I had just been strangled half to death and perhaps I wasn't thinking very clearly. Maybe I was seeing things. How can I trust myself? How can I trust my own thoughts when they are all fuzzy anyway? It could be that when Bryan choked me he cut the airway to my brain just a little too much and I have to regain some type of mental strength back. Or perhaps it was the trauma. The trauma of all that I've seen Willow go through with me since I've met her. All that I've gone through with men for my entire life and of course the trauma of just being choked nearly to fucking death by Bryan the psychopath. Maybe it was all getting to me and I was starting to suspect any man of being anything less than a pile of garbage. My faith in men is microscopic at this point, to be honest and to be fair I have earned those feelings. But for all I know, the guy in the hoodie watching through the window could have just been some nosey passerby taking a video or snapping a picture to post and gloat on Facebook or X or Instagram or whatever the fuck people gossip and share news on that's none of their damn business to begin with.

And that settles it. I've convinced myself that there is one less creep on the streets to worry about. I put my phone back into my bag, toss it over my shoulder, push my chin up in the air with confidence and step inside the coffee shop so I can watch Bryan get handcuffed. Then Willow and I will go celebrate the victory at my house with a feast that I know my mom will make for us because of what we have just been through. Comfort food. Lots of swirly pasta, warm cookies, and a bottle of wine.

We can get wasted with a ten year old bottle of wine that I've been holding onto for my and Ronnie's tenth wedding anniversary. He's not coming back. There is no use in waiting to devour this bitch any longer. Now is the perfect time to drink the pain away in the best way possible.

CHAPTER TWENTY-NINE

HIM

There it is. Again. I was really hoping I wouldn't have to be burdened with this as much as I have been since moving here, but as I walk through the complex to get to my door, it echoes. Loud and haunting. His fucking stupid sounding laugh lingers in the air between us as I get to my front door. God. Shoot me now. I am not in the mood, Sandy. I'm really fucking not.

"Nooooo. It's my turn. You already had your turn and you're slobbering all over it. Ewwww." Sandy lets out more laughter at this. He's flirting with her. Playing, but being honest at the same time. A nice way for people to get a point across. Nobody likes a slobbery blunt.

He sits halfway in and halfway outside the front door to his apartment—I'm sorry, let me rephrase. I meant his mommy's apartment—and side by side with a woman who looks old enough to be his mom. Wait, is that his mom? Maybe his sister? His aunt? I can't imagine any woman in her right mind would date this loser, but hey. Everyone deserves love. Her hair is light brown and she has over the top tan skin that looks like it comes straight from a daily tanning bed visit. Much different than Sandy's pale skin. In fact, everything about her is different from him. Maybe they aren't related after all. Perhaps Sandy really does have a lover. How can he keep a lover and I'm fighting to keep mine? The cards in this deck just don't sound right.

The wrinkles on her face are leathery like her hands and no doubt also from the tanning bed. Not just her age. That shit will age you faster than time itself. She wears a black beanie on top of her head but it's lopsided. Obviously it's not on purpose for a fashion statement. She's probably too high to even realize how stupid she looks. Surprisingly, she's not wearing a ton of makeup. Most women with leathery tanned skin from a tanning bed do. Her eyelashes are extremely long, black, goopy and look like spider legs sticking out from her eyes. Only much darker and thicker. They each wear a Beastie Boys t-shirt. I wonder if they planned that before she came over or if they made a shopping trip together and bought them at the same time earlier today. They're crisp and clean, looking brand new. She's twice his size, but just about anybody is bigger than Sandy. He's a scrawny little shit. The size of a middle school boy going through puberty. She leans away from him as he reaches for the blunt she holds up to her mouth, and swats at his arm with her free hand.

He laughs again. A little too hard. A belly laugh like he can't contain himself and it's really not that fucking funny, Sandy, but then again he is stoned out of his mind and I'm sure she is, too.

"Okay, okay. Fiiiiiiine," he replies to her reaction. Even though his eyes are already bloodshot red and he's squinting without even trying, he catches me before I can walk inside without small talk.

"Heyyyyy buuuuuuddy." They both giggle at the way he's approaching me. Like stupid little high school kids on summer break smoking a doobie before their mom gets home to catch them higher than a kite and toying with the neighbors.

"Oh my God. Sandy, you're so fucking high right now." She grabs his face and squeezes it with one of her hands like you've seen the more harsh parents do to their kids to get their attention. Aggressive. She moves his face to be eye to eye with her. She sways her free hand in the air, to move the thick weed smoke out of the way. Does she even realize that that's the hand she's holding the blunt in?

"Look at me. Were you already high before I got here?" she asks as she yanks his face with the same hand she's holding it with. I wonder why the fuck I'm still standing here watching this other than for entertainment purposes. He still squints—not on purpose—and tries to hold in his laughter. He swallows to gulp it down like a forkful of spaghetti he just took a big bite out of, but he fails and cackles out loud right in her face. When he does this his lips curve in a heart shape rather than a normal smile because she is still holding onto his face and squeezing it.

I laugh a little, softly, quietly because shit that was kind of funny. While Sandy is annoying, immature and a loser, he's a little bit funny. *A little.* I laugh at him. Not with him. There is a big difference between the two. I can't really imagine holding a conversation with him that would involve the two of us having the same sense of humor, but that was funny. She shoots daggers at me with her eyes. I look away. Not wanting to make eye contact.

"Something funny to you, neighbor boy?" *Neighbor boy?*

Really? Ooooh got me there! Couldn't you possibly do better, Leatherface?

She lets Sandy's face go with a force and places her attention on me. Like an animal caught eating its prey but hears another noise and stops to look up and gauge what sound that was.

I answered her. "Well, I mean, it's just." I sigh, scratching the back of my head and gaze down away from her eyes that are way too serious right now while I'm trying to contain my laughter at everything I just witnessed in the last four minutes since walking up to my front door. "Are you his mom?"

"What?! No! I'm his… I'm his…" She tries to find the right words to describe this fuckery.

"She's my probation officer," Sandy interrupts. Finishing off the sentence for her and answering my question. "And my girlfriend." He wiggles his eyebrows at me like he's hit the jackpot with Leatherface. Her jaw drops in shock like the old school cartoon characters you watched as a kid. Then she folds it right back into place.

"You idiot!" She screeches and punches him right in the gut. I raise my eyebrows at this. A probation officer old enough to be the offender's mom is getting high with and fucking her client. Only in the city. Okay. That's not true. This could happen anywhere, but come on, really? This is the city for ya. Not the kind of people I want around Willow.

Sandy lunges straight forward. Like her punch filled him up with air and he's a pool floaty. Instead of grabbing his stomach where she punched, he grabs his chest. His heart, as if it's broken. "Trishia! What did you do that for?" He makes his fist pump up and down over his chest where his heart is and whines, "You broke my wittle heart."

And God, that is so fucking annoying that I want to punch him again. Let him really feel it. It won't only be his heart that's broken if I get ahold of him in a fit of annoyance.

Trishia puts the blunt out the way you do a cigarette on the concrete in front of them, stands up and grabs Sandy by the collar of his shirt and pulls him inside. As his body drags along with her, he makes his legs crab walk to keep up with her. "Women." He laughs as if it's no big deal that he just told on his probation officer. As if what they're doing isn't completely illegal and immoral. "Am I right or am I right?" He jokes.

The door slams closed behind them and a little black and white sign that reads, 'Welcome to the shit show' that hangs on a hook on the door rattles back and forth. Welcome to the shit show is right. That didn't go the way Leatherface Trishia had hoped their date would, I presume. If I didn't have anything better to do, I would report her for 'abusing' her authority and dating one of her clients. That would definitely put the cherry on top. It's what she's scared of for sure. She'd probably even make the front page of the paper getting caught up in something so scandalous like that. Okay, maybe not the front page, but she would make it in there, for sure. Today is her lucky day because Sandy, Trishia and their fucked up little role playing relationship is the least of my concern. They aren't even on the list of my top ten. Not even my top hundred.

Willow holds that place for me. She's my number one, and everything that has to do with her takes their place below the number one on my list. I turn the knob to my front door—diagonal of Willow's—and I wonder what she has in store for me today.

CHAPTER THIRTY

HIM

To my surprise—and boy am I fucking surprised—the show I immediately get upon entering my apartment is that of someone pounding their fists on Willow's front door. I drop everything in my hands to the floor—mail, keys, gloves—and I jog over to my Nikon camera. I zoom in the closest I possibly can on his face. It is a he and this fucking pain my ass is just so lost without Willow. Give me a damn break. He barely knows her enough to be this heartbroken. Willow has that effect on people, though. I know best. Why does he act like he was in my shoes? The bigger question is how the fuck is he already a free man? With a blown mind, I zoom my camera lens in closer just to make sure it's really him.

It's Bryan. But how? What the fuck? It's only been three days! Surely! Possibly! My eyes have got to be playing a trick on me. It can't be him. It can't be. You can't just fucking choke a woman in a public fucking place, a coffee shop, and only spend three Goddamn days in the pen. No way! This can't be real!

I set the Nikon camera down on the table. I rub my eyes because hey, maybe something is caught in there that makes this guys' face just look like Bryan's face. Feeling anxious, I pick the Nikon back up and sure enough, it's still Bryan. It's. Still. Bryan. But how? And why? Who in their right minds would let him out after almost killing a woman? He strangled Mya nearly to death! If we were anywhere else but New York City he wouldn't have been able to bail himself out, especially not this quickly. But shit like this happens all the time here. I mean, I wouldn't go as far as saying women get choked out by men in public every day in New York City, but the likes happen frequently.

People get mugged in broad daylight and nobody bats a fucking eye. A man once raped a woman who was walking by herself in the back alley of some neighborhood, outside at night. I know. I know. The cliche' of it all. It does happen, though. Any-fucking-ways. People heard her scream. "Rape, rape, rape!" and "Help me!" Nobody helped her, and she had to hail a fucking taxi afterwards to get to a hospital.

Do you know what happened next? I'll bet you can guess. The hospital staff and cops instructed her to scream, "Fire, fire, fire!" next time as if there should even be a fucking next time. The man was caught because the victim was great at identifying him in the lineup due to a very distinct visible tattoo on his face. Also, one of the houses had a camera pointed towards their back driveway and it just so happened to give a great description to the investigator. Still, it was the woman who was raped that saved the day.

That, apparently, wasn't enough trauma for her.

Do you know what happened after that? I'll bet you know this one, too. The man was put behind bars like the animal he is. Hooray! However, after he was apprehended it wasn't long before he was let go and back out on the streets. He got out on a twenty thousand dollar bond—come on NYC, you can do better than that—and you guessed it…He raped again and again and again until he was caught another time. I heard he's still in jail awaiting trial, but at this point they just give guys like that probation. A slap on the fucking wrist.

Speaking of probation. I wonder what my neighbor Sandy did to earn that title. And speaking of men who rape women in public, I wonder if Willow is home, hiding from Bryan. Who chokes women in public. Because the cops don't do shit, so I'm assuming that saving Willow will have to be up to me. I'm going to have to kill him. The shit this woman gets me into. I really do put one hundred and ten percent into our relationship, and what do I get back? Watching her get fucked by some felon. At least she broke it off quickly with this one.

I snap my neck around to have the Nikon zoom focused inside of Willow's apartment. I can see all of her living space. It's a pretty wide open concept. Just a studio apartment and all of it flows together. The bedroom, kitchenette, bathroom, dining area are all linked in one. If she is hiding I would know because I would definitely see her. She isn't there, though. Not a shadow in sight.

She isn't even home, and he is pounding his fists so hard into her front door over and over again like she'll eventually open the door for him. His fists might be bloody now. Who would open the door to that shit? I wonder why nobody has called the cops for a noise disturbance or poked their heads out of the door to shoo him off or at the very least out of curiosity. Only in the city. Only in the city. People here are just so used to this kind of shit.

I point my Nikon camera back towards Bryan. He's still going at it. Knowing what I have to do if he doesn't stop, I zoom in on his face and watch him plead to Willow. I'm able to read his lips. "Willow!" a slap on the door with one of his open palms. Hard. I can see it shake the door knocker. "Please!" Another fist onto the door. It rattles the door knocker again. He slaps the door another time and keeps his open palm pressed on it this time, sliding it down with his forehead laying against the door while his face is scrunched up in agonizing pain. Not physical pain. Although I'm sure his palms and fists won't be thanking him later on. But the kind of pain that pierces the center of you. Right into the heart. I've been exactly where he is and regarding the exact same woman. I get it. I really do. But the difference between me and Bryan is I'm not a six time felon. I'm not choking women in public. Also, I've known Willow and have been with her way longer than he has.

I picture his mugshot from his recent arrest. The one from him choking Mya. A defeated looking Bryan stood in front of the camera three days ago with his mouth turned down. Sad face. Poor Bryan. Now, I imagine what the new mugshot will look like when someone, maybe I, call in for a noise complaint against a guy harassing a woman that I can say is far too scared to come to the door. They'll believe me because how in the hell would they know that I know she's not even home? While I fantasize about pulling his guts out, I have to be careful. This is his last chance before I continue to do the right thing about his stalking and harassment of Willow. The next time I have a run in with him like this, he'll be facing me head on.

"Yes, I'd like to report a noise complaint," I tell the woman dispatcher that answers the 911 phone call. She seems annoyed by the reason I'm calling, like it's petty and they have other more important things to worry about. I suppose they do, so I fill her in on a little more. "My neighbor is too scared to come out or answer her door. I've seen him here harassing her before. He's banging on her door and," I pick up my camera to make sure he's still there causing a fucking scene. I hope he is. I need him to be. I'd love nothing more than to see his lame ass go back to jail today. The camera is still zoomed in, and is he really fucking kicking her door now?

"Now he's kicking her door in. Please hurry! She must be terrified!" I describe with urgency in my voice so they send someone quickly.

She asks me to come out when I hear the sirens, so I can officially meet and greet the officers to explain all that I've seen and heard, but I tell her I'd rather remain anonymous. Plus, my son is with me, and he's just so young. I'd really rather not put him through all this. It works. Nobody wants a kid involved in drama like this.

CHAPTER THIRTY-ONE

HIM

Willow didn't have a show to put on for me today, but I sure did get a damn good one out of him! The pitiful look on Bryan's face when he was handcuffed was priceless. Although Willow is still my favorite episode through and through every single day for the rest of my life, I really enjoyed watching him make a fucking fool out of himself. He squirmed around and wiggled like a damn worm to get free, so that's another charge piled on top of what he already has for the day. How many charges does that make for Bryan?

Let's count the charges together. Shall we? What a fun little game this is! One charge for resisting arrest. Another charge for harassment. I knew he'd get that thrown in there. Another harassment charge piled on top of his others. I have only myself to thank for this one! That makes two for the day so far. Another charge for public intoxication. I guess he was too drunk to realize what an absolute tool he was being. That seems to be his pattern. Some type of substance use—in this case, alcohol—and harassment. So anyway, that makes three. Another charge for disturbing the peace. That makes four. Four charges! Four charges for the day! Try to bail out of that, especially resisting his arrest, Bryan.

When Willow gets home she rushes to see what all the ruckus is. My favorite show begins. She jogs up to her apartment with her book bag and purse falling down and off her shoulder every few seconds. She would slow down each time and yank them back in their place. The cycle would continue until she gets to her destination and plops the bags down on the ground. Enjoying the foreplay, I zoom in on her body to watch what is mine as she jogs. Her perky tits bounce up and down getting me hard. I snap a quick picture—or two, or three, or four—for pleasure as her cleavage pulls out of her shirt more and more.

I know what I'll be doing later on tonight.

When she drops her bags to the ground I zoom out to get the big picture. The whole picture. Like it's a movie I'm watching and Willow is the star. I suppose that's exactly what it is. My favorite movie of all time. Willow.

Mya had come along for the ride with her. She is right by her side, consoling her the way friends should. I'm pretty sure she's also happy to see him get arrested again because when one of the cops grabs his arm and twists it behind his back, Mya grins. She doesn't even try to hide it. It's not a little smirk either, like she has self-gratification and just smiles to herself. No. This is a full on wide, presenting her shiny white teeth type of smile. Also showing just how much pleasure she is getting from his discomfort. Truthfully, she deserves it. She deserves to witness this. She really does. Willow does too. They both do. Hell, so do I. Justice for all! This is something we can all bond about after Willow and I get back together and she introduces me to Mya because I'm that important to her. Still, there is something about Mya's smile that seems a little…. odd.

Or off. It's wicked. It reminds me of The Joker. A slow rising from ear to ear grin. Her eyes match the grin that shines across her face. I shudder, getting chills up and down the spine of my back. It creeps me the fuck out.

All the sudden I find myself wondering if Bryan was telling the truth just three days ago when he accused Mya of spitting on his face. I'm not excusing his behavior. I'm not saying he doesn't have a spit-on-able type of face because he very much does. I'm also not saying she deserved to be choked. Women should be treated better than that. A lot of men could take notes from me. I protect Willow like a man should. Maybe Mya doesn't have that in her life. She did not deserve to be choked even if she had spit on his face or his shoe or his arm or wherever, but I have to wonder if there is a dark side to Mya that Willow doesn't know about. If so, does this mean she isn't safe around Mya anymore? I don't like hurting women, but I'll do what I have to do to keep Willow safe. I really hope it doesn't have to go there.

Goddamnit Willow. Why does she always have to pick the weirdest, creepiest, most fucked up people to surround herself with? Does she really think they're alike? Because while Willow is a very stupid girl to invite such a cluster fuck into her life over and over again, she's also a very smart girl. That leads me to think that maybe she doesn't exactly know that Mya has a dark side because really, she smiled that way behind Willow's back. And just a few days ago, nobody, not even I believed that she actually spit on Bryan's face when he seemed so adamant about it. Stomping his feet all around, throwing a temper tantrum like a fucking toddler, that she was getting away with it. He's the victim. Poor Bryan.

While the police drive off Bryan, no doubt about it, sulks with his head hung low in the back seat of the police car. Just like he did at the coffee shop the other day while waiting for them to show up. Mya pulls Willow into her arms and scoops her up into a big best friend hug. She strokes her hair while moving her lips, appearing to give her comfort. Curiously, I zoom in close enough to Mya's face. So close that I can read her lips perfectly.

"Want me to kill him for you?" That's what she says. A possible true intention disguised as a joke.

Willow laughs as she wipes tears from her eyes. She shakes her head yes.

They laugh together like they aren't being serious about it. But I wonder, just how far will Mya take this 'joke'?

CHAPTER THIRTY-TWO

WILLOW

As soon as I step into my apartment I drop to the floor with the back of my head pressed against the wall. Overwhelmed, I lift my head so my chin is up in the air, like people do when they praise their Gods. Although, I do this to think without any interruptions or people in my ear giving me unasked for advice or their opinions about my life and the shitty decisions I make.

I get it. I'm a mess. I am no good to or for anyone anymore.

That may be a bit dramatic, but I'm drained. Drained from all the energy I've put into the relationships surrounding me. From the people that suck the energy right out of me and use it as their own like energy vampires. I am drained from just being here. Alive. It's almost too much to handle. It's almost too much to even bear the thought of being alive. I'd rather sleep it away. That's safer than dying at the hands of my own guise. I never thought my body could be anything except bruised and mangled. My chained and locked door. My gruesome haunted house. The unlearning of abuse is taking so long. So very fucking long. I don't want anyone knowing about my past. About Neil. About Brock. About me. I want to take that key to my gruesome haunted home and lock the door.

Then throw it the fuck away. Bury it while I'm drunk, so I won't remember where it's at. Burn it. Toss it in the sea to be lost forever.

Too many people have taken from me while they are pretending to give. Who can I trust? What gives? Can I even trust myself?

I think about dying. I think about taking a razor blade to my dainty little wrist and cutting it the right way. The way that actually ends it all. No fucking around and cutting it horizontal to get attention, like so many people do as a cry for help, and they do need help. So, help them, Goddamnit. I think I already have enough unwanted attention right now as it is to be cutting my wrists horizontally only to end up still alive and left with whatever lingers behind. Mental anguish. Deep scars over my wrists. A possible permanent disability. No. I won't cut them in the fake kind of way. I'll cut in the real, no fucking around kind of way. Vertical. A straight line down both of my wrists. Deep into the veins as I lay in a bathtub full of water, so whoever finds me won't have to clean up too much of my blood. It'll go straight into the water, linger, and turn it red. A dark red. Rose red. The crimson color of my blood. Whoever finds me will just pull the drain and down the bloody water will go. And there you have it. Nice and easy for them. No blood spatter on a wall where I've shot myself in the head. No vomit to clean up after taking pills and having my body reject them. Just a quick slice to the wrists will do.

The aftermath will be the hardest part to clean up once my body is pulled from the bathtub. The nagging smell of my death. The blood stains that unfortunately will have to be cleaned up with bleach in the porcelain white claw bathtub. The surviving memory of finding me lifeless in a pool of bloody water draining from my body. Whoever the unlucky person is that finds me will be burdened with it all. A lifelong lasting burden. I wonder who it'll be. Who will be the one to find me like this?

Will it be Mya? Will she come running to my rescue too late? Will she come because I haven't been answering my phone calls and texts from her? Will she be standing at my door, biting her nails with anticipation as an apartment manager unlocks it and they plug their noses from the stench of my decaying body? I'd rather it not be her. She is still coping with the suicide of her husband.

I wonder if it will be my stalker? Will he or she get sick of waiting for me to come out of my apartment and finally bust the doors down? She's mine, dead or alive!

Would it be Bryan? He's already kicked and dented my door to get me to come out when I wasn't even home. He doesn't take no for an answer, so I've learned. That's a huge problem. So many men have that problem, don't they?

Perhaps it will be Diego Cold Hands, The Famous Bearer because he is the stalker. Is he my stalker?

Will it be Mr. and Mrs. Grey? Will one of them text me and realize I haven't texted back in so long that they get worried and find me. They still don't know my address, only that I live in New York City. I still haven't texted them back about Thanksgiving. Or will they send someone over for a welfare check?

Maybe it will be my parents. Will they have some type of mother's or father's intuition and go to the ends of the earth to find me because the thought of losing me would be too heavy on their hearts? Would they finally realize the damage they caused that can't be undone? That can't be unseen.

Possibly it'll be Pauleen. Will she get a *real* mother's intuition that doesn't sit well with her and finally leave her house to come find me? She is the main one I wouldn't want to burden with this. She's already lost a daughter. I don't want to put her through any more hell than she's already endured.

Will it be my landlord who will put up the apartment he finds me in on the market the very next day?

I'm not really going to kill myself. A woman can fantasize though. Right?

CHAPTER THIRTY-THREE

WILLOW

A knock on my door wakes me up. I've been sleeping for three whole days. A hazy dreamland consumed me. I don't want to answer the door, just like I haven't wanted to answer any of my texts and phone calls.

Even from Mya. I am not answering anything right now. It's time to keep sleeping instead of dying.

But the knock is the same kind of knock that came the day the bag from Lucky's Charms was by my front door. It's a persistent, daring knock.

Knock

Knock

Knock

The three knocks beat slow but loud against my front door, just like it did that day. A whole five Mississippi seconds in between each one. It reminds me of the charm on my necklace I'm wearing that I haven't taken off since I laid down in my bed three days ago. I have only gotten up to pee, drink water, pour more vodka into my cup laying on the nightstand, and to eat a few crackers with peanut butter one of the days. I'm clearly in no mood for visitors. Demanding my attention, the knock gets a little louder.

Who is on the other side of my front door? I wonder. I've laid here long enough to the point they have probably gone away now.

Knock

Another one? That's different. The last time it was only three knocks. Now it's four. Whoever it is, is still here. I sit up slowly, toss my legs over the side of my bed and push myself up to force myself towards the door. My fingers run through my hair, brushing it as I tiptoe. I creep slowly up to the door like I did the last time. I'm definitely checking the peephole before I open it up. *If* I open it. I stop right in front of it and point my toes like a ballerina, so I can be eye level to see what's out there before making any rash decisions because let's face it, I am not the best at judgment.

Nobody is there. Not a single soul in sight. Not even my neighbors are outside. Unless, whoever knocked is hiding where I can't see them from the peephole, which is totally possible. I step down in a normal position to stand with my feet flat on the floor. Leaning my body against the door, I let out a sigh loud enough that anyone standing right on the other side would be able to hear. I slap both of my hands over my mouth.

Shit. Did they hear me? Is it a he? Is it a she? Who the fuck is doing this?

I don't hear any shuffling or movement. That's a good thing. Maybe that means they're finally gone. I creak the door open with the chain still on, holding the lock in place. Just like my heart. No more people can get in. I look through the opening and I can see much more than I could through the peephole. I was right. Nobody is here. Maybe this time it was just some stupid kids messing around and perhaps…

My gaze drops down beside my door. I notice another little gift bag waiting for me and close the door. Quickly. I click the deadbolt lock. *Click.* Bye asshole. Stop fucking with me.

I guess because I'm finally up and have blood pumping through me and my heart is beating faster than it has in the last three days, I should go ahead and take a shower to wash the depression off. Sniffing, I take a whiff of my armpits. I reek of body odor and sadness. Don't worry, I won't take a razor blade to myself just yet.

I'm out of the shower now, alive and not bloody. Not a lick of red goo has poured from or out of my body. Surprised? Are you proud of me? I thought about it. Killing myself. While I was bathing. Every time the loofa caressed against my wrist and forearms the thought of the razor blade replacing it ran through my mind, but I survived!

I'm here. I am alive. Hopefully you're proud of me for not dying today.

I guess now is as good a time as any to see what this gift bag outside my door holds inside for me. I creep up to my door again, like the boogeyman is still out there and waiting to snatch me up and chain me to his bed like Brock did. Like I imagine Diego Cold Hands, The Famous Bearer wants to do to me in Dubai. My heart pounds inside, flopping around like a fish.

Anxiety and anger fuels me. Who the fuck is this piece of shit?

Once I get to the door I swing it wide open—I'm done feeling scared—and toss my arms in the air. Come and get me! I'm ready to die, you asshole! But am I really? I think I still have a little fight in me. I hold my arms higher up and with more passion. With confidence, I bob my head forward. Come with it, bitch. I got you. Motherfucker.

Nothing. Nothing happens. He—or she—but most likely a he, possibly Diego Cold Hands, The Famous Bearer doesn't come to my beckoning. I drop my arms to my sides, then step outside. Over the threshold I go. With curiosity, I swing my head from side to side, looking in all directions to find the culprit. Nobody is here. Nobody but me and my thoughts swirling around in my fucked up little brain.

I grab the bag off the ground and head back inside my apartment and lock the door behind me. Then I place the gift bag on my kitchen island. This one doesn't have a name brand on it. It doesn't show fancy writing with a swirly heart like the last one did. It's blank and bare and red. Like blood. Red as the color of my blood that I just fantasized about pouring out of me. I stand there for a while, just gazing at this blood red bag and I wonder what the fuck could be inside it. I'm scared to open it. I have no idea what's waiting for me. The other one was a nice gift. Albeit intrusive, but I loved it. *Love* it. I wear it every day. I'm wearing it right now.

I had someone with me the last time this happened and I could just fall into his arms if what I pulled out of the bag was something dreadful from my past or a dead animal. I gain enough mental strength to open it up, doing it the same way as before.

Slowly.

Slowly.

Slowly.

That's how I pull out the pink sparkly tissue paper that covers what's inside. Red and pink. Like Valentine's day. Colors that represent love. Does this person think they love me? I shiver, chills running through me from getting the creeps of it all. Before I pull out the last tissue, I pick the bag up and shake it. It's light. Really light. There's no way a dead animal could be in there. A small blessing. I pull out the last sparkly tissue paper, taking my sweet ass time doing it. It drops to the floor with the rest of the tissue paper I've pulled out equally slowly.

What the actual fuck?

My fingerprints stain the picture of me that I'm holding. It's the side of me, my profile from top to bottom with my blonde curly hair crowding my face that holds the expression of pure anger. I have a look for a lust of danger. Do I always look like this? Bryan sits with his head in his hands while Chelsea stands with her hips out and her hands placed on them as disgust smears across her face. The other customers at The Charming Coffee Delight are all staring at the drama that unfolded before their very eyes. In the background of the picture, I see Mya. She is a little blurry but she's there, standing outside looking through the window with her cell phone in her hand and looking straight at the camera. She looks dizzy and confused but concerned. Her face is frozen with her eyebrows furrowed and her mouth slightly open.

He was there. He is here in New York City, where I am. This isn't just a visit. He is living here. Day in and day out. I know he is, and I do think my stalker is a he. He followed me. He is stalking me for real. Not just a little bit, not just sort of, but on a very real level of stalking. I can think of only one person. Diego Cold Hands, The Famous Bearer who has not stopped harassing me since I broke up with him before I moved here. I'm not sure who else it could be. While I feel like I'm going insane, I'm positive that he's the culprit.

It's not Bryan. He's in the picture, so unless he can be in two places at the same time, in which he cannot, it's not him. Maybe if I leave for just a few days I can come up with something. Something to make this stop without having to get the cops involved because while I'm on their good side right now, I haven't exactly earned it and I don't want any suspicion to be raised my way. I like staying in the dark.

I think it's time to make a little visit to Pauleen.

CHAPTER THIRTY-FOUR

WILLOW

Before I head to Texas, where Pauleen was born and raised, I make a little pitstop to The Charming Coffee Delight. I grab myself the biggest vanilla latté that they have with two extra shots of espresso and *no milk.*

"Where have you been?" Chelsea asks. I'm sure she wants to know because I'm usually here every morning with either my phone or a book or a friend in my grasp. This morning, I moved fast and took my order to go.

I don't give her much information, "I've been packing for a trip out of state." Explaining, as I quickly head towards the door.

I have no time for small talk and when she calls out, "Where to?" I don't bother answering. I can't risk my stalker knowing where I'm going if he is here right now and there's a good chance he might be. Besides, I already have my back to Chelsea. I'm close to being out the door, so she might mark it off as I just didn't hear her. I hope she does, anyway.

This latté is a punch in the gut and just what I need for a long road trip in a rental car. A fucking Audi. A sharp, electric blue Audi. I usually pour a little vodka in my cup to give me an extra boost for the day ahead of me, but today I am driving and how fucking ironic would it be if I were to drink and drive on my way to see Pauleen, who lost her daughter and husband in a drunk driving car accident that was no fault of her own or her husband or her daughter. Karma would take care of me. I wouldn't even have to kill myself then. The universe would do it for me. So, I don't pour vodka in my cup this time.

The drive to Texas is a breeze. I got here within a snap. I mean, you would think that after driving for sixteen hours that I would say boy, that was a doozy! But I don't because it wasn't. I had so much time to think, and I mean really think about my past. About my future. I forgot to think about my present, though. The thoughts. The memories. The ideas kept popping up one after another. Remember when… What will happen if I… How can I…

Not wanting my brain to go there, I slapped the power button on the radio and let the music carry those thoughts and feelings away. Far, far away from me. And guess what? It worked. I jammed out to some of my favorites. Jack Johnson, Alanis Morissette, Linkin Park, John Lennon. A random little mix. During the day, a few times I had the window rolled down to let the pressure of the air pull weight against my hand. I swung it out there specifically for that very feeling, just like when I was kid. I've always enjoyed that feeling. The fight against the air. Something I can't see, but I can feel and I win the little battle. I win.

Feeling eager and excited at the same time, I roll the borrowed Audi up to Pauleen's home. It's a cute little brick house with raised up flower beds in a row lining her front lawn. Purple, pink, orange, red, yellow, green and blue perennial flowers peek above the raised up wooden flower beds. They're barely showing colors and practically dead with fall in full swing, but the color is there and Texas allows this year round basically.

I can only assume that because today is cold, tomorrow I'm supposed to dress like it's summertime. That's what Pauleen said. The colors of the flowers remind me of Pauleen's daily nightgowns. I wonder if she still wears them every day. I wonder if she ever leaves her home, or if she stays cooped up inside like she did at the apartments. I wonder if she was the one who built the wooden flower beds. I can picture her outside, wearing her pastel pink nightgown and matching slippers with the bows, kneeling down on a floral knee pad over the flower beds. I wonder if she still pops pills like they're candy.

As I open the door of the Audi the cool air frosts me immediately, like Diego Cold Hands, The Famous Bearer. It's not as cold as New York City, but I've been driving and have gotten used to the heater blowing on my face the last sixteen hours. Keeping me nice and toasty inside the Audi I enjoyed driving so much that I'm now thinking of looking into buying one of my own. It would be nice to have a car to come and go as I please, instead of grabbing taxis every time I need to go somewhere. I miss having my own car, but it was the first thing I sold upon moving to New York City. Finishing up a song before turning the car off, I set my phone inside my purse and swing it over my shoulder. I step out of the car and stretch my body like a damn Armstrong stretch man. Pauleen's front door swings wide open and she takes one step outside before I can even get to the trunk of the car to grab my luggage.

"Willow!" She stands at her open front door, waving her hand back and forth with excitement. A larger than life smile is spread across her face. She's not wearing one of her nightgowns today. I'm assuming it's because she has been expecting me. I'm company, and I can't really picture Pauleen being the type to wear one on the first day that I'm here, but the rest of the days she probably will. Instead, she wears an oversized orange sweater with brown leaves that look like they're falling from a tree, brown leggings and matching brown boots. She looks like Autumn spit up on her. Her hair is still gray—no hair dye for her—and piled on top of her head with at least thirty bobby pins holding it all in place. She has on makeup today. Just a touch. And she glows with natural beauty and pure happiness.

I've missed Pauleen.

Stepping out from her doorway, she speed walks my way like she can't get to me fast enough.

"Oh my gosh! Willow! It's really you. You're here!" She beams at me and snatches me up to give me a big ol' momma bear hug. I hug her back, equally as tight as she is holding me and suddenly my feet are no longer touching the ground. She's got me up in the air and swinging me back and forth.

"It's so good to see you," I say as she sets me down, then holds her hands on my upper arms. Her eyes fill up with tears, so I hug her again hoping she won't pick me back up. Thankfully, she doesn't. She pats me on my back as we embrace each other.

"Let's get you inside and all warmed up, kiddo," she prompts as she goes to grab my bag out of the trunk of my car.

With a full heart, I realize right that moment that I need to be here and I am most definitely not letting her carry my things inside when I am fully capable and she is in her sixties, so I put my hand on top of hers as she reaches for my luggage. "I can get it." She smiles at me like she's proud, and then leads me into her home.

A picture of Tillie, her dead daughter, is the first thing I'm greeted with as I step into her living room area. It's the same one she's had hanging up in all of her apartments over the fireplace since I've known her. She is in Texas now, so I don't think she felt like she needed to rent a house with a fireplace even though outside begs to differ. So, Tillie's wide smile when she was still alive hangs on a gallery wall Pauleen created that sits by her television set instead of over a fireplace.

Feeling a tinge of jealousy, I step over to admire the canvas of Tillie. Like a God to be worshiped. Pauleen takes a place right beside me. We admire the pictures together. The picture of Tillie—the same one that's been hung above the fireplaces in the past—is the largest one and parked in the middle of all the rest. It demands your attention. It has mine for sure. Tillie wears a flowy floral sundress, like the kind I wear in the summer and springtime. She sits upon a giant rock with one of her bare feet kicked in the air and the other one flat on the surface. Her head slightly tilted back. It must have been a windy day wherever they were that day because her blonde curly hair isn't laying on her back or shoulders, instead it's swaying in the wind. She glares at the camera with a hint of innocence in her eyes. On her face. That's the moment I realize that Tillie and I are really not the same at all to be honest. In fact, we are polar opposites aside from the way we look and the way we dress.

Ding! My phone chimes at me, interrupting my stare down with Tillie. I turn around to face my luggage and purse I placed on her coat rack at the entrance of her door, upon entering her house. I wonder who that is? Is it Diego Cold Hands, The Famous Bearer? Is it Bryan? Is he still in jail? Is it my stalker? Who is my stalker? Is it Mya? I miss Mya. I need to call her.

Pauleen wraps her arm around my shoulders, bringing me back to the present. To what's happening here and now in this house instead of on my phone. The warmth of her hug is like medicine. Curing my sadness. "Let's get you something warm to drink. How about some coffee? Or actually, I do have tea I can put on the kettle, too. Would you like that? Or I can do hot cocoa. Which do you prefer? I have all different kinds of teas. I have green tea, black tea, oolong tea, white tea, herbal tea, earl gray. Earl Gray is one of my favorites! Which would you like?" She smiles wide and steps a little closer to me as if we weren't close enough already. I don't take a step back because I think it would hurt her feelings.

I smile warmly at her. "Let's have some earl gray tea." I remember when I promised her tea and girl talk. We can actually do that again and for much longer this time.

"Okay!" Pauleen sounds chipper as ever. She claps her hands and rubs them together. "Let me just show you to your room real quick, so you can get all settled in and I'll put the kettle on while you unpack!"

With a calmness flowing over me, I grab my bags——just a purse and an overnight bag-——off the coat rack by the front door and follow her down the hall to the bedroom where I'll be staying while I'm here for the week. When we get to the bedroom my eyes have to adjust to how many Precious Moments posters are hung on the wall. They stare into my soul with their big, sad eyes. I wonder how many nightmares this will give me for the week. Knick knacks are covering almost every inch of the dresser with Precious Moments characters. The bedspread isn't Precious Moments themed to my surprise, but it definitely matches with the color choices of the quilt Pauleen has chosen. A few Precious

Moments dolls are propped against the pillows, and I know that I'll be putting them in a drawer away from me as soon as she walks out that bedroom door. I wonder if this is how Tillie had her bedroom decorated. I turn to her with a smile. It doesn't match the way I feel anymore. I feel a little uneasy and creeped out by the dolls, but hey, Precious Moments was a big thing back in her day. Everything in here looks twice my age. I set my bags on top of the bed and dust flies in the air. Maybe I won't stay a whole week.

"Thank you, Pauleen."

"Oh honey, you don't have to thank me. Thank *you* for coming all this way to see little old me. It means the whole entire world to me." Pauleen perks up. She gives me another big ol' momma bear hug. "I'm off to get the kettle steaming for that girl talk and tea that will be even better than our last one." And I swear, as she walks away, I see her click her heels in the air with excitement like a little leprechaun that found the gold at the end of the rainbow.

CHAPTER THIRTY-FIVE

HIM

The cold breeze of the crisp night air fights the pressure against my hand as I hold it straight out the window of my rental car. Just like Willow. I followed her to Texas because I fear she'll get herself into a mix of something she can't get out of just like she always fucking does.

It wasn't long ago that I left for three days—only three fucking days—- and she made a friend that is far too involved in her life when she—Mya— should just be worried about taking care of her son and mom at home. She's not a Caseworker anymore. There is no need to stick her fucking nose into what's not any of her business. But alas, Willow attracts people like that everywhere she goes. Like flies on honey. That makes me think of the way she smells. I fucking miss the way she smells. I stick my hand in my hoodie pocket and pull out the red lacy panties that I stole from her bedroom floor. I breathe her in because fucking Goddamnit I miss her. And that leads me right back to my very thought of Willow attracting the wrong people. Not me. Of course, not me. But Mya, people like Mya, yes. People with questionable intentions.

So, no. I don't allow Willow to just hop in a rental car to take a detour to Texas by herself. She obviously cannot be trusted.

I didn't go all out and get myself an Audi, though. I settled for a black Toyota that won't stick out. It blends right in with the hustle and bustle of the highway. She had no clue I followed her here. Even when I passed by Pauleen's house and saw Willow standing at the Audi rental driver's side door. Stretching her body from the long drive she just endured. I slowed down to get a good look.

It never gets old. Watching her perk her tits out like that. She puts on a show even when she doesn't think anyone is around to enjoy it. I love the show. I love those tits. Those tits are mine and that pussy is mine, and at least at Pauleen's house she won't be giving out free samples of it. She no longer has that right. I'm making it stop right the fuck now. I fear she'll meet some good ol' Texas boy while she's here. That she'll think she's in love at first sight, and she'll cheat on me again. I can't let that happen. There's no way I can watch this go on any longer. I can't stand to see any more men take advantage of her, spreading her legs for any dark haired, smooth talking son of a bitch. She is mine and she fucking knows this. This little game she's been playing is ending right the fuck now.

***

The hotel I'm staying at is only five miles from Pauleen's house and it's definitely not anything special. It's not diagonal from Willow's. It's not close enough to where I can just pull out my Nikon camera and see what she's up to. To do that I'd have to park in front of Pauleen's house. That is way too risky. They might see me. No. They'll definitely fucking see me. Instead, I wait until it's late and dark outside to make a little visit. I just want her to know that I'm here. I need her to be aware I'm watching her. That I'm right here with her wherever she goes. I'm always here for her. I can't wait to see the look on her face when she opens up my next gift after her visit with Pauleen is over and she gets back home.

Click

I've zoomed in on Willow's face. She sits paused with her head tilted back and a big toothy smile on her face, laughing with Pauleen, who is wearing a mint green mew-mew nightgown with a little bow sewn into the top. Not much has changed. She reminds

184

me of my grandmother, who also popped Xanax after Xanax to calm her ass down. I zoom the lens out.

Click

Willow sits on a gray couch with her fluffy sock feet propped up on the matching gray ottoman. She holds a mug that reads 'Dog Mom' even though neither one of them have a fucking dog.

Click

Willow's face turns into concern as she moves her body more to face Pauleen. She curls her feet underneath her ass. Pauleen grabs her mint green mug—come on woman, does everything have to match your fucking nightgowns?—off the end table beside her and reaches for the prescription bottle with her other hand. I zoom in to get a look at the name and yep, it's still Xanax she's popping like candy. She opens the bottle up and pours four little bars in her shaking hand, pops the lid back on, sets it back down and drops all four of those bitches right into her mouth, then sucks it down with whatever she's got in her mug. She purses her lips afterwards and instantly wears a look of satisfaction. Just the thought of those jagged little pills swimming in her stomach makes her smile. Everyone knows Pauleen is a pill popper.

Click.

I captured three pictures of the act. One of the pills plopping down on her tongue. Another of her guzzling them. The last one is a close up of the lustful look on her face after they disappear into the abyss of her stomach.

Watching Pauleen gulp down her pills to get high makes my stomach growl. Instead of eating, I've grown an appetite for beer. I feel like letting loose a little bit before my big day tomorrow. I place my Nikon camera into its little black case that hugs just right, so it can't get away or broken or scratched. It keeps it safe. Like I keep Willow safe. I am her little black case.

I've done my job for the night. I drove back to my temporary home, even though I could watch Willow for hours. She's still my favorite show, my number one episode to watch. I try to figure out what the two of them are talking about. I can even make a little game out of it, but I'm sure I have already been brought up a time or two. I know I will be soon if I haven't been yet. Right now, it looks like it's Pauleen's turn to talk, but when it gets to Willow's turn, I know she'll talk about me. She can't stop thinking about me. She talks about me all the time.

***

After I grab a six pack of Bud Light, I pull up to the shit hole motel that I'm staying at and that pisses off the people outside because my headlights are too bright. It shines onto their faces and interrupts their oh so important conversation as they drink their moonshine and pretend to be drunk. Fucking get over yourselves. They flip me off when I get out of the car and I don't really give a shit, but I wave to them in a friendly manner with a closed smile that I'm hoping says fuck off instead of hi.

I'm on the third floor, so I take the stairs, skipping every other step. Room three o' eight! I just had to make sure I got that room number. It makes me feel close to Willow.

I plop down on the bed and imagine her beside me as I scroll through the pictures on my Nikon camera. Thinking of the days when the pictures had me in them with her, I grab a bottle of beer and chug it. The memory of being right there with her eats me alive, like a flesh eating beetle or a leech that pulls at my skin and sucks harder when I try to get it off. There is just no moving on. I don't care what anybody says. It's not that easy. The thought of being right beside her where I can smell her, not just the lingering of her from her string thongs that she wore the night before, makes my imagination run wild. Oh, the days that we pillow fought on the bed and it led to one thing, which led to another and afterward we were naked with only bed sheets covering our bodies, feeding each other strawberries, just like you see in romance movies. The memories of snapping one picture after another of her as we were together, instead of hiding to do it consume my thoughts.

186

Our relationship isn't natural anymore. I do this all behind her back because she doesn't give me permission anymore. But why does she get to say when it's done? When it's over? She doesn't. She won't. We aren't over. This isn't over. Not even close.

***

The next day is bright and shiny and much warmer than it was yesterday because the weather here is bipolar and fucked up. Texas people don't really get an autumn season and that's a damn shame. I wasn't prepared for this change, so I went about the day wearing a winter outfit I had packed. All black, casual, soft black gloves to keep my hands warm and not leave any fingerprints, a hoodie so I can pop it over my head if she looks in my direction. But Willow and Pauleen don't go out for the day. They don't get out of the house and tour the state that Willow has never been to. Instead, they stay inside wearing their pajamas and watch movies together. They cry together, laugh together, and eat together, cheering with mugs full of whatever—together.

I have a very important task I need to do today, and because they have chosen to stay inside, this is my perfect opportunity to do it without getting caught in the headlights. I won't feel like I have to watch over my shoulder. It's exactly six minutes to drive back to the hotel and get it all together.

I have a notebook paper folded over the picture, so nobody around me can see what it is.

"They all cost the same." The woman behind the desk at the post office tells me as I stand by the shelves of envelopes. I'm not gauging their prices. I want it to be bubbled wrapped inside so the picture is safe, but I don't want all this stupid shit all over the envelope like balloons or confetti or flowers. It doesn't match my message.

I turn my head to face her. Act cool. She doesn't know. I nod to her as if I understand. I found a brown one that's bubble wrapped inside. Perfect. I hold it up in the air to show her I found it. "Thanks." God, how I wish other people would walk in here so

187

I wouldn't be the only customer right now, but that's a small town for ya.

I walk over to the island in the middle of the post office where the markers and pens are stationed. She watches me the way a dog watches its person. Curious of what my next move will be. Please lady, do anything else but fucking stalk me. I place the picture inside the envelope and keep the paper wrapped around it. She watches me do this because of course she does, and because I don't want to be suspicious I don't take the paper off the picture. She would get curious to see what it is and perk her face up even more at what I'm doing. Stop watching me and get a fucking life. I pull out my phone from my pocket and search for his mailing address. I glance up and her fixation is finally off me and onto her phone. Fucking finally.

I scroll through the history on my phone. Dammit! It's three weeks of history to go through. I glance up at her again. I'm taking too long. She's going to get curious again. She still watches something on her phone. TikToks maybe. Got it! My shoulders relax and I accidentally sigh with relief aloud. She looks up from her phone. Shit. Fuck. Damnit. Leave me alone!

"Finally find the mailing addy?" She asks me like it's a normal question in my situation. Lady, you don't know the half of it.

I give her a warm smile like she's used to over here. "Yeah. My sister moved and I couldn't remember her address." You're talking too much. Stop it. "I had to go through all our Facebook messages to get it." Shut the fuck up! "Finally got it after going through three weeks of conversation." Shoot me now. Get it over with. I'm positive she'll remember my face in a line up.

She chuckles and looks back at her phone as if I interrupted something and she is glad I stopped talking. "Happens all the time." She comforts me with that.

I write down his mailing address with the boldest blackest marker I can find here. Instead of giving her the envelope to mail it off for me I pay for it as I hold it in between my armpit and forearm. I pay for a book of stamps, too. She doesn't find this peculiar, as I expected. I did it! I step outside and instead of walking up to the mail slot I go to the Toyota rental and finish it up. I place two stamps on the top right side. Flowers and butterflies were my only choices out of the book, so I chose butterflies to signify a fresh start that I'll have with Willow. One pink butterfly and one blue butterfly. I don't write a return address on the left side. Driving away, I head to the next post office only ten minutes away in the next town over. I slide up to the mailing slot in this black Toyota that blends in and makes me look normal. Reaching up, I slip the envelope into the slot of the mailbox.

Willow isn't the only one that gets surprises from me. This is for both of them.

CHAPTER THIRTY-SIX

CHIEF PHILL

Chief Phill gets to his work building bright and early—as he does every morning—and stumbles into the building with a half-eaten glazed donut in one hand and a to-go coffee cup in his other hand. He pushes his back against the door to open it and steps inside. Tipping his cup, he takes another sip of his coffee, half the cup already gone—black with two sweeteners. He feels ready for the day of work ahead of him that will no doubt be a hard one.

As the head chief of missing person's cases in the district of Chicago, he has seen his fair share of brutality, of how ugly the world can be, but it doesn't make it any easier. He hasn't become a jaded chief of police that can see a woman's dead body and mark her down as a case number. No. Each time he takes it to heart. He pours his heart and soul into his career. It's the reason he is a divorcee. His wife couldn't handle it any longer and he wasn't about to let his work go. Not for anything, or anyone. Not even for her. He is devoted to his very important job of getting the monsters off the streets. One by one. He has a hunger for it. Every day he wakes up ready to take on the Ted Bundys of the world.

"Morning!" he calls out to the front desk the same way he does every day and nods with his hands full, heading to his office. The building is old and there are a few moldy spots on the ceiling, but he wouldn't have it any other way. He loves doing the dirty work in Chicago that other people step over. Like spilled milk on the floor that nobody wants to clean up because it takes too much effort. The smell of fresh coffee lingers in the air as his department pours their doses into their mugs to give them fuel for the day because dammit, they're gonna need it.

Chief Phill gets to his office and sets his belongings down on the computer desk that's become his second home. He turns the computer on, types in his password, pulls up the case file he's currently working on and heads to the staff room. It's a small room with only one table to sit at and eat lunch, basic with no welcoming signs hung on the walls, a refrigerator and a sink are to the left side of the room, and the mail slots are to the right. Chief Phill pulls a set of keys out of his pocket and unlocks his mailbox slot, grabs what has filled up in there and turns to lock it. He grips the few envelopes, all three brown and plain and heads back to his office. He doesn't have a second thought about the mail he's received. To him, it's just a normal Tuesday morning.

When he plops down in his desk chair, it leans back and rolls a little bit. He catches his balance and then picks up each envelope, squinting his eyes to read who they're from. He puts his reading glasses on and is able to see better. One is from the state of Florida letting him know inside is a case file that's transferred because a loose cannon he's searching for originally started his killing spree over there. And now he's terrorizing the streets of Chicago, but he hasn't been found, and Chief Phil is determined to save the day. Getting one less creep off the streets is a milestone for him.

Another envelope is from a district over, just ten miles away. This one is concerning a missing child's case. A fourteen year old girl—who of course was deemed as a runaway case before they suspected foul play. Chief Phill was notified about her twenty-three year old boyfriend who lives in his district. He is ready to tear that guy a new one. The thought of a grown man preying on a teen girl fuels the fire he needs for the day. He's ready to turn that loser's world upside down and inside out.

The third and last envelope he holds up doesn't have a return address. This immediately piques his interest. He's only had a few envelopes with no return addresses sent to him throughout his career and he knows that usually means something sinister is waiting for him inside.

He shakes it first. It feels light, like nothing is in there, but he can hear the swoosh sound inside. So, of course there is something. Things like this worry him because people have been known to put rat poison or fentanyl on the paper inside to harm the receiver of the mail. He can think of a few people who would want to harm him.

Chief Phil opens up a drawer to his desk and pulls out a pair of rubber disposable gloves, places them on his hands, draws in a long sigh, and then tears open the envelope. He doesn't just tear it from the top. That's not a chance he would take. He doesn't want to have to stick his whole hand and arm inside to grab whatever is in there and have a chance at any substance rubbing against his skin. He tears it wide open and lays it flat on his desk. His eyes are met with a notebook paper folded over a picture that he only sees the corner peeking out as if to say hello, but he can tell it's a picture by the crisp sharp corner of it. Unsure of what action might be paused on this paper and sent to him for a reason, his heart skips a beat as he picks up the picture first and examines it while he holds it away from his face first. Front and back. He moves it closer to his face. Concerned it might be a picture of a child forced to pose as they're demanded to do the unspeakable, he's relieved to find there aren't any children in the picture. Instead, it's a woman. While he feels relieved that his eyes aren't violated from the innocence of a child being taken away, he still wonders why someone would send something so vile to him.

The woman in the picture looks familiar to him. A case he worked on a year ago. A young missing woman who was found in a field beaten, bloody, muddy and barefoot. The picture shows just that. There Willow lay in the damp cold grass with her wet hair covering part of her face, but he could tell it was her for sure upon looking closer. Willow lay frozen in a position of sleep to almost death with her black floral sundress hiked up to see the panties she wore and the lower part of her stomach. A telling of the blood and where it came from with her upper thighs and in between her legs smeared with the dried up blood. Bruises covered both of her arms, black and blue, up and down and all across like sleeves of tattoos. Boot print marks stained her upper legs and crawled up to her abdomen. Mud, grass stains and blood surrounded her once pretty floral sundress.

Willow practically looks dead.

Chief Phill furrows his eyebrows in confusion and holds up the picture to the light as if there was more to it. He places it down on his desk and opens up the folded notebook paper hoping there would be some type of gesture there. A reason. Nothing. It's blank. He held that up to the light to examine, too. He can clearly see that there is no deadly concoction on the paper or picture. The sender's message isn't to harm him, but simply to confuse him. He takes off the gloves and tosses them in the trash. Picking up the picture of Willow again, he studies it as he leans back in his squeaking rolling office chair.

***

"Willow," Chief Phill utters as he holds the phone up to his ear with one hand and taps the picture of her on his desk with his other hand. "This is Chief Phill." He pauses to conduct what he'll be saying beforehand even though he knew he should have done that before he called her. "Something—interesting came in the mail to me today and we need to talk. Please give me a call back. 972-555-0505. I hope you're doing well." He clicks the end button on his work cell phone and sets it down on his desk along with the picture. Side by side.

"We're gonna need to run fingerprints on these." Chief Phill tells his team as they peer over at each other with knowing eyes because they all remember this case so well. How could they not? Who forgets a case of a missing woman who was held captive in chains and forced into pregnancy? A case where a young woman's freedom was taken away from her just for simply being her, instilling trust in the wrong people like she did when she was a child. With a narcissistic mother. And a father who was around,

193

but not really. He was cold, distant, and calculative, like Neil, the man Willow married. A mixture of her parents is who she found in Neil and Brock. She paid the ultimate price for believing in them. For believing in her mother and father when she was far too young to even understand the tools they carried around on their belt to make her sacrifice. She was so afraid of becoming them, but she fell in love with them through the men who mirrored them. Longing for unconditional love, like the love she had to win with her mother, but you can just forget about it with her father.

Chief Phill understood this all too well, and it reminded him of Patricia, another one of Neil's ex-wives, or victims should we say. He wondered if she ever got her happy ending. Was she safely tucked under a covered porch, drinking her coffee, waving to neighbors as they checked the mail, while her kids ran rapidly in the house as her husband cooked them all breakfast? He thought about calling her up, having a little chit chat and asking her the usual questions that would get to his answer—are you okay now?––but he knew that just hearing his voice would probably set her up for a trauma response. He didn't want to be the reason why she might spiral downwards. He settled on his last memory of her. The very fact that she was still alive is enough to suffice him for now. His primary focus is on this package and who sent it to him and *why*. The fear he feels for Willow's safety is like that of a father and daughter. He feels protective of her.

This all sends a jolt straight to his heart.

Someone was watching her. Someone else was there. Someone is *still* watching her.

CHAPTER THIRTY-SEVEN

MYA

Can you think of anyone else who would do this to you? I mean, it's possible Diego had been following you before you met him." I clasp my hands together in front of me like I'm talking to a client when I was a social worker. Willow clutches the charm on her necklace and rolls it against her chin like she does when she's nervous or in deep thought. I lean forward and make eye contact with her. Think Willow. Think. Come on. Think hard. Dig deep.

"Is there anyone else who might be doing all these things? The gifts. The stalking. Knocking on your door. I'm talking think back to as far as when you were in high school even. Any enemies? Any ex boyfriends that stuck around longer than you wanted them to?" I poke around in her head, trying to get down to the bottom of all this.

Willow clasps the pictures of her and Pauleen from her recent visit in her hands and accidently wrinkles them. She's thinking. "I don't know. I can't think of anyone who would go to this extreme, Mya."

The picture of her lying vulnerable, muddy and bloody on the ground lay on the coffee table in my den in front of us. She closes her eyes and shakes her head a little each time she happens to look at the picture.

"Can you think of any guys from your past?" I dig, trying to get her to think of any and all suspects.

Sometimes the past comes creeping up to bite us when we've long forgotten it. At a time we're oblivious to it. When we least expect it. I take a sip of my coffee and maneuver myself on my couch to sit Indian style. "Are there any guys that you didn't date that came on a little too strong, maybe?" We've all been through this one. I know she can think of someone.

Willow drops the charm on her necklace and it sways back and forth in front of her chest as she leans in with an aha expression on her face. "Oh. My. Gosh. Mya." She makes eye contact with me now. Her eyes are glazed over. "There was this one guy." She shivers as if she got a chill up and down her spine. She probably did. "I was basically forced to be his partner in a science lab experiment. That's all it was. A science lab project. But he was determined that we were together. Like, as in a couple. Together like that. He was a total creep. A stage nine clinger. A stalker. A freak show." She shuffles in her seat. "I can't believe I forgot about him. He ruined my senior year in high school. I forgot all about him. He's been like a… repressed memory."

"He was so weird." She shivers again and shakes her head.

"What kind of things would he do?" I want to know. Not just because I'm nosy. I need to know because I have to help her.

She hugs herself without realizing it. A trauma response. She needed comfort and love at the time this happened. But she did not receive it, so she saved herself. She is stronger than she thinks.

"He would stalk me everywhere I went. If I was out with friends, you can bet your ass he was at the same place. Just watching. Watching me. And he didn't even care that I could see him do this. You know how normal people stop looking at you when you notice they're watching you?" She didn't stop and wait for me to answer. She kept going.

"Well, when I would catch him there, looking at me from across the room, he would just continue to stare. Sometimes even smile and wave at me."

Ah. The first guy to cross her boundaries—unless it was her father— and she became an addict. An addict to the toxicity of it all. To the attention. She didn't realize how dangerous this can be.

"I never dated him. I never kissed him. I never even led him on. But in his sick little twisted mind he thought we were together."

"So, what happened?" I ask, urging her for more.

"He left. One day, just poof, he was gone." She snapped her fingers.

"Gone. I never saw him again. He never bothered me again. Unless…"

I let this linger in the air between us because we might actually be getting somewhere. She grabs her phone off the coffee table and types in his name on Facebook. Albert Caldwell.

***

Albert Caldwell is nowhere to be found online. We search on Facebook, Instagram, X, TikTok and more. He has essentially disappeared. I think to myself, this could be our guy. He doesn't want to be found because he is a nobody. A nobody that is stalking and harassing Willow. He wants to be undetected so he can continue to do what he's doing and not be caught. We take it a step further and search his name on Google along with the town and state they went to high school with… and nothing. It truly is like he disappeared. Just poof! Like Willow said. Gone. But how? And why?

Ding!

Willow picks her phone up off the table. "The unknown number left me a voicemail." Her eyes go wide, like she's scared to listen to what the message is.

"Let's listen to it," I suggest.

What? It's not that intrusive. I'm her friend. I'm her best friend.

"I'm not ready just yet." She exhales and puts her phone back down on the table.

I let it slide, knowing I can't push her.

"I gotta go." She stands up and dusts her pants like there is something on them when there's not.

197

"Wait." Immediately, I realize I said this a little too desperately. I straighten myself the fuck up because *no mam*, I am not crossing boundaries.

"Why? Is something wrong?" Stupid question. Of course, something is wrong. She's dealing with a stalker. A psychopath, possibly.

She looks at me with sadness in her eyes. "I'm just tired. I need a nap."

"I understand." I tell her as she pulls her coat on and buttons it up, then swings her purse over her shoulder.

Reluctantly, I walk her to the front door and to her car. "Call me if anything else happens."

"Of course," she agrees.

Relying on her words, I head back inside. I lock the door behind me even though it's daytime, because when you have a friend who has a stalker, you can't be too careful yourself.

***

Putting my hands together in front of me like I'm praying, I intertwine my fingers and push my arms forward to crack my knuckles. I have work to do. Ryder is at the park with my mom and I have free time to do whatever I please because I'm privileged like that. I know this and yes, I do have survivor's guilt. Instead of painting my pretty flowers or mushrooms with my over the top scenery, I choose to do something in a different kind of productive way today.

I've forgotten to replace my husband's office chair with one that's more to my taste, so brown cracked leather is my option. It'll do for now. I place my hand along his desk and slide it across the siding. Smooth. Like when you pick a freshly grown tomato and feel the skin against your hands. Dusty. That's another thing I forgot. To dust in his office. I haven't been in this room for a year.

I caress the desk, making my way to a picture frame and pick it up. It's a photo of me, Ronnie and Ryder in the hospital just after he was born. I slouch sitting up, wearing a hospital gown with

198

my hair and makeup done like I didn't just give birth. My smile is big and cheesy, but you can see the pain. The idea of getting my hair and makeup done was his. I was exhausted, as most women are after giving birth. Ronnie had paid a makeup artist to doll me up for after birth family pictures. I could only assume that the raw, real me, sweating after pushing a ten pound baby out of my vagina was not enough. The asshole wanted me to look perfect doing it. But he could never accept reality for what it was no matter what.

I set the picture back in its place. Just like Ronnie would have wanted it to be. The dark wood shows a line without dust, so I know it belongs there. I won't lie. Panic swirled in my gut before I realized how easy it was to find the exact place the picture was before I picked it up. My lips pinch tightly together. I suppose that's my own trauma response.

Because Ronnie…. Well, he would have needed it in the right place or else.

CHAPTER THIRTY-EIGHT

WILLOW

"Things happen. It's called life. I can't be perfect, Willow."

"I told you I was in something deep so many times in so many different ways, Mother!" I spout through gritted teeth, holding my phone up to my mouth. It's so close I can almost taste the speaker.

"So, I'm supposed to be a mind reader now?" My mother asks. She doesn't say this in a mean way. The question all by itself is enough to hurt. She asks like it's a simple question. Like she is about to go to the grocery store and she's asking her husband if he wants white or wheat bread when she'll come home with gluten free bread instead.

"Well, it's not that hard to see something is going on with your daughter if you really take the time to get to know her," I snap with confidence in my voice instead of anger. Growth.

She pauses and takes in a breath. "All you had to do was tell me and I would have done something to help. In fact, I *was* helping you. I was always helping you. I was a slave to you." She sighs and I stay quiet. She continues. "Always picking up after you, changing your nasty diapers, cleaning up your spilt apple juice, wiping the food off your filthy little face every time after I fed you. And you never appreciated any of it. Instead, you only complain. That's all I got for a thank you after giving up my entire life just to care for a needy, spoiled, ungrateful little brat like yourself!" The words stung. I won't lie.

"Wow," I mutter with disgust. "You have resentment towards me for being alive." She doesn't respond. Because in my heart, I truly feel like she is the most selfish woman in the world, so I get off the phone with her. "I have to go." I can't handle another second of listening to her rant about having to be my mother, so I hang up on her. I don't wait for her response because I know it will only be one full of hate towards me.

I know who my people are. I know who I can trust. I know who I can confide in. Mya is my go to person. That's who I will stick with in my time of need from now on.

***

"I don't have anything else to add. I just wanted to make sure I had the last word. I think I've earned that." A quote from Gone Girl on the page I'm reading. It feels so… familiar. The air of it. It demands you to pay attention to it. This is what my stalker wants. The last word. The true narcissist feels this way. Like my mother. Who did not get the last word. Finally.

I text Mya.

Willow
Feel like having company?

While waiting for her to respond I make myself a cup of coffee. I spin my k-cup holder on the counter in my kitchen and choose the one my finger lands on as it stops. It's like someone choosing their next destination on a globe. Even though my k-cups are all the same, so are the places in the world. Full of people not to be trusted.

Ding!

Mya
Always!

Willow
I'll be there shortly!

201

Before heading over to Mya's place, I finish making myself a vanilla latté with two extra shots of espresso and *no milk*. I grab a hold of the handle to my cheetah print coffee mug—my favorite one—and breathe in the smell of my drink. Then, I take a sip. Because it's steaming hot, I blow on it over the rim. I continue the process over and over while sitting in my green reading chair beside my back balcony window. Anxiously, I read on to what happens next in Gone Girl. Even though I already know what happens next because this is my third time reading it.

My head begins to throb. With tears in my eyes and determination to get rid of this headache, I massage my temples like I always do to slow my thoughts. Drying my tears—because I know that crying only makes it worse—I lean back in my chair and close my eyes. As I pull my head forward, I notice how heavy it feels. Like the bowling ball your fingers are too small for and the weight of holding it pulls you down towards the ground. Surely, another swig of this latté will do the trick, and wake me up as I'm suddenly starting to feel like curling up for a long nap. I take a big swig in one big gulp. *Gulp.* Slowly, I flip through the pages of Gone Girl and try to continue reading. As my eyes begin to droop, I down my latté like a vulnerable schoolgirl that snuck out on a Friday night trying to impress the boys. Licking my fingers, I flip another page and begin to nod off.

***

The squeaky sound wakes me out of the—almost—deep sleep, but only a little bit. I'm too loopy and groggy to stand up. Knowing that I need to get up to go to Mya's house, I just want to shut my eyes and go back to sleep. My front door glides open. While my heart thunders through my chest, ramming against my rib cage, I'm too fatigued to do anything about the intruder. As the intruder glides towards me, I notice that his feet are familiar and panic swims through my veins.

This can't be. His steel toe boots make their way slowly in my direction. They're like the ones Brock wore when he kicked my stomach over and over again to force my already wanted abortion. I just didn't want it so violently.

The memory of the blood forming a puddle in between my legs sends me right back to that place, like I was placed in a box and mailed priority overnight. In a rush to send me to that never forgotten destination If I could just cut that memory out, like photoshop, maybe I'd be alright. Maybe this wouldn't be happening right now. Is this another bad dream? Is my imagination playing a trick on me again? With my heart palpitating wildly, my body shivers and beads of sweat drip from my forehead at the same time. A fever has set in and I can't move. Trying to catch a glimpse of the intruder, my eyes fight to stay open. I pull myself up and try with all my might to stand up and swing at the intruder who has his face covered with a blur, but I can see that the person is a man because his hair is short and his stature is masculine. His blurry face meets my eyes. He resembles Neil, but with the boils and burns I remember seeing on Brock's face. A mixture of the two monsters from my past. Who is he?

As soon as my feet touch the floor, I fall flat onto it instead of attacking the intruder like I intended. With a heavy body, I try to push myself up with my hands pressed against the floor and my face falling slack against it. I can't budge. I'm paralyzed, like morphine has settled in the IV stuck in your arm as you lay in a hospital bed. The high has taken over. I wish I could say that this high was a fun one, where I mumble funny, questionable things before passing out. Instead, it's a war to stay awake because if I fall asleep, who knows what will happen to me. I hear sex and organ trafficking are a hot business right now. My mind wanders off to the most gut wrenching places. The hardwood floor is cold against my cheek, relieving some of the fever I've caught.

His steel toe boots step right in front of my face, slowly and one after the other. The sound of his boots against the hardwood floor is enough to make me quiver. Stopping in his tracks, he bends down, and glares into my eyes. I can't see the color of them or even the shape of his nose. His face is still blurry. Damnit.

"Don't worry, Willow. You're going to be safe now. I promise." His voice is gentle, contradicting how I feel.

CHAPTER THIRTY-NINE

HIM

Nobody took a second glance our way. Which isn't exactly surprising to me. I got away with it! I wrapped Willow up in one of her fuzzy throw blankets, so she wouldn't be cold while I carried her out to my car because unlike her other exes I actually care. Her eyes were open as her head rested against my shoulder. I held her delicately in my arms, and walked to my car, parked in front of her building.

It's New York City. People probably thought she was just drunk. She's young and it's a Friday night, after all.

Actually, being able to smell her and not just her lingering scent is exactly the medicine I've been needing. Craving.

***

"Where are you taking me?" Willow mumbles laying in the back seat of my car. This one isn't a rental, but I wasn't about to take my real car out of state. Not a chance.

I adjust my rearview mirror so I can see her. She looks so comfortable curled up in her fuzzy blanket with her hands pressed together in a prayer position underneath her cheek. She is right where she is supposed to be. With me. Finally.

"Home," I remind her. Doesn't she realize yet?

I hear her fumble around a little back there. Usually, I would panic under these circumstances, but I don't panic for even a full second because the child locks are on and she is far too drugged up to get out the windows. For a split second I think of stopping the car and filling her arm up with more drugs. Tap, tap. The morphine swims through the veins. But I don't want to kill her. So, I continue driving us home because that is just not part of the plan.

***

"We're home, Willow." I park the car and open my door. With just a twinge of panic in my gut, I gaze around first to see if anyone is watching. We are secluded, but you can never be too careful. It's better to be safe than sorry. Right? One car passes by, but they don't seem to suspect anything because our tiny home is miles from the road. Everyone drives slow here because it's a little bit of a bumpy road. Still, I don't move until they're gone. I have to be smart about this.

Eager to start our future together, I open the car door, grab her arm and pierce her skin to add enough morphine to keep her asleep, so I can escort her through the front door of our new home together. I finally get to carry her over the threshold. It's practically like we're coming home for the first time after our honeymoon.

Willow is out like a light, so it's easy to get her inside. She's also light as a feather. I walk through the small kitchenette and into our bedroom, laying her down on the bed with her soft, fluffy blanket wrapped and tugged all around her like a burrito. Sitting down next to her on the bed, I watch her sleep. Like I've done many times before.

So peaceful. So perfect. So very much mine.

206

CHAPTER FORTY

WILLOW

As I awaken from a deep sleep, the only familiar thing in my vicinity is a throw blanket I keep resting on my couch. Fixing my gaze around the room I'm stricken to, the rustic chain circling my wrists rubs against my skin, and I begin pulling at it with no surrender. Panic creeps up my spine with the fear I might die here. The chain is harsh and heavy. Much heavier than the chain I was bound to in Brock's apartment. Whoever did this to me has done this before. They have practice. They know what they're doing. I could only wish they would be a sloppy kidnapper. Pulling myself together, I stand up, feeling a little wobbly and lightheaded, but not too much to stumble around a bit and take in my surroundings. Where the fuck am I?

As I stroll around the dungeon I'm forced to be in, the chains clink together behind me. Tears spring to my eyes, stinging as I embark on a journey that's all too familiar to me. Why is this happening again? What have I done to deserve this? What will happen this time? Is it possible to be the woman that escapes two kidnappings in her lifetime? I'm not sure I can be that lucky. Putting my fears to the side, I take another step while holding onto the wall.

The walls are that fake kind of wood, like the ones you saw in your childhood friends' homes in the 80s and 90s. Fake wooden walls narrow in on me as I tour the small place I'm trapped in. Fake wooden walls everywhere. Every single wall is covered with it. A sloppy job. My eyes peer around, looking for a window or a door to escape from. There are no windows in here and the only door is covered with locks and bolts to keep me here.

Is it my stalker who kidnapped me? Are there other people here? This place is too small for anyone else to be here without me seeing them. Still, I look around and call out, "Hello?!" just in case. I don't get a response.

I am alone.

Feeling more awake now, I have the energy and I am ready to get the hell out of here before anything else bad happens to me. Taking in a deep breath, I let it out to get ready, then, I charge towards the front door. My feet clomp against the floor, like a stampede of wild animals. When I get just a few feet from my destination I'm halted by the chains wrapping around me, like vines swirling on the branch of a tree. I fall back against the small dining table and quickly dust myself off. He knew what he was doing. He measured the length of the chains. Who would take this amount of time to give me just enough distance from the bed to barely get to the front door of this shack?

Because I have nothing else to do and my kidnapper isn't here, I keep trying to get to the bolted up door. I know I can get out of here. I've done this before. I've been a prisoner once. I won't be again. My strength is back like a hulk. Get out of my way, bitch. I am stronger than ever, and I will get the fuck out of here no matter what it takes.

I step backwards until I get to the end of the wooden planked walls and once again, I bolt towards the door to try and pull these chains a little looser. I go in headfirst, like a bull ready to do damage. I continue to do this repeatedly. It doesn't work in my favor. Not even in the slightest. The chains don't loosen. They are far too heavy and I am starting to get hungry and tired again. That was a workout.

Out of breath, I take a seat on one of the chairs in the kitchenette dining room area of the shack I'm forced to stay in. Gazing around the room, I take a mental note of how much I don't want to be here. There isn't much to it. I couldn't imagine my life stuck here, with the bare of bare necessities. There are a few cabinets, a small refrigerator like you see in a classroom, a countertop stove and some framed pictures hung on the walls. Like 'Welcome to our diner', as if me and my stalker will be cooking together. Another one reads, 'We dance in our kitchen', and I assume my stalker believes that we will actually be dancing in this piece of shit kitchenette.

My stomach growls at me, demanding to be fed. I listen to its demands and go through each cabinet and the small fridge to find something to eat. I don't trust the chocolate pie he has in the fridge, even though my mouth waters looking at it. It's homemade and there might be drugs in it. Or poison.

This is a trick. He might kill me and I'm searching for food. *Great.* There is a bowl full of fruit sitting on the counter that also makes my mouth water. Bright red apples dare me to take a bite. I pick one up and press it against my nose. I close my eyes because it smells crisp and sweet, like summertime. I put it back in the bowl because I don't know if I can trust eating it. I'm not trying to create another Snow White moment. Just one bite and I fall to the floor. No. I can't trust anything unpackaged.

I go back through the cabinets again and end up choosing a Little Debbie snack because it is store bought and packaged. Opening it up, I shove it in my mouth like I haven't eaten a crumb in days. Maybe I haven't. How long have I been here? As my stomach yaps at me again—*I'm trying, damn*—I grab an unopened box of crackers and devour them all until I hear footsteps outside the locked front door.

Like a deer in headlights, I stop in my tracks and wide-eyed stare at the door, then gaze around the rest of the shack. What the fuck do I do? There is no back door or window to escape out of. I already know this. Quickly, I wipe the crumbs off my mouth and run to the bed and cover up with the blanket because I don't want him to look at my body and be tempted. I'm scared of what he might do to me.

Clink. Clink. Clink.

The shuffling of keys outside the door is almost an answer to my question. Who is he? Then again, I don't want to know. It's bittersweet. The keys are loud and this place is small and crowded, but clean. So very clean. I wonder what will come of the crumbs I dusted onto the floor. The door slowly opens and the back of him is all I see—he does this on purpose—as he bolts up all the locks to ensure that we stay here… and only here.

I study the room, looking around for something, anything, to knock him over the back of his head with. I should have done this before I ran to the bed, but my instinct was to hide. There isn't anything. Not even a lamp. The black beanie he wears covers his entire head, so I can't even see what color his hair is yet. *Yet*. Every inch of his clothes are black like that's a camouflage to him, so he can blend in with whatever crowd he's in. Those steel toe boots are the only thing that aren't black. They're the same ones I remember being kicked with. Tan. I shake my head to get those thoughts out of my mind.

Live in the now, Willow. Get the fuck out of here.

Anticipation crawls all the way down my spine as he turns to face me, pulls off his black beanie, and *no fucking way*. It can't be. It *can't* be him. Am I dreaming? Am I hallucinating? Is this real life? Violently, I shake my head to make him go away. He doesn't, though. He stays put.

His face isn't blurry this time. It's clear who he is, but I am not accepting it. I back away from him on the bed against the headboard and pinch my eyes shut, covering my face with a blanket.

"This isn't real. This isn't real. This isn't real," I say to myself over and over in a whispered tone.

"Willow," he says, his voice gentle. Like he didn't just drug me, kidnap me and chain me up.

I hear his footsteps as he walks slowly towards the bed I sit on and the mattress sinks in at my feet that are huddled against me because I have my knees up to my chest. He sits close enough that I can feel his body against the blanket. He sighs as he rests his hand on my knee. I shudder with disgust and angst from his touch. This cannot be fucking happening. Trembling with fear, I move my body away from him.

"Don't touch me! Go away!" I yell. I think I sound dominant when really I sound frightened because I am. I am so very much frightened.

He sighs again. "Did you at least get enough to eat?" *He saw the crumbs.*

That voice. His voice. I can't believe I'm hearing it again.

"Go away! Get away from me!" I screech, with my eyes still pinched closed and my hands covering my ears to block him out.

He sighs once more, like he's trying and I'm being difficult. "Okay then. I'll be back later. I'll bring more food. Okay?" He places his hand back on my knee and quickly takes it off like he remembers that I don't want to be touched by him and he's doing me a favor. Like he's a 'nice guy'. "Okay?" he asks again, as if I'm supposed to respond, like this is a normal situation and I'm still being too difficult.

"Willow? Can you at least acknowledge my existence?"

And because I know he is not going to give this up I answer him, whispering, "Okay."

"Good girl." He grimaces.

"That's good. That's very good." He adds.

CHAPTER FORTY-ONE

HIM

Click.

I lock the door behind me and shiver against the cold as my body protests it. I was only inside for a few minutes, but it was nice and toasty in there, and that's where my family is, so it's where I want to be. Baby steps. Baby steps, I remind myself. She'll eventually get used to this.

Shivering against the cold, I turn the heater on in my car to warm up and cup my hands over my mouth to breathe hot air onto them to speed up the heating up process. I take my phone out of my pants pocket and pull up the video app. I click the play button, watching as Willow paces the floors of our new home, talking to herself. The color is in black and white and there's no sound. I opted for the cheaper way to go and that's okay because it gets the job done.

She begins frantically taking everything out of the cabinets in the kitchen and the bathroom areas. I grab a sandwich out of the bag beside me on the passenger side seat, open it up and take a big bite. Then I wash it down with the gas station fountain drink in my cup holder. I haven't taken my eyes off my phone screen because Willow is my favorite show to watch. After she gets done throwing things all over the place and completely destroying our new home, she begins screaming. Her eyes close tightly and her mouth opens wide as she yells at the top of her lungs.

Now *that* I can hear as I roll the car window down. I need her to shut the fuck up, even though we don't have neighbors. I can't take any chances. Quickly, I grab the bag beside me that holds her sandwich and bottled water, then I head back inside.

***

"Get this shit cleaned up," I demand of Willow. I feel one eyebrow raised at her.

She sniffles, reminding me of a child that just got done throwing a temper tantrum, with her puffy tear filled eyes and rosy cheeks as she wrinkles her eyebrows at me. Willow shoots me a look of pure hatred. She bends to the floor and begins picking things up as she cries. She cries *again*. I am trying to be patient with her. Can't she understand? But, for the love of all that is holy, if she doesn't shut the fuck up, I might lose my shit.

Breathing in and out a few times to calm my nerves, I set the bag down on the table to take out her dinner. I grab a plate from the cabinet and set the sandwich beside it. I dare not open it because she won't eat it if I do. I need her to get some real food in her stomach. Not the crap she stuffed her face with earlier. Sadness beams out of her as she picks up the mess she made.

Guilt washes over me. I feel bad for being annoyed with her when she is only trying to take in her fate of being here when it's not as fancy as or decorated the way her apartment is, so I help her get the rest of the mess cleaned up.

"Your dinner is on the table." I pull out a chair like a gentleman to make up for being an asshole. She blinks at me like I'm stupid. I suppose she doesn't have to forgive me right away. I have all the time in the world for her. Really, I do. She hesitates, and to let her win this time, I back away with my hands up in the air like I'm showing free hands to a police officer. Once I've stepped away from the table she sits down in the other chair. Not the one I pulled out for her. Before she opens up the sandwich, she examines the package for anything suspicious. I can't help but chuckle a little at this. She shoots daggers at me with those brown eyes of hers.

213

Quickly, I look away because I guess she's right about this one. I shouldn't be laughing right now. She wins this fight. I got the war.

I sit down in the chair I pulled out for her, across from her. "Willow. I've missed you so much." I place both of my hands on the table and close to hers. She quickly backs away. The chair she sits on screeches against the concrete floor as she moves. I have got to carpet these floors. I make a mental note.

Folding my hands together in front of me, I look down. This is going to be hard work, but she is worth it. She is worth every agonizing second of it.

"It's been a long time. Hasn't it?" She doesn't answer me. I try again. "I would ask how you've been, but I gather you know that I already know." I chuckle a little again, trying to make things lighter. She doesn't pierce her eyes towards me this time. Maybe she's already starting to accept it. She is motionless, though. Showing no emotion to my comment.

Nothing. Not a peep. She just sits there, fiddling with the necklace wrapped around her pretty little neck that I bought her.

"Aren't you gonna eat?" She has only taken a bite out of her sandwich. She glances at it, then her eyes meet mine. They pierce into my soul this time.

"You aren't really here and I'm not really here and this is all a dream. A nightmare," she whispers with her eyes glazed over and still looking into mine.

She repeats, "You aren't really here," over and over again.

"Willow, come on now. Stop that."

She continues. When I stand up, she gets louder. I ask her nicely to stop, several times, but she won't shut up. My heart pounds with anger. My jaw clenches. Heat surfaces to my face. This is what she does to me.

"Stop it! Goddamnit!" I yell as I slam my fist down on the table and her plate of food shakes. She flinches and turns to face away from me. She rocks herself back and forth in the chair. Making me feel guilt once again. "Shit," I mutter. "Look. I'm sorry. Okay? It's just, you kept saying it and for so long that's how I've felt. Invisible. I am here. Dammit. I'm here!"

She sniffles. I can tell she is starting to cry again. Not knowing what else to do right now, I take the keys out of my pocket and start walking towards the door. I want to hold her and console her, feel her skin against mine, touch her and taste her, but I know I can't because she will only recoil from my touch.

"I'll be back shortly," I tell her as I'm unlocking the door, instead of what I really want to do. What I should be doing. What I have earned to have now.

Just as I have the key in the hole a *swoosh* sound fills my left ear and air slaps my cheek. I don't flinch, but when my eye meets the knife that she darted into the door, I am intrigued. "Where the hell did you get a pocketknife?" With a quick yank, I pull it out from the door. She stands there, quietly staring at me like she just messed up because she missed my head or back or wherever she was targeting.

"Good throw, but not quick enough." I let her know, through a sarcastic laugh. I point the sharp edge of the knife her way. "You stay right there, Willow." I rummage through the drawers and cabinets to look for anything else she might find to use as a weapon because I'm sure that's where she found this. One foolish mistake and I'd be dead. She would be gone to run into some other guy's arms. Not gonna happen.

"It was you, wasn't it?" She interrogates.

Halting my movement for a minute, I turn to face her with a can of corn in my hand from the cabinet. I toss the can back and forth between each hand. The silence between us is so thick I could cut it with that knife she threw at me. Even though this is an accusatory question I am happy to be having a real conversation with her; one where we both join in.

"What are you talking about?" I ask, knowing exactly what she's talking about. I just want to hear her use her voice directed at me, gazing into my eyes as she chatters away.

"You raped me that day. Didn't you? You drugged me and you raped me and I thought it was a dream. A nightmare."

Wait a second. She *is* accusing me. A nightmare? How daunting. It isn't rape when you're the husband.

"That wasn't rape, Willow. You're my wife," I remind her.

She grits her teeth. "You are *nothing* to me." She spats.

"I know you don't mean that." *I know she doesn't.*

"Oh, but I do. You see? I do mean that. I meant it then and I mean it today."

Ouch. "Time will change that. You'll see." She will see.

She backs away from me and plops back down in a chair at the dining table. She looks defeated and exhausted from fighting, but she tries to seem stronger. "How did you get away with it?"

"With what, exactly?" It's my turn to question her. "Shouldn't you be asking yourself that question?"

She shakes her head no. "You are unfuckingbelievable." She shakes her head again like she can't believe this. "How did you get out of the fire, Neil?"

Smiling, I reply, "I've been dying for you to ask this question." Rocking back and forth on my heels with my hands in the front pockets of my jeans, I dance around the question.

"Magic." My face grimaces and I snap my fingers.

One of her eyebrows lifts high up on her forehead. She doesn't seem amused, but I'm not here for her entertainment. I'm here to make her see that I'm the one. I always have been. I always will be. "Brock didn't stand a chance, lying there already dead before the house caught on fire, with his face boiling off. You did a good job, Willow."

"I'm not a murderer!" She screeches.

"Oh, yes you are," I reaffirm. "Need I remind you how you didn't think twice about killing not one, but two people in one day?" Pacing the floors of our new home, I glance at her with a tear falling down my cheek. "You killed your husband." Sniffling and slurping back the tears and snot, I shake my head and laugh a little again. "You thought you killed me. Your husband, Willow! *Wake up!*" I belch, slamming my fist down on the table again for

216

emphasis. It's time for her to understand the damage she caused. She flinches and begins to cry with me.

"What do you want me to say? You were so controlling and abusive. It was either me or you. I had to pick myself for once."

Raising both of my eyebrows, I blink at her a few times. "Abusive? You're joking, right?"

"You don't have to put your hands on someone to abuse them." She sniffles. Big, fat teardrops drip onto the table in front of her. "I've been struggling with this every day. Knowing that I locked the door when I could have let you live."

I want to believe her, but I'm not sure if she's faking remorse. There's only one way to find out. Stepping towards her, she doesn't back away. We're getting somewhere. Once I stand in front of her, I lean down and in for a kiss. She recoils from my touch. Like she's done so many times. Fumes of anger fuel my body and I can't help myself. Grabbing a hold of her neck, I take her to the bedroom and have my way with her.

"I love you." Whispering in her ear as she sleeps has always been a comfort for her. She used to toss and turn all night, but once I rested my hand on her back and whispered in her ear, she'd fall asleep and stay asleep. I miss those days. While I have them back—because I have her back—I know things will be different this time, and a lot of work from both our ends.

"How long have I been out?" she asks, rubbing her eyes as she pulls her legs up to her chest. I had to dose her up just a little bit because she was too shaken up after our first time making love in our new home. It's not rape if she's your wife. Willow is still my wife.

"Just one day," I answer.

She glares into my eyes. "I deserve to know. Please tell me, now. How did you get out of the fire?"

Sighing, I concede. I guess she's earned the right to know. "I waited."

Pacing the floors again, I continue. "I knew the smoke would rise to the top, and I waited for my time. I wasn't about to let you kill me, Willow. When the fire busted the windows open, it burned the pieces of wood nailed across them, and I climbed out the window without a scratch on me."

"So, you're the one who took a picture of me, laying bloody, nearly dying?"

Shaking my head yes, she blinked back tears. "Why?" She sits up. "Why not just move on with your life and find somebody new?"

"As a dead man?!" This time I shook my head no. "I had to start over. Change my name. Hide away inside. Pretend like I was dead. I did it all for you. For us!"

"You've been harassing me for months! Taunting me! I thought I was going crazy!" She belches. I have nothing to say back. I've already told her that I did this all for us. I saved her ass from not going to jail for murder. What more does she want out of me?

"And how long have I been here?" She sits on the bed with her knees up to her chest.

"You've only been here three days, Willow. Not long." I pull the paper towel off the sandwich I covered up for her. "Come sit at the table."

Silence fills the air between us. Without turning to face her, I tell her again. "I know you heard me. Come sit at the table." Demanding her through gritted teeth. I can't help it. She pisses me off more than anyone I've ever met.

The chains clinking together lets me know she's being a good girl. She plops down in a chair and sighs. "I hate you!" She screams at me. She won't win. She's already lost. She knows this.

I grab an apple from the plastic fruit bowl sitting on the counter and toss it her way. It lands in her lap. She pulls her eyes down to the apple then back to me.

"Eat up." I demand. It's a game. I saw her smell it yesterday on camera. She wants to eat it, and she's barely eaten anything since she's been home. I want to know how desperate she is. How far I can take her down on just day three.

She picks up the apple and throws it at me. I duck. It hits the kitchen cabinet behind my head and falls to the floor. "You are dead!" she screams. "DEAD!"

The doorknob on the only door to our tiny home wiggles and we both dart our eyes that way.

I pull the knife out of my pocket that she threw at me the other day and put it up to my mouth like a pointer finger. "Shhhh," I mouth to her while I pull up my shirt a little to show her the gun in the waist of my pants. Her eyes dilate and she backs away from me all the way to the end of the tiny house and onto the bed. Stupid girl. If I was going to use it on her, I would have already done it. I don't want to kill her. I want to fulfill my duties as her husband. That's why she's here. Not so she can end up dead. I'm protecting her. But if it works as a scare tactic that much, I know what my last resort is. I won't make a habit out of threatening my wife with a gun.

Now that I have her situated, I can go investigate what that noise was. I unlock and open the door. Curiously, I peek around the corner of the house. Not a soul can be seen. Not even a squirrel in sight. I close the door behind me and I walk around the house to make sure nobody is lingering. That's when she starts it again.

"HELP ME!" Willow yells out, banging her fists on the walls. I let her do this because I have to make sure that we are alone. I can't take any chances. I've worked too hard for this.

I step around to the back of the tiny house. The leaves crunch under my shoes. I hear something move and grab a hold of the gun at my waist.

CHAPTER FORTY-TWO

WILLOW

Two people go back and forth. Muffling sounds of an argument between a man and a woman fills my ears. The man is Neil, but I don't know who the woman is. Curiosity gets the best of me, and I hop off the bed and step closer to the door. It's closed, so it's hard to hear what's being said.

Pow!

A gunshot goes off. More scrambling and a sickening muted thud. Silence follows behind it. Who won? Was it Neil? I hope not. Was it the woman? Who is the woman? Are they both dead?

"Help me!" I yell out again. In hopes that someone is here to set me free. I continue to beg in mercy, in the case someone, *anyone*, can hear me. I stop mid yell when the door swings wide open. In comes Mya. MYA!

She holds a sledgehammer in both hands and the weight of it pulls her down some as she walks towards me. Blood spatter is wet and fresh on the hammer and her clothes. Reminding me of the movie and main character, *Serial Mom*. My heart shakes against my chest. I am too freaked out to ask her what happened. To ask her what she did. She finally gets to me, to the bed I sit upon, and raises the blood spattered sledgehammer high in the air. Please, no!

Before I close my eyes, so I don't have to witness what she does next, I notice the Resist tattoo on her left forearm creeping out of her white, bloody sweater that she has pulled the sleeves up to her elbows, like she's been doing yard work. The blood spatter is sprinkled all around the word Resist, making it look like it was an added affect to her tattoo.

"You fucked with the wrong person this time, Willow." The light above us makes a reflection in her eyes. Her face is grimaced and her long, thick pretty auburn hair is even more pronounced under the light. Shiny, like the commercials daring you to buy Pantene.

Down the hammer goes. No, Mya. Please don't!

I flinch and guard my face with my hands and my eyes pinched shut. I lay there, frozen in fear. My heart beats faster than it ever has. I might have a heart attack. This isn't the way I'm supposed to die. I'd rather go quick and painless. Not a slow painful beating with a sledgehammer by someone who said they are my friend, but of course you can never really trust anyone. Can you? What did I do to her? Why would she kill me? And so violently?

Clink!

The blow she made was hard, but it barely made a sound. My head isn't beat-in and I am not in any new pain. I squint at her through my fingers over my face. She stands at the edge of the blood spattered sledgehammer that rests upon the lock of my shackles. She picks it back up. *Bam!* She hits it again. I look over at the door hanging wide open. There is no sign of him.

"Don't worry, darling." Mya grins at me. She looks menacing smiling like that and holding onto a blood spattered sledgehammer. "He's dead. I *crush*—" She said as she slammed down the hammer onto the lock again. She is filled with adrenaline. "I crushed his head in."

My jaw drops and I cover my mouth, in shock at how violent she can be when it's needed. The locks and chains finally separate from each other. I rub my wrists and ankles once again, like an inmate that just got released from jail. My prison sentence is finally done. She sets the sledgehammer against the tacky, fake wooden wall and with heavy breathing she plops down on the bed next to me.

"How did you know I was here?" I can't help it. I need to know. My question came out before I could thank her for literally saving my life.

She sighs. Not because she's annoyed, but because she is still catching her breath. "When you didn't show up at my house the other night I knew something was wrong, so I came to your apartment and I saw him carrying you out to his car. I followed you two here and waited for the right time."

"Why didn't you call the cops?" Once again, I am curious and thankful at the same time, but showing my curiosity more than my gratitude first.

"Because." She turns her head to face mine and looks me right in the eyes. "What can the cops do about a man who is already dead?"

She is right. But how did she know?

"Wait," I say and sit up on my knees. "What? How did you know?"

"I saw him the day that Bryan choked me at the coffee shop. He was there, Willow. He was taking pictures of you and watching you. I thought my head was playing tricks on me because of what Bryan did to me, but when I saw him at your place and carrying you to his car, I realized it was him. I realized that actually did happen at the coffee shop." She closed her eyes and pressed tightly, rubbing them with the sleeve of her shirt and then tucked her sleeves back up to her forearms.

"But more importantly I did my research. I looked you up, so I could find any clues as to who this guy could be. I saw your story on Google. It was the first thing that pulled up along with Neil's and Brock's pictures. I found that out last night before I went to your apartment, but I remember seeing it in the news before. A long time ago. I knew you looked familiar. So did he. That day at the coffee shop. I knew he looked familiar, too. I just couldn't remember where I saw his face before. Now I know."

"Thank you," I say to her, even though she deserves more. So much more than a subtle thank you.

"We need to bury his body and get the hell out of here."
She sits back up.

"I saw a shovel outside when I got here," she reminds herself out loud as she stands. "Come on. We need to hurry."

I do as I'm told.

His blond hair is tinted with the blood red pouring out of his head. It's no longer standing like a perm the way it used to. It's slicked back and wet. His dark eyes look more fierce than ever before. Even in death he tries to intimidate me. Before we push his dead body into the hole we dug up, I close them so he can't watch me anymore. I want to make sure he's really dead this time, so I pick up the shovel and crush his skull in until I'm breaking a sweat in the November cold of New York.

He. Is. Dead.

We take turns digging the hole. It is much harder work than I expected it to be, but it feels victorious when we finally get it dug deep enough. I think back to the days he threw me into a hole to rot. I think to myself how ironic it is to get to do it back to him. Except this time, it isn't metaphorically because he is dead and going into a real hole to rot.

Forever.

Mya hands me the shovel. "You get the honor."

His bushy eyebrows, closed eyes, pointy nose and thin lips are all that is left to cover with dirt.

"Goodbye, Neil. For good this time." I push the shovel with my foot into the dirt pile and toss it over his face again and again until I can't see it anymore. Then, I pat it with the back of the shovel, making it smooth. Relieved, I drop it to the ground and wipe my nose from the cold I seem to be catching and look over at Mya. A true friend will help you bury the body. So, the saying goes.

CHAPTER FORTY-THREE

WILLOW

"This is Chief Phill," he answers the call. He sounds the exact same. An old man's voice, a little raspy, reminding me of Mr. Grey.

"Hey, there! It's Willow. You called?" I say to him like I'm oblivious as to why.

He explains, telling me all about the picture he got in the mail. The one of me lying bloody, beaten and muddy in a back field.

"Are you okay?"

"I'm okay."

"Has anything weird happened lately?"

"Like what?"

"Has anyone been lurking around or watching you or have you received any pictures?"

I pick up the charm to the necklace Neil got me and move it across my chin. I'll cherish this gift forever. My forever lost crutch. My husband's memorabilia. Bittersweet.

"No. Not at all. I'm happier than I've ever been. If something happens I'll let you know," I pronounce with a chipper voice, that's anything but fake. It's not a forced chipper. It's a real one. Neil is dead. Just like he already was reported to be. I have nothing more to say to the chief about this.

Chief Phill tells me, "I will keep the investigation open and please keep a lookout. Watch your back."

"Yes, of course," I agree and disconnect the call. I glance over to Mya who has been listening with the phone on speakerphone as we sit in her car.

"You know we have to get rid of all the evidence now, right?" She probes.

And I know. I do know.

***

Splash!

The sledgehammer hits the deep waters of Lake Travis here in New York. The blood seeps in to blend with the green murky water and whatever else that's been tossed in by criminals, loiterers, and lazy pedestrians walking by.

Splash!

The shovel hits a different part of Lake Travis, so the two don't ever meet again.

Splash!

We drove a little further up the lake to dispose of our last piece of evidence. Neil's gun sinks to the bottom, never to be seen again.

***

Mya is glowing. I've never seen her this fresh faced and happy before.

"Those can go in the supplies box," she instructs as I try to figure out what to do with Ronnie's things on his old dusty desk. A moving box labeled Office Supplies settles on the floor beside his desk chair. I pack up his hole puncher, stapler and then I pick up the family picture of him, Mya and Ryder. I study it. Trying to find any discontent in Ronnie's face. They're in a hospital and Ryder was just born. Ronnie has his hand on Mya's shoulder, holding her down underneath his thumb. He had a hold of her. His face shows it. Mya looks drained of life, but with a face covered in makeup and every inch of her hair in its perfect little place. Like a mortician did their job right.

Dead and beautiful. Beautiful and dead.

"Hey. So how did your husband die, again?" She never told me exactly. She only told me he committed suicide.

"I told you already," she exclaimed after a pause. There was a pause.

I ask, "How?"

She shakes her head. "I really don't want to discuss it."

But I know. I know what she's hiding. We're the same, me and her. I don't press. I can't until she's ready because even though we both killed our husbands, it doesn't mean we never loved them. I need to let her mourn while we pack away his office for her to turn it into a playroom for Ryder.

It's time to pack up the past and leave it behind anyway.

Mya changes the subject. "I wanted to wait to show you this because you've taken a break from social media, but I feel like you have the right to know."

She holds up her phone. There Bryan is in an orange jumpsuit. Another mugshot. A newer one. His eyes are dilated and his cheeks are sunken in. When I got back home after we buried Neil, I found my phone to have twenty one missed calls from Bryan and over one hundred text messages from him threatening me, begging me, you know… all the things. So, I blocked him and got a restraining order on him. Which was not hard to do considering the evidence he left behind.

I looked up the definition of stalking and found out that by law it means more than three unwanted contacts by an individual. By that definition I was being stalked by Neil, Bryan and Diego Cold Hands, The Famous Bearer, although, there's been no word from him. I think he finally caught on. I didn't realize the severity of it all. How, even though it tore my life apart at the time, I thought that was love. In a way, I did. I think that's what I was taught at an early age before I could comprehend what healthy love looks like. Now it's time to unlearn that and heal from all the trauma that I never took seriously before.

Not only are Bryan's eyes dilated, but they're dark. Not the color. It's the intensity. They're soulless. I read onto what booked him in this time and my heart drops to the pit of my stomach. For a second, I think I might puke, but I don't. I am stronger now. I can stomach much more than I could before.

A suspect, Bryan Winters, in the murder of Diandre Klaire, a twenty-two year old woman whom her family and friends say they just started dating. Bryan Winters' ex-girlfriend, who wants to remain anonymous, stated he moved to Chicago from Texas to be with her and shortly after began abusing her and cheating on her with the victim. She confirmed the address he put on his license was not his address anymore. He was staying in his car for months. The family has a Gofundme link below for any donations for Diandre's funeral. Trial will be held in February.

-The New York City Weekly News.

"You better count your lucky stars, girl. That could have been you." Mya puts her phone in the back pocket of her jeans and walks back over to the moving boxes.

She's right. That could have been me. But it's not. I am here. I'm alive. I am ready to have that fresh start in New York City. This time, though? I can spot a predator from a mile away. I'm writing a book to tell the story of my life in my own words. I'm not letting anyone else tell my story for me again. Only I can get it right.

***

"They judge me like a picture book by the colors, like they forgot to read." Lana Del Rey sings in my ears as the cool breeze pierces my face like a thousand needles against my skin. She is right about that. People put their noses in the air or look at me with pity in their eyes. It's so easy to make up your mind about someone just by hearing a small portion of their life. They don't dig deeper, only surface deep. I hope where I'm going is different.

My chin quivers because I'm so cold. I open the double glass doors and step inside the small, kempt building. The warmth

227

hugs me, wrapping itself around me like a blanket. I'm welcomed here. I don't even hesitate. I walk right up to the front receptionist who is wearing red scrubs with Santa Clause faces all over them to be festive for the holidays. She has short gray hair, wears thin glasses with trim that are the same red color as her scrubs, and greets me with a friendly smile. I pull the Airpods out of my ears and tuck them in the pocket of my purse.

"Hi." I smile warmly at her. "I'm here to see therapist Jeffrey Thompson."

She hands me a clipboard with papers tucked in to fill out for this new journey of mine. This is my healing journey. The one where I save myself.

The one where *I* am the knight in shining armor.

Acknowledgments

It's time to thank all the people who worked zealously to bring this book into your hands. My editor, Nicole Mullaney (check out her books), spent countless hours editing, answering emails and text messages about every little detail. Your patience is like no other! Thank you for pushing me to be a better writer with your commentary.

A massive shoutout goes to my husband, who listened to me read Willow's Crush out loud to him multiple times and showed excitement and support each time. He also gave many honest opinions that helped shape this book. He is my rock and best friend. He is the absolute best. I also thank my daughters for tiptoeing through sometimes while I worked day and night on writing and rewriting, as well as showing just as much excitement and support for me as I do for them with their endeavors. They are the best daughters a mother could ever ask for.

To my twin brother, earth parents, and friends- You all helped me so much throughout this journey of Willow's Flame. Thank you for picking up my phone calls to ask, "Do you think this sounds good?" and answering honestly. And I thank you for clapping and cheering me on through social media, as well.

Another huge shout-out goes to all of my readers for believing in my book and for your honest and lovely feedback. You are what makes me want to keep writing.

Finally, I raise a glass to all the Authors out there who inspired me with your own words of wisdom and praise.

Other Work by Stephanie Fields

Willow's Flame (Book 1 in Willow's Wounds Series)

369 Damn, You're Devine (Spirituality journal/book)

Mirror (Short paranormal/suspense story)

Deflated (Short dystopian/suspense story)

Under (Short sci fi/suspense story)

Ellie Goes To Kindergarten (Children's rhyming book)

Let's Connect

You can find me on the social media accounts below.

TikTok 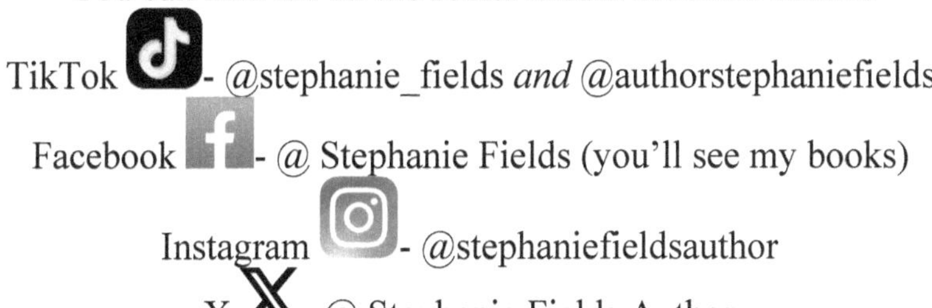- @stephanie_fields *and* @authorstephaniefields

Facebook - @ Stephanie Fields (you'll see my books)

Instagram - @stephaniefieldsauthor

X - @ Stephanie Fields Author

I want to thank you, the reader, for coming along on this ride. I hope you had as much fun as I did. If so, please take a moment to post a review and tell a friend.